THE HOSPITAL

It promises its patients the finest care that modern medicine can provide—while it delivers something dangerously different. Some of its staff work around the clock to save lives—while others never stop their efforts to enrich and advance their own.

THE HOSPITAL

Each day brings new life-or-death medical dramas to the operating rooms and intensive-care ward, while behind the scenes, lust, hatred, and betrayal riddle an institution that desperately needs shock therapy. One doctor fights for his professional life while another pulls strings and twists arms to save his medical skin. One woman makes men her sexual toys while another uses her body and brains as weapons in a vicious vendetta. One perfect nurse finds out the terrifying truth about her daughter, while a perverse millionairess does not even suspect the truth about hers.

THE HOSPITAL

The scorchingly suspenseful medical spellbinder that continues that drama and intrigue at Chandler Medical Center.

The
HOSPITAL

Tyler Cortland

A SIGNET BOOK

SIGNET
Published by the Penguin Group
Penguin Books USA Inc., 375 Hudson Street,
New York, New York 10014, U.S.A.
Penguin Books Ltd, 27 Wrights Lane,
London W8 5TZ, England
Penguin Books Australia Ltd, Ringwood,
Victoria, Australia
Penguin Books Canada Ltd, 10 Alcorn Avenue,
Toronto, Ontario, Canada M4V 3B2
Penguin Books (N.Z.) Ltd, 182–190 Wairau Road,
Auckland 10, New Zealand

Penguin Books Ltd, Registered Offices:
Harmondsworth, Middlesex, England

First published by Signet, an imprint of Dutton Signet,
a division of Penguin Books USA Inc.

First Printing, October, 1994
10 9 8 7 6 5 4 3 2 1

  REGISTERED TRADEMARK—MARCA REGISTRADA

Printed in the United States of America

PUBLISHER'S NOTE
This is a work of fiction. Names, characters, places, and incidents either are the
product of the author's imagination or are used fictitiously, and any resemblance
to actual persons, living or dead, events, or locales is entirely coincidental.

For Gatz,
champion of my Dr. Samantha Turner mysteries

Chapter 1

Ellis

Ellis Johnson, riding shotgun in the ambulance, looked through the heat vapors rising above the gridlocked Interstate 10 to make out faint red lights ahead. A runaway horse that had been struck by an eighteen-wheeler, had turned this lonely stretch of the highway west of Houston into a steaming bottleneck.

Riding up front was Ellis's dubious reward for coming along with Cole Morgan, Chandler Medical Center's emergency room doc. Ellis didn't make many ambulance runs, but the call from the Department of Public Safety said an on-site amputation might be necessary. Ellis specialized in thoracic surgery and was stepping into his partner's arena with this one, but Patrick had been in the middle of an appendectomy and Cole couldn't wait. Besides, they were most likely overreacting. Field amputations had gone out with the Confederacy.

Pokey, their fallaciously named driver, catapulted the ambulance off the right shoulder onto the steep bank of the bayou and rode the bumps for two hundred yards. He pulled back onto the shoulder, dusting scavengers scuffling over cases of beer, damaged cargo from the jackknifed eighteen-wheeler.

"Watch out!" Ellis yelled over the siren.

Pokey swerved a hard left to avoid the horse's carcass. Cole Morgan took a frenzied pitch into a gurney.

"Somebody oughta move that horse," Pokey said by way of apology.

Cole picked himself up off the floor, mumbling his agreement. He leaned over the front seat to have a look. "What a mess!"

The left shoulder was crowded with official cars and fire trucks from Harris County and neighboring Waller County. Chandler Medical Center's ambulance represented Fort Bend County.

Rubberneckers had all but stopped traffic on the other side of the Interstate. They had the best view of the overturned tractor in the median and the attached twelve-foot-wide mower that stood on one end like the leaning Tower of Pisa. A red Subaru station wagon, with North Carolina plates, was crushed under the mower. The bush-hog mower, as locals called it, had seen the last of its weed-cutting days. Nor would the Subaru be taking any more long trips.

"Pretty obvious where the pinning is," Cole grumbled. "Ellis, you go left. Pokey and I'll see about the eighteen-wheeler."

Pokey pulled up next to the sheriff's car. Ellis jerked the door open, getting a good blast of blinding dust and blaring siren. He clutched his surgical kit and jumped out into the August heat, leaving Cole and Pokey to their own devices. He sprinted over the mowed field, slowing where the tumbleweeds and cockleburs hadn't been sheared. A county worker was sitting on the tire of the overturned tractor, a towel to his head. Ellis pulled the towel away. The worker's leathery face was skinned and bloodied and he had a nice goose egg at his temple.

"How you doing?"

The man shrugged. "I've had better days."

Ellis held up a finger. "How many fingers do you see?"

"Four."

"Four?"

"One up, three down. Got anything in that bag for a splitting headache?"

"No, but sit tight. Someone's on the way."

"You the doc?" a deputy wearing a Harris county uniform called from the other side of the tractor.

"The surgeon. The doc's checking out the trucker."

"He's fine, but we've got one over here. Pinned between the two blades. He's in pain like you wouldn't believe."

Ellis rounded the tractor and worked his way to the back. The front end of the car wasn't touching ground, but had managed to wedge itself between the two jumbo pie-plate blades of the bush-hog. The car was precariously supported with jacks, as was the tilting monolith.

"You can crawl in over here, or in the back. This'll get you closer." The officer motioned with his flashlight to a black hole between two jacks.

Cole was headed this way, leaning hard on Pokey's arm as he hopped on his good leg and dragged his cast down the freshly mowed slope. It would be another couple of months before Cole's femur mended from being gored. Cole had been a damned fool to think he could ride a bull in the yearly Chandler rodeo. He was a big, burly man, a good fifty pounds heavier than the wiry cowboys who rodeoed professionally.

His injury had taken its toll. Cole looked every minute of his thirty-eight years. His sandy hair was still full, something Ellis envied him for, but his rugged face was etched with lines that had not been placed there by time alone, and his shoulders sagged under the weight of the world.

Ellis decided not to wait. He took the flashlight and crawled under, trying hard to avoid shattered glass and oil slicks.

The male victim was little more than a boy. Mid-twenties, maximum. His only noticeable injury was a nasty gash above his left brow. He was trapped behind the twisted metal that had once been a steering wheel, one blade of the bush-hog perilously at a tilt above his head, the other poking through his door. "I'm one of the docs. How are you doing?"

"Okay, Doc."

Doing a somersault in a coffin would have been easier than maneuvering in this cramped oven. "What's your name?"

"Skip. Skip Jones."

He seemed to be in command of his faculties. "Can you feel your legs?"

Skip shook his head, splattering blood and sweat on Ellis's cheek. "Only part of me that doesn't hurt."

That was the wrong answer. "Can you move your legs, Skip?"

"They're pinned."

Pinned just below the thighs. Ellis needed to find out how much pressure was on the kid's legs. "But can you wiggle your toes?"

"Don't know."

Ellis slithered over what was left of the hood and hung like a bat over the dash to see the legs. They didn't appear severed, but were unnaturally twisted like shoes on the wrong feet. When he touched them, they felt cold and clammy. Skip's pulse was weak and thready. The kid was going into shock, a true emergency. Where in the hell was Cole?

"You going to cut off my legs?" he asked between rapid shallow breaths. "Someone said you were going to cut off my legs."

"Naw, too hard to sew them back on."

"Can you really sew legs back on?"

"A microsurgeon can. It's a lot of bother, though. Much easier to pull you out in one piece." The smile on the kid's face would haunt Ellis as long as he lived if he had to take the legs.

The car rocked as Cole shimmied over the rear seat, his cast clanking. "It's got to be a hundred and ten in here." Pokey's arms reached through the rear aperture to hand over the emergency medical case. The ice packs came next.

Ellis took the oxygen from Cole and put the mask over the kid's mouth.

"Skip, Dr. Morgan is behind you. He'll give you an injection of morphine . . . and Levophed," he added to tell Cole that the kid was going into shock and needed something to raise his blood pressure.

They worked fast, Ellis packing the ice around the kid's legs, Cole taking his vital signs and setting up an IV line.

Cole gave Ellis a conspirator's look. "A crane's on its way. ETA six hours."

Six hours! Where was it coming from? The third circle of hell? The kid didn't have that kind of time left, and they both knew it.

Ellis nodded.

Cole craned around to where Pokey was looking on. "Call Houston. Tell them to send the helicopter and alert the microsurgery team."

"Skip, remember what I said about reattaching severed limbs. Houston has one of the finest teams in the world."

He fought his mask to say, "You're going to cut off my legs."

"Sorry, Skip," Ellis said as he refitted the oxygen mask, "we've got to get you out of here."

Ellis worked his way into the passenger's seat. He opened his instrument bag and walked through the procedure in his mind while Cole put their patient under. "Looks like it'll have to be the guillotine technique." It was not the definitive technique, but this was not the best operating room he'd ever been in, either.

"Wait," Cole said, "you know how when you skin a rabbit there's almost nothing left?"

"What's your point?"

"Let's skin his seat. See if we can take out enough padding to free his legs."

Ellis looked at the bucket seat, and then at the dan-

gling blade. Rescuing Cole from the Brahma bull had
cost Ellis an injured shoulder and a week of work. This
folly might cost even more. "We're sitting in air, waiting for this bush-hog to crash down around our ears
and you want to start pulling out the seats?"

"The stuffing. You're going to saw through bones,
why not saw through the seat first? There's got to be a
good three inches of padding. What harm would it
do?" Cole propped his cast up on the backseat and
looked under the driver's seat.

"Besides the obvious?" Ellis motioned to the blades.
He depressed the passenger's seat and then looked at
the kid's legs. He wasn't all that sure three inches
would help and they couldn't do anything about the
springs. It was the memory of the hope in the kid's
pain-glazed eyes when he told him he was going to
pull him out in one piece that made him decide to act
like a damned fool. "All right, we'll give it a try. Fifteen minutes. That's all."

Ellis drew his scalpel across the front rim from the
inside seam to Skip's right leg. He handed the scalpel
to Cole so he could work at the back. They were knee
deep in cotton stuffing by the time Pokey came back to
report that the helicopter was on the way.

"Tell 'em we might be needing the antishock trousers."

Ellis gave Cole his best you're-the-biggest-optimist-
I've-ever-known glare. They would need the antishock
trousers only if they could get the kid out in one piece.
Inflated, the trousers constricted internal bleeding and
kept the blood from pooling in the compromised ex-
tremities so that it could circulate through the rest of
his body.

"We've suctioned as much fat out of this baby as
we're going to. Moment of truth." Ellis put a knee on
the seat and pressed for all he was worth. The kid's
legs were still dented above the pulverized femurs.

Cole twisted in behind the driver's seat. "Damn this
cast." He snaked his hands around the sides of the seat

and pressed down. The springs gave a couple of centimeters. "Give him a tug."

Ellis pulled the legs toward him with everything he had, snapping the tibia plateau like a brittle twig.

"Harder!" The springs sunk farther as Cole bore into the seat.

"There is no harder!" Ellis yelled as he pulled.

They both froze as the bush-hog groaned and shifted.

"Take it easy in there!" someone yelled from outside. "It's about to give way."

"Okay, let's try this," Cole whispered as he wiped sweat off his eyelids. "Climb on top of him. Put a foot on either side of his seat. I'll pull."

"From the backseat?" Ellis could hear the whirling of helicopter blades.

Cole moved the IV line out of his way and nudged a shoulder through the two front seats. "Satisfied?"

Ellis turned around and slipped his right leg between Skip's body and the blade poking through the door, shifted his weight slowly and dragged the other over. The car creaked.

Cole nudged his upper body between the seats and stretched out as far as he could.

"Can you reach his legs, Cole?"

"Not quite."

A flight nurse appeared at the back. "We're not quite ready for you," Ellis said with more dignity than he showed. She didn't budge, only stared. "We'll call you when we're ready for you." She still didn't take the hint. "Go away."

"Yes, Doctor."

Cole and Ellis exchanged knowing looks. This had better work or they'd be the joke of the Texas medical community.

"I've got one leg," Cole said, straining. "I can't reach the other."

One was better than none. "Ready?"

"Wait a sec. Okay, I'm ready."

Ellis tunneled into the seat. Cole grunted and yanked. Skip's right leg doubled back at a right angle. Cole's hands climbed up the leg until it circled it above the knee. Ellis moved his feet to the very edge and bore down. The right leg popped free, squirting blood like a geyser.

Cole wormed through the opening to his hips and reached the left leg as Ellis tore off his shirt sleeve to fashion a tourniquet. "Okay, Ellis, one more time." Cole walked his hands up the kid's leg until he had the knee. Ellis pushed the thigh as Cole pulled from the other side. A spring in the way kept the leg from budging. "Okay, Ellis, just relax."

"Relax! He's bleeding to death and we're drowning in blood."

Cole turned away, throwing the leg over his shoulder like a knapsack. "Ellis, has anyone told you that you have the makings of a first class asshole? Now, push that seat to the floor!"

The cracking sound came in spiraling slow motion until the rag-doll leg was freed. The kid was a mess, but he was in one piece.

"Let's get the hell out of here."

Chapter 2

Emma

Next to nobody was out and about on Thursday morning, Emma Chandler realized as her granddaughter Allison drove her through Chandler Springs on the way to her hospital. And no wonder. Emma had been right about the weather—it was proving to be a very hot and miserable summer all over East Texas. A big fat moisture-laden Gulf cloud would be a welcome sight about now.

She untwisted the tight, sweat-drenched, green silk sleeve, and pulled it away from her underarm with a sucking noise. She knew she should give up the pretense of being a size fourteen, at least during the dog days of summer.

On Main Street, Hillary Johnston was visible through her storefront window as she changed the book display. Emma shifted uncomfortably under the confinement of her seat belt, hoping Dr. Johnston's wife hadn't seen her. The woman was making a fool out of herself petitioning the school board to add another cheerleader—her chubby daughter—to the high school squad. Not only was Hillary a laughingstock, but Emma feared her revolting behavior was tarnishing Dr. Johnston's fine surgical reputation, and therefore, Chandler Medical Center by association. If Ellis Johnston hadn't come from such good stock and wasn't one of the leading thoracic surgeons in the country, she wouldn't hesitate to ask for his resignation. Anything to get rid of that cackling wife of his.

Emma pulled down the visor against the glare off the water tower. When would it ever cool off? And why hadn't she insisted on riding in the Cadillac instead of this incessantly bouncing Jeep. "Slow down, Allison!"

Allison laughed and floored the accelerator. More for the benefit of the Texas Ranger behind them than in defiance of Emma's wishes. The Texas Ranger had no jurisdiction within the city limits of Chandler Springs. And they'd passed that bean-pole lady police officer out by the highway.

"The light's turning red!"

Allison raced through the intersection as she laid on her horn. A cowboy in a white pickup returned her honk with a quick wave. "Hey, Allison!" he bellowed.

"Who was that, Allison?" Emma asked after they'd returned to a more-or-less tranquil speed.

"Just somebody, Nana." Allison adjusted the volume of the music to compete with the blaring car radios of the local hoodlums hanging out at the ramhackle Dogs and Suds Drive-In. Emma's late husband, Caleb, would never have sold the land had he known what an eyesore it would become some forty years later.

Emma reached over and turned off the radio and rode the rest of the way to the hospital in peace.

Humidity poured over her like thick gooseberry syrup as Emma struggled to get out of the Jeep. She never should have allowed Allison to buy such a car. She'd been taken in by the girl when Allison insisted that it would be easier to get up to the ranch line in a four-wheel. Emma had been hoodwinked; the only part of the ranch Allison was interested in was the elegant ranch house. Her other granddaughter, Margaret, was the one who had a knack for running the ranch. Emma had given her practically a free rein since her grandfather Caleb's passing.

Emma took a moment to admire the six-floor, red-brick hospital building she and Caleb had built twenty-five years ago. It was impressive then, and still was. A construction road obliterated a good deal of the landscaping on the bayou-side of the hospital. But by fall the industrial-size Dumpsters, port-a-potties, mountains of building material, and heavy equipment would be gone, and the grass and shrubs would be replanted, and everything would be back to normal—until a spurt of growth was again demanded in order to continue to be a state-of-the-art, full-service hospital.

The lobby of the hospital was empty, save for caterwauling voices of two admitting clerks. They were planning a Tupperware party. "Perhaps we need only one admitting clerk if there is so little work to keep them busy," Emma mentioned as Allison and she passed.

The board room was nearly empty, too. Other than Allison and herself, the only board members present were Dr. Richard Bell, chief of staff as well as her longtime friend, and Marcus Laurence, the scrawny Yankee hospital administrator. Her other granddaughter, Margaret, had gone off to California with Dr. Rosa Sanchez at the beginning of the summer and still wasn't back. Sanchez had returned in a few days, but Margaret found something that made her want to stay in California. "A surprise," was all Margaret would tell her over the phone. It was more like something Allison would pull than sensible Margaret.

Dr. Sanchez also refused to tell her anything except that Margaret was staying in Beverly Hills. That seemed respectable enough, but Emma didn't trust Dr. Sanchez's judgment. The cardiologist hadn't worked out as well at Chandler Medical Center as Emma had hoped. The hospital's well-being should be the prime concern of every doctor on the staff. And Dr. Sanchez's vendetta against Dr. William Martin was completely uncalled for. It was not her place to say that he should be sanctioned for doing seemingly unnecessary testing on Jacob. Jacob McQuade was Allison and

Margaret's other grandfather. And he had been Emma and Caleb's best friend and neighbor for over fifty years. No one had wanted him well more than Emma had. Maybe Jacob would have lived if he'd had more tests. Besides, Dr. Martin's radiology department generated a great deal of money for the less profitable areas of the hospital.

Emma had been able to nip in the bud the notion of having the medical staff sanction Dr. Martin, but if Rosa Sanchez persevered in this unhealthy endeavor by going to the county medical society like she threatened, Chandler Medical Center might be forced to pay off her contract. Emma had already instructed Marcus to have the figures computed. The hospital attorney had looked over Rosa's contract, but found that a moral clause was the only grounds for her termination. A detective agency Emma had hired had come up empty-handed on that front. If Emma were to believe the report, Rosa Sanchez lived the life of a monk and spent almost every waking hour either in her office or at the hospital.

Emma refused to let this Sanchez thing get her riled up. She had enough to worry about. Margaret and Allison's spa, now being referred to as the Houstonian Health Retreat, would have its grand opening in early September, with the girls bringing in the best caterers and musicians in Houston. There were so many loose ends to tie up; so many arrangements to be made.

Buying the ramshackle motel across the street from Stephen F. Austin Hospital and turning it into a spa had been the biggest coup for CMC in years. The Stephen F. Austin board thought they could buy the motel and turn it into a guest house for the relatives of out-of-town patients, namely from Chandler Springs. They sure got that wrong!!

That was another reason Emma wished Margaret hadn't gone gallivanting off to California. The grand opening was seriously close to fall roundup. Jacob's will left the Rocking M to the girls. It would need Margaret's constant attention if she intended to keep it running as smoothly as Jacob had. Of course Emma would give the girls as much guidance as they needed.

Emma glanced at the clock on the wall as Allison got up and twirled around for Richard in her newest creation—a denim split skirt that came to the ankles of her turquoise boots. The rhinestone vest was worn over an ivory Victorian blouse. A matching rhinestone clip held her heavy black tresses at the nape of her neck. Allison would put any fashion model to shame. And, except for the dark circles under her tired green eyes, she had flawless features.

The circles and tired eyes were surely from staying out all hours with Dr. Joshua Allister. How Allison thought she fooled her old Nana tiptoeing up the stairs at four this morning was the only mystery. Apparently the girl didn't realize Emma could hear her Jeep zoom up the dirt road and over the cattle guard.

Enough socializing, Emma decided. It was time to start the weekly board meeting. She opened her briefcase and pulled out the hospital admitting records. "Marcus"—she looked down the long mahogany table at the little administrative weasel—"I've noticed a disturbing pattern with the surgery patients. As we all know, the more difficult surgeries are done first. The surgery schedule"—Emma held it up—"shows that those are usually Ellis's cases coming from the Intensive Care Unit. The simpler surgeries are usually on people who are admitted to the hospital only for the surgery."

Marcus nodded.

"So why is the general surgeon admitting his patients to the hospital the night before? Why can't he admit them the morning of their surgeries? That way they won't have to sit around all morning worrying."

It was not like the old days when the hospital was reimbursed for its expenses. Medicare and many of the insurance carriers had set a fixed fee according to diagnosis. Chandler Medical Center received the same amount of money for a day's stay as it did for a twenty-day stay. The less time the patient spent in the hospital, the less it costed Chandler Medical Center.

"Patrick's usually in surgery assisting Ellis," Richard volunteered for Marcus, as he took off his glasses and rubbed the red marks on the bridge of his nose with his jittery hands. "If his patients aren't admitted until that morning, he won't have time to round on them." Richard was the last of the country doctors. He had brought Emma's Tommy into the world, and was there for her when he died. He was there for her when Caleb died. And he was there for her when Jacob died. She could hardly stand to see him looking so old and tired. She would have to make a decision about his replacement as chief of staff too soon, she feared. Either Dr. Martin or the psychiatrist, Meredith Fischer.

"Surely he's seen them in his office or they wouldn't be coming in for surgery," Emma reminded Richard. "Let him address their fears in his office."

"Or have a nurse do it," Allison offered.

Marcus cleared his throat. "I'll speak to him."

"Good." Emma turned her attention to the chief of staff. "Richard, have you a report for us today?"

"Well, Miss Emma, Cole Morgan has returned to work full-time." That was good news. She was still undecided about discontinuing the Chandler rodeo. She just couldn't afford to have her doctors hurt. The temporary doctor, who had been covering for Dr. Morgan in the emergency room, had run up a substantial tab at the motel. If she ever had to bring in temporary help again, she'd put them up in the hospital. There was always an empty bed somewhere.

Richard shuffled through his different reports, got up, and carried them to her. "All of the committees met this week except the surgical committee. Ellis had to work in an emergency coronary bypass. He's rescheduled the meeting for tomorrow."

"Thank you, Richard." She took the reports, which

she would read in detail later. "Marcus, have you a report for us?"

"By the way, Marcus," Allison stated, "the girls in Admitting don't have enough to keep them busy."

The hospital administrator nodded acknowledgement, cleared his throat and squared his papers. "The hospital census was up seventeen percent last quarter."

That was because of all the pediatric patients they admitted after a school bus overturned into the river. The incident was very unfortunate for everyone concerned, but the community was very lucky to have the full-service facility that Caleb had built after their son's car crash twenty-five years ago.

"I'm pleased," Marcus went on, "to announce that the Jacob McQuade Radiology Wing will break ground next Monday. I have the contractor's assurances that it will be completed by October."

"In time for the annual mammogram clinic, I hope?" Allison asked, checking the polish on her red fingernails.

"Absolutely," Marcus assured her.

"And there won't be any problems with a garage for the mobile CT unit?" Allison asked, voicing Emma's concerns. Emma hadn't liked the blueprints of the attached garage, but a mobile CT unit would provide a great service to the doctors in the smaller communities of Fort Bend and Waller counties. The truck was far too valuable to be left out in the parking lot.

"The electrical hookups will be moved to the north side of the building as you suggested."

Emma glanced down at her agenda. "The financial report, Marcus?"

Marcus was nearly finished with the financial report when the door burst open and Coral May McQuade came strutting through.

"Why—"

Emma put a hand on Allison's arm, stopping her before she forgot she was a lady and called Jacob's widow "white trash" or something worse. "Coral

May," Emma said calmly, "we're in the middle of a board meeting."

"Like I didn't know that," Coral May said in her usual uncouth tone as she continued to advance on her silver stilettos.

Even worse than breaking into Emma's sanctuary, Coral May was staring up at Caleb's portrait with unadulterated hate. "What is it you want?" Emma asked, acting much more civilized than Coral May had reason to expect.

Coral May stopped next to Emma and dug into her flashy designer purse, her heavily madeup eyes nothing but black slits. She came up with something that looked like a legal document. "I wanted to give you this personally," she said as she slapped the paper on the table in front of Emma.

Emma's resentment of the slut's audacity was off the Richter scale, and she wouldn't give Coral May the satisfaction of touching the paper.

"Aren't you going to look at it?" Coral May said heatedly.

There wasn't anything Emma wanted more than to see what Coral May was up to this time, but she would look at it when Coral May was gone. "I'm busy, now." Emma thumbed through Richard's reports, letting Coral May cool her high heels.

"Well," Coral May said after a moment, "bet you'll be all the more busy now." She turned and sashayed out.

Emma opened the document.

"What is it, Nana?" Allison asked.

"A wrongful death lawsuit against the hospital and Ellis Johnston."

Chapter 3

Pam

Pam Roberts looked over the counter of the nursing station to the activity around one of the examining tables. Except for Dr. Cole Morgan, pedicatrician Sarah McNamara, and the visiting Green family, the emergency room was empty.

"Twenty-two inches!" Cole hooted. "Twenty-two inches?"

Pam's headache wouldn't quit. Cole was being exceedingly irritating, and despite the air-conditioning streamers fluttering like battleship flags in a gale, Chandler Springs in August was living hell.

"The tape measure doesn't lie." Sarah pulled the tape measure away from the Green's baby and held it in front of Cole's eyes for his closer inspection, to the delight of the new parents.

Pam was working for Dennis Green, the regular day-shift nurse, while he took a week's vacation time to help out with his new baby. Why he wanted to bring the baby in for everyone to breathe germs on was beyond Pam. If he liked it here so much, why didn't he just stay? She preferred being charge nurse on one of the floors upstairs. Even working peds was better than being Cole's gofer. Cole was as bad here as he'd been when he was her patient in the intensive care unit after he'd been gored by a bull. And now that he was almost over his injury, he made more work for her when he tried being helpful. Who cleaned up the IV pole he tan-

gled with? Or the pint of blood that slipped out of his
sweaty palms? It sure wasn't Cole. No, his modus was
to lose his temper to frustration. Lose it more than he
cared to admit, or apologize for.

It was amazing that Sophie Drummond, the director
of nursing, wasn't here. She was always snooping
around Cole. Sophie and Cole were childhood friends
and his bull-goring accident had brought them together
again. Pam would hate Sophie until the end of time for
not giving her the evening charge-nurse position in
ICU. The stupid, stupid woman. How could the woman
not realize that she was the best nurse for the position?
So what if she had the least seniority?

Pam had half a notion to take up with Cole just to
see how Sophie would handle it. Sophie had a boyfriend, but Pam wasn't all that sure she didn't have de-
signs on Cole as well.

It wouldn't be all that hard. Many times Pam had
felt Cole's gaze on her. She knew he was interested.
And why not? She was young and pretty. Queen Bee at
CMC, if truth be told. She was petite and didn't have
an ounce of unwanted fat anywhere on her body, unlike big-boned Sophie. Pam could have Cole with a
snap of the fingers. Cole just didn't suit her. He didn't
have that worldliness, or polish, or spark, or whatever
it was Dr. William Martin possessed. Nor was he political like Bill. No, she'd set her nurse's cap for the right
doctor. When she was Mrs. Doctor William Martin, she
would have the power she needed to bring Emma to
her knees.

Aunt Emma. Emma was Pam's great-aunt, being her
granny's sister. Not that Emma knew. She'd broken all
ties with her Appalachian kin when she left home at
fifteen and made her way to Dallas where Caleb Chandler met her just after World War II. He brought her
down to the family ranch near Houston, married her,
and made her rich. Something the old woman lorded
over everyone in the community, especially those who
worked in *her* hospital.

Pam would never forgive Aunt Emma for causing her granny's death. The miser has more money than she knew what to do with. She could have sent the five hundred dollars to bail Pam's father out of jail when Granny begged her for it. It wasn't like she was going to embarrass Emma by telling everyone in Chandler Springs who she really was. All Granny wanted was bail money so Daddy could take care of all of them. Granny walked all the way into town in the dead of winter without so much as a coat on her back to use the phone at the country store and Emma pretended she didn't know who she was, and then hung up on her. Emma was going to pay plenty now. Pam would see to it.

She knew just how she would do it, too. Radiology was the only lucrative department at Chandler Medical Center, thanks to outpatient films and radiation therapy. Without it, the hospital would soon have to close its doors. And that's exactly what Pam intended. She would convince Bill to set up an outpatient radiology clinic. There was an empty lot across the road. That would be the perfect place to build their clinic. Yes, that way Pam could watch CMC crumble.

Cole ripped the tape measure out of Sarah's hands, to Betty Sue and Dennis Green's wild delight, and re-measured their week-old baby boy. "We've got ourselves a big one here."

"He's a keeper," Dennis announced with fatherly pride.

"Long and scrawny, just like his father," Betty Sue cooed as she cozied up under her husband's arm.

"Pam," Cole beckoned, "come see the little fellow."

"Long fellow," Sarah corrected.

Pam pulled at the skirt of her uniform as she got up and started over to the jolly group, a big smile on her face. She hated babies and didn't know why everybody made such a fuss over them. Babies were a lot of work. Her mother had had enough of them for Pam to know that.

"Isn't he the most precious thing?" Sarah asked in an odd mixture of baby cadence and grandmotherly pride. She wasn't the baby's grandmother, though she was certainly old enough to be. The Greens were just eating it up.

Pam smiled broadly and cocked her head to line up with the baby's. For some reason, everyone always did that when looking at babies. "My, he's a handsome fellow." She stroked its bald head. "You're going to break lots of hearts, I suspect." The baby had big ears; Pam doubted he would grow into them anytime soon.

"Well," Dennis said, hugging his wife lovingly, "we should get going. It's a long way to Grandma and Grandpa's."

Betty Sue held her enlarged midriff and belly laughed. It would be a while before she lost that gut. Pam had met her only three months ago, just after Pam graduated from nursing school and started working at CMC. Maybe Betty Sue had always looked like a butterball. "Don't think your mom and dad are going to want Willis calling them Grandma and Grandpa."

"Sure they will," Sarah guaranteed as she twisted the teddy bear's arm to play that dreadful lullaby again. Pam, for one, was getting a little sick of hearing it.

"It's like a hormonal grandparent thing," Cole said.

Pam left Sarah chastising Cole for his less-than-astute medical analysis when she noticed Coral May at the inside double doors. She didn't think anyone else had seen her. She hoped.

She guided Coral May back through the doors and looked down the corridor to make sure no one was around. Coral May was the last person she wanted to be caught talking to. "Coral May, how nice to see you."

Coral May smiled, and said in little more than a whisper, "Just wanted you to know that I served the papers on Emma."

Pam motioned for Coral May to follow her into the

waiting room. Coral May still had her obnoxiously loud Texas twang, even when she was trying to be clandestine. The television was blaring in the waiting room, though no one was there. Pam switched it off. "Tell me all about it."

Coral May leaned against the doorjamb and crossed her arms under her enormous breasts in great satisfaction. Surely, they were silicone. She must have thought they made her look sexy, but they just made her look like a cow. Pam would take her small perky ones any day. "You should have seen her, sitting at the head of the table like she owned the world."

Aunt Emma did own it, at least around these parts, and until Pam had the chance to bring her to her knees. "What did she say when she read it?"

"Didn't say anything. She was just so stunned and everything. Wish she'd had a heart attack like my poor Jacob. Wish she'd had of died right there on the spot."

No, Pam wanted Aunt Emma to suffer a slow, torturous death.

"The only thing I worry about is not suing Bill, too."

That's all Pam needed! It was hard enough trying to get Bill to divorce his wife. Having him worried about a lawsuit was going to make it a thousand times more difficult. "Coral May, now you listen to me, I'm your friend. Would I steer you wrong? Didn't I copy Jacob's hospital file for you? Didn't I show you who caused Jacob's death? If you had let your lawyer list Dr. Martin as a . . . what did he call it? . . . a correspondent, who'd testify against Dr. Johnston?"

"But he said we should have listed everybody," Coral May whined. "That we could always drop them, but we couldn't add them."

"Listen, Coral May, I had a look at those reports myself before I gave them to you. Bill had nothing to do with Jacob's death. It was that skunk Ellis."

Jacob was an old man who had had a coronary and died. So big deal. But if the widow wanted to sue his surgeon, along with the hospital, Pam would be happy to help. The pompous ass, Dr. Ellis Johnston, could stand to be knocked down a couple of pegs. Pam hadn't liked him since her first day at work when he had yelled at her for not taping Jacob's monitor lead to his chest. The lead would have been fine if stupid Coral May hadn't tried to make the old guy more comfortable. How could anyone be so stupid?

Even Coral May's sigh had a stupid Texas twang to it. "I just don't know what to do."

Pam turned on the charm. "I overheard Dr. Martin talking about you, Coral May, to Dr. Morgan."

"What did he say?" Coral May asked, trilling an octave. Strong emphasis on the last word seemed to be the Texas way. It wasn't the only thing Pam hated about Texas. Actually, there wasn't much to like. Certainly not the weather that hung around her like stringy gum.

"He was telling Dr. Morgan what a nice lady you are, and how Jacob's death had hurt you so much on account of how nice you are." Pam could have come up with something better than that if her head wasn't throbbing like a kettle drum. "Then he said how awful Ellis Johnston and Emma Chandler had been stealing your ranch that way." That should do it. Jacob left the ranch to his granddaughters. But according to Coral May, he'd sold the ranch to a housing developer just before he died. According to Ellis, who was the last doctor to see him alive, he was comatose at the time he supposedly signed the bill of sale. The court believed Ellis over Coral May.

"They done me wrong, and that's a fact!" Angry gutturals poured out of the woman's mouth. "And the high-and-mighty princesses! Did he mention those two bitches?"

"He sure did. Dr. Martin was so angry, you wouldn't believe it."

"Oh, I'd believe it, all right! They took the Rocking M like they thought they had every right in the world. Jacob wanted it to be a planned community and all,"

Coral May jabbered foolishly. "Those two are the most awful girls."

She'd give the woman that. Coral May was their step-grandmother. Pam assumed Coral May still held the dubious honor of step-grandmother even though she was now Margaret and Allison's maternal grandfather's widow. Emma was the girl's fraternal grandmother; her precious son, Tommy, had been their father. Jacob McQuade's daughter had been their mother.

Pam needed to get back before she was missed, but she didn't want to offend Coral May. She wanted Bill's name to stay off the list of correspondents.

Coral May reached under her short knit skirt to pull the tops of her nylons up. She didn't have panties on, Pam noticed before she looked away. Not only was it unsanitary, but a forty-year-old woman trying to look like a sex kitten was obscene.

"Emma and her two granddaughters think they can get away with anything. Well," Coral May said, shimmying down her tight skirt, "they stole my ranch, and they swindled the Steven F. Austin Hospital out of its motel, but they aren't getting away with murdering my poor Jacob!"

Pam's ears perked up. "What did you say?"

"They aren't getting away—"

"No, about the Steven F. Austin Hospital."

"You know, that high-priced spa the girls are opening."

Pam had read about the new venture in the *Houston Chronicle* a couple of weeks ago when they did a feature on Allison's Houston and Galveston designer dress shops, but what did that have to do with CMC's nearest competitor? Steven F. Austin Hospital was on Houston's west side. Lots of Chandler Springs's residents were willing to drive the fifty miles to be seen by big-town doctors, especially if they'd had a bad experience with CMC.

"What are you talking about?" Pam asked.

"So you don't know about that little scam." Coral May pushed away from the doorjamb and crossed to the floral couch, where she flopped down and crossed her legs and made no attempt to cover herself. "Well," she said as she pulled out a gold cigarette case and a matching lighter, "it was the day my poor Jacob had his heart attack." She opened the case exposing a row of pastel-colored cigarettes. She pulled out a green one and torched the tip, taking great pleasure in inhaling the smoke deeply into her lungs. Pam didn't know whether the gratification was from nicotine dependence or defiance of the hospital's nonsmoking policy. "I just knew he was out of sorts so I went with him to the weekly hospital board meeting. That's where I heard it. Jacob warned them that if people found out what they were doing, they'd be madder than all get out. The girls just twisted him right around their little fingers and said they were personally buying that shack of a motel with the money Jane left them." She looked up at Pam and rolled her eyes. "Jane was my Jacob's first wife. A saint, according to Jacob. Now they're laid out side by side."

As Coral May started looking around for an ashtray, Pam tried to put the woman back on the path that would do Pam the most good. "What does this have to do with the other hospital?"

"Well, they were going to buy it and turn it into a nice place where the relatives of out-of-town patients could stay."

"And Emma bought it first."

Coral May puckered lined lips around the cigarette and nodded.

Pam would look into this further. But she'd pretend disinterest in front of Coral May. Pam liked to keep her own counsel. "I should get back to work before Cole misses me."

Coral May got up, sending ashes flying. "I need to get going too. I'm meeting Salty for lunch. He's the land developer Jacob sold the ranch to. He'll want to hear all about it, too. He's still sore about the judge saying Jacob didn't sign over the ranch when he was in his right head. That was all Ellis's doing. Testifying in court like he knew what went on in my house when he wasn't even there."

Pam held the door open for Coral May.

"Boy, am I going to get even with Ellis," Coral May added as she started out. "You were so sweet to copy Jacob's records for me."

That was when Pam saw John McNamara standing by the ER doorway, a witless grin on his Down's syndrome face. Pam waited until Coral May disappeared around the corner, then started toward the boy.

Pumpkin Head held out the mail.

Pam gave him her best smile, but didn't take the mail out of the stubby nineteen-year-old's hand. "How long have you been here, John?"

John shrugged.

Long enough to hear every word Coral May had spoken, she suspected. Well, he wasn't going to sabotage her plans by innocently repeating whatever he might have overheard.

"I was just goin' in to see Cole," John said. "I want to tell him I'm buying a Stetson next Saturday. With three 'X's, just like his has. Mom said I finally saved up enough money. It's one hundred and seventy-five dollars plus tax. That's twenty-five dollars an 'X.' They don't start until after a hundred. But you can't get a Stetson for under a hundred, anyway."

"It's not nice to eavesdrop on other people's conversations."

He looked down at his scuffed shoes. "I didn't mean to. I just ... I brought...." He held out the mail.

"What exactly did you hear?"

"You mean that about copying Jacob's records?"

Pam curled her fingers around his necktie, and then

slammed him up against the wall. "You so much as open your fucking mouth about what you heard, and I'll cut out your fat tongue and make you eat it! Do you understand me?"

Chapter 4

Josh

"There's the man with the brogue," Josh Allister said as he shoved the X-ray film of an ankle in its jacket and tripped the off switch to the light box. "Must be lunch time."

Psychologist Sean O'Neill shuffled his feet in vaudeville tradition and then raised his pant legs to reveal very big shoes. "My brogues could use a wee polish."

"What?" Josh asked with bona fide confusion.

Sean threw back his head and laughed mightily. Coming from the six-six, two-hundred-and-fifty pounder, it was meaningful. The red hair and freckled face contributed to his youthful look, though Josh at twenty-seven was somewhat younger than the Irishman. "The shoe is on the other foot. Now you know how I felt not long after coming to America and someone mentioned my brogue. Brogue is the Gallic word for shoes."

Josh threw his light sports jacket over his shoulder. Sean was in shirtsleeves, but Josh hadn't been in Texas long enough to be comfortable going out without his jacket. Even on the hottest days, New Yorkers wore jackets. "Then how did it come to mean Irish accents?"

Sean shrugged. "Don't ask me. I can barely understand anything these Texans say."

"You can't blame that on Texas. It's a national saying." Josh reached up and put a hand on the giant man's shoulder. "But I know what you mean. I'll take Manhattan any day. Even Long Island."

"I'll be making a present of Ellis Island."

Ingratiated, Josh ushered his friend out the door. "Come on. Time's awasting and I need a curbstone consultation."

Sean looked down at the linoleum. "Curbstone is it?"

Josh sighed. "It's non-Gallic for cornering a colleague in the hall to get some free advice."

"Ah," the big man said with a nod, "as long as you realize my advice is worth about as much as you pay for it."

Josh didn't believe that for a moment. Sean was about as levelheaded as anyone he had ever known. Josh didn't have the greatest respect for psychiatrists— the five most screwed-up people in his medical school class, who would have benefited the most from psychoanalysis, became psychiatrists—but Sean wasn't a psychiatrist. He was a clinical psychologist specializing in dependency rehabilitation. Most of all, he came from a small rural village in Ireland and still had his family's values intact.

"Well," Josh said as they started down the hall, "if I don't like your advice, I won't pay for lunch."

Sean threw up his hands in mock anguish. "First they close down the steak house upstairs, now I have to sing for my supper."

"Life's a bitch, Sean."

"Your cornball—"

"Wait a minute." Josh stopped in front of Bill Martin's office to tell Bill that he was going to lunch. He opened the door, his mouth poised to speak, then suddenly realizing his faux pas, pulled the door to. He latched it slowly and quietly.

"What's wrong?"

Josh shook his head and hurried down the hall and out of the department, Sean a step behind. It took him half the length of the parking lot before he realized he was not the guilty party. His coming upon Bill and one of the nurses in a compromising embrace was similar to the time he was on a beach in Kauai and all the people were nude. He had felt somehow guilty for being dressed until he was back in his rented car and read the no-nude-bathing sign posted by the road separating the sugar cane field from the beach. Bill and Pam Roberts, the new nurse from Colorado, were in the wrong, like the nude sun worshippers. Josh had no reason to feel ashamed. But next time, he'd knock.

"Want to tell me what prompted this?" Sean asked as Josh backed out of his parking space.

He assumed Sean's use of the word *this* referred to his pensive mood over seeing Bill fondling the nurse Sophie had tried to set him up with before Allison had laid claim to him, but it was Allison he wanted to talk about. "At lunch, my dear friend. An expensive one because I want my money's worth."

It wasn't to be, Josh realized as they walked into the Damn Yankee Inn, Chandler Springs's only decent motel and restaurant. Allison and Emma were sitting in the corner booth having lunch. Allison waved them over.

"I thought you said you couldn't have lunch with me, that you had to work?"

Josh had become used to Allison's demanding tone over the last couple of months. It was part of what he wanted to talk to Sean about.

"Don't be upbraiding the lad," Sean chided blithely. "Surely you wouldn't have wanted me taking my noonday meal alone?"

"Of course not," Emma said with the ingratiating smile Josh had grown to realize was more of a lie than Sean's misleading statement. "Please join us."

Josh slid in beside Allison, leaving Sean to share Emma's side of the booth.

Allison tweaked his sleeve repentantly. "You look a little tired, sweetie."

Of course he looked tired. He *was* tired. Energetically tangling sheets with her every night wasn't doing his body much good, nor his spirit. If only she could ease back a little and give him some space. He reminded himself that she was compulsive and obsessive in all her undertakings, not just about their relationship. If she could only be more relaxed, like her sister, Margaret.

He wondered how much longer Margaret would be away. Even though he knew she didn't approve of him, when he was around her, he found the solace he needed to balance his life. He missed her and wished she would come back soon.

Josh couldn't blame Margaret for disapproving of him. He was becoming all the things he didn't want to be. Coming to Texas and working in this small-town hospital had been his attempt at being the dedicated, principled country doctor. If he wanted to make big bucks and hobnob with the rich and famous, he would have stayed in New York, gone into plastic surgery and shared his brother's Park Avenue office.

To make matters worse, he was coerced into radiology because he showed some talent reading films when he was an impressionable intern headed for family practice. All he really ever wanted was to help the sick—the noble call that drew him and almost every other candidate to medical school. It was once he was in the system that his goals became confused. As a radiologist he hardly saw the patients. He spent most of his time in the reading room looking at black-and-white shadows of other doctors' patients. That's what he was: a doctor's doctor.

Ordering X rays was one of the attending physicians' favorite things to do when they were in a quandary over a diagnosis. A missed diagnosis might mean a malpractice suit, something every doctor feared. No doctor was infallible, and with every error he felt remorse, despair and anxiety. There was no profession with a higher suicide rate. Ordering lots of X rays and lab work was good, defensive medicine. After all, what defense was there if a test would have detected the ailment and the doctor failed to order it? But reading X rays held almost no reward, other than black ink on the accountants' ledgers. When he found an interesting lymphoma, that's all it was, interesting. He didn't think about how the life of the patient who has the lymphoma would be changed forever. Josh was a big disappointment, even to himself.

Josh felt Allison's hand stroke his thigh. He held it steady as it threatened to move into his lap. With his free hand, he opened the menu the hostess had brought and gave it a perfunctory glance. "Well, Sean, what looks good?"

"Don't have the special," Allison said, giving a disgusted nod to her plate, "it's awful."

"A club sandwich," Sean vocalized when the young waitress came to take their order.

Josh perused the page one last time. Heat and fatigue kept hunger at bay. "A hamburger on sourdough," he declared as he closed the menu and slid it across the table to the waitress.

He looked across the table at Emma. Allison had a penchant for exaggerating the truth, but she might have been right about Emma being worried sick about Margaret being away. He was worried himself. It was so uncharacteristic of her to go away. She stayed pretty close to the ranch and didn't like being around strangers. Josh suspected it was because of the keloided facial scar, a burn she'd gotten in the car accident that had killed her parents. It had been all Allison could do to persuade Margaret to fly them to Galveston one Sunday last spring. And it was obvious that Margaret had hated every moment of it.

Josh was somewhat concerned that Jacob's death might have sent Margaret over the edge. Rosa insisted that she was fine. He respected Rosa's judgment, and knew she wouldn't have said it if not true. Still he worried. "Any word from Margaret?"

"No," Emma replied with a sigh. "Don't know what to do with that girl. She's so willful."

Allison giggled. "She's gotten so weird since Grandpa died. And to go off with Rosa after all that woman—"

She stopped abruptly when Emma kicked her under the table. Josh knew that for a fact because he caught a piece of Emma's *brogue* himself.

"With weather like this, we should all be in Los Angeles," Sean offered to ease the tension. "I've never known such heat."

They all had to agree. Hades couldn't have been much hotter. At least they could look forward to the end of summer and a little relief from the mugginess.

Not until they were on their way back to the hospital did Josh have a chance to share some of his misgivings about Allison's and his relationship, mainly her possessiveness. Allison wanted more of his time than he could give. She expected a play-by-play of every moment they were apart.

"Clinically speaking, obsessive-compulsive disorder is an incapacitating illness. Although it affects as many as four million Americans, I wouldn't include Allison," Sean explained in his best English. "It's characterized by uncontrollable obsessions and unwanted thoughts, such as repeatedly checking the doors and windows to make certain they're locked."

"Then what would you call Allison's behavior?"

"Charming. I should be as fortunate to have a woman who wanted to be with me every moment of the day and night." He laughed. "But, seriously, one behavioral therapy used for the obsessive-compulsive disorder patient might work in your situation. It dictates placing the patient in a stressful situation and showing him no harm will result. A patient who has a fear of dirt and washes his hands compulsively might be asked to touch something dirty." Sean gave a swipe to the dashboard and held up dusty fingertips. "With support from the therapist, the patient will refrain from washing, and then he sees that no harm comes to him."

"What would Allison's fear be?"

"Rejection? Fear that you don't really love her?" he shrugged. "Pure speculation, you understand, but let's say it is. Explain that a solid relationship is based on faith. That you each have your work, which dictates the need to be apart, that you trust her unequivocally, as you know she does you, and that the time you spend together is that much more precious."

Josh didn't love her and, at times, didn't even like her. He was feeling more and more trapped in a relationship that was only physically fulfilling. "But what if I don't really love her?"

"Do you or don't you?"

Josh shook his head.

"Then cut her loose, for both your sakes."

Chapter 5

Margaret

"Don't be so discouraged, Margaret. It'll look wonderful." Visitors were not allowed at the Beverly Hills clinic, but Rosa was given a professional courtesy, if not a personal one. And Margaret was so happy to see her again. Spending the summer cooped up in the clinic had been awful.

Margaret gave Rosa a tiny smile, and a facial muscle, which had previously been numb, began to tingle. She leaned forward, feeling the satin of the posh clinic's pillow fall down her back, and studied the red scar in the golden-framed mirror (only one of the many amenities the private clinic offered). She had complete faith in Rosa, and there was nothing she wanted more than to be rid of the ugly burn on her face, but she'd had lots of corrective surgeries and lots of disappointments. "It looks like raw meat."

"That's what they all say." It was Dr. Jensen's voice.

Startled, Rosa swung around. Margaret knew Rosa had specifically waited until her ex-husband had made his rounds so that she wouldn't run into him.

Instinctively, Margaret found her glasses and held them to her eyes to have a look at Dr. Jensen in the doorway. She couldn't wear them because the area over and behind her ear was swollen and throbbed from the hair transplant. A pity Allison wasn't here. Allison hated her fish-eye glasses. She called them that because they were so thick, they made her eyes look twice their size. She tossed her glasses to the bed. Even without them she could see that Dr. Jensen wore his favorite tweed sports jacket over hospital greens.

Margaret found him pleasant enough, but she sympathized with Rosa. He had left her for a local television news anchorwoman, and like any person who had been rejected, Rosa was still very bitter.

"Heard you've been over at UCLA Medical School, Rose. Coming back?"

"I was visiting friends," Rosa said cordially, betrayed only by the red anger that had climbed to her cheeks. "You look tired, Sterling. The *baby* must have kept you up all night."

He gave an embarrassed laugh. "That's what nannies are for. To walk crying babies in the middle of the night. Have you been away from civilization so long you've forgotten these things?"

"You never gave me cause to have a nanny, if memory serves."

Dr. Jensen crossed to the bed as if on parade, gave Rosa a little hug, and Margaret a big smile. "Raw meat." He nodded. "Yes, we like that look. It means we've done our job." He was as golden-boy handsome as Rosa was Latina beautiful. Margaret had watched the new Mrs. Jensen co-anchor the L.A. nightly news. She was sprightly and cute, but she lacked the elegant sophistication Rosa possessed.

"Feel it, Margaret," Rosa challenged.

Margaret touched her face gently. The only feeling was in her fingertips, as if she were touching someone else's face.

"Smooth?" Rosa asked.

Yes, it was smooth. Margaret hoped they were right about the red going away. And even if it didn't, it was a thousand times better than having all those hideous veins covering the side of her face like the branches of a dead tree.

"Smooth as the proverbial baby's butt," the proud surgeon, and new father, added.

Rosa looked at him as if, given another time and place, she would deliver a suitable repartee of her own. Instead, she traced her hand along the line of Margaret's chin. "The texture is good." She craned around to address her ex-husband. "What about the hue, Sterling?"

He shrugged. "Wait and see. There's always cosmetics, which will go on like butter now, or tattooing. She'll definitely want tattooing at the junction of the graft, near the angle of the mouth."

Margaret wasn't at all sure she'd wanted tattooing around her mouth, or anywhere else.

Rosa nodded. "That's an idea, isn't it? Define the outline of the lips."

"Well"—Dr. Jensen clapped his hands together—"I should be going." He paused a moment and then smiled at Rosa. "Maybe we could get together for a drink this evening."

Rosa smiled sweetly. "Thank you, Sterling ... but I don't drink with married men."

"Well—" he said with another clap of his hands, "I'm off."

Margaret was the only one who watched him leave. He looked back when he reached the hall. Margaret detected a whiff of regret.

"Rosa, I know it's none of my business, but I think he misses you."

"He never could make up his mind about anything." She sighed, and then smiled at her. "But he's a fine plastic surgeon and his laser treatment has made you look wonderful." She pushed the one-armed bed tray away, careful not to disturb the mirror on top, and sat on the side of the bed. She tilted Margaret's head to look at the hair transplant above her ear. Rosa tried too hard to look pleased with the welted mass of hair plugs taken from the back of Margaret's head. "I think you'll be happy with the hairline."

Margaret shrugged. "Anything would be better than the bald spot I had." She had worn wide headbands most of the time to hide the hair loss, but it didn't make any difference with her face the way it was. She was ugly and knew it. She'd been foolish to think that anyone could change that.

Rosa took her hand. "Margaret, give it some time. You really will be happy with the results."

Margaret nodded.

"Now you're being patronizing. Margaret, you are one of the nicest people I have ever met in my life. You're kind, caring, sacrificing, courageous, and loving to everyone around you. The only person you don't like is yourself. And that's a shame because you're my favorite person in Chandler Springs and I'm hoping we can be great friends."

As hard as she tried, Margaret couldn't hold back the tears. Except for her two grandfathers, no one ever made her feel special.

Rosa gathered her in her arms and rocked her. "It's all right, sweetie," Rosa whispered in her ear. "You are going to be as beautiful on the outside as you are on the inside."

The doctor wouldn't think she was so beautiful on the inside if she knew her thoughts about Josh. She felt so guilty. She had agreed to the laser surgery because of some ludicrous notion that Josh would magically fall as in love with her as she was with him. She was evil and despicable for having such thoughts about her sister's boyfriend.

Rosa gave her one final pat on the back and released her with a sigh. "I wish I could stay longer, but two days was all I could manage."

She wished Rosa could stay. Margaret felt such an overwhelming loneliness here. She longed to get back to the Circle C and Rocking M. Today was Friday. "You can't stay through the weekend?" Margaret asked softly, hoping she'd kept the desperation out of her voice.

"No, there isn't anyone to cover for me. Richard's going into Houston for his granddaughter's birthday and Tilton's on vacation. I have to get back to cover the weekend for them."

"Wish I were going. Texas gets in your bones."

Rosa patted her hand. "Give it another week."

Margaret looked back into the mirror. Perhaps a week could make a difference in her appearance, but it couldn't heal her soul.

Chapter 6

Sophie

As Sophie Drummond slumped into her chair behind the antique oak desk in her cubbyhole office, both she and the chair gave a sigh. Some days she hated being CMC's director of nursing. On this particular Friday, she simply hated being a nurse. She'd just come from Three North where a member of her church was in the end stage of carcinoma of the lung. Ellis had removed the solitary metastatic lesion a little over a year ago. Now Carl Reese was back to die.

Carl and his wife were pretty pragmatic about it, as well as courageous. Ellis had given him an extra year of life. A year in which Carl saw his oldest grandson graduated from high school and his youngest daughter married to the man she'd been living with in Houston for the last four years. Yes, they could be thankful for that, but little else.

He was emaciated, unable to eat, his urine output was low, and morphine seemed to help less and less with each passing day. It was only a matter of time.

She picked up the phone and dialed maintenance. "This is Sophie over in nursing. Will you send a recliner to room 310A?"

"Hey," came a voice at the door.

Sophie looked up to see John McNamara. She gave him the wait-a-minute sign and turned her attention to the phone. She hung up after being assured that a reclining chair would be sent up for Mrs. Reese, who had been spending every waking moment with her husband. She ushered in her visitor. "You must have mail for me, *hey*, John?"

His smile widened. He advanced in a shuffling gait and laid a ragtag collection of letters and periodicals on her desk. His smile vanished as he stared at her. "You look sad, Sophie."

Out of the mouths of children and other innocents comes such simple wisdom. Sophie gave him a reassuring smile. "I'm a little tired. That's all."

His smile returned in full force. "I saw Lisa just now. She sure is pretty."

"Thank you, John. I think she is." It had been a trying year with Lisa's rebellion, but her daughter was finally coming around. She was a hospital volunteer and she seemed to be enjoying passing out books and magazines to the patients. Sophie was happy just knowing where she was. And with both of them working in the hospital, they had something in common to talk about over dinner.

"Most of the ladies in the pink coats are old like my mom. Lisa sure is pretty in her pink coat."

Sophie wasn't quite sure how to respond to that. She didn't think it was her place to chastise him for calling his mother old. Although Sarah was somewhere in her early sixties, she had the vitality of a teenager and was by no means old. Though Sophie at thirty-seven probably seemed old to the nineteen-year-old boy. "Older women usually have more time to give to service organizations. Lisa won't have as much time when she starts back to school."

"She won't be here anymore?" he asked, as if he would sorely miss her.

"Yes, she'll come in after school for a couple of hours."

"Good, otherwise she'd miss us." He opened his mail pouch for Sophie to see. "I have to go deliver the rest of the letters." She picked up the pile of mail as he started out. "See you tomorrow." He stopped. "I mean

Monday. Tomorrow's Saturday." He sighed. "I'm buying a Stetson tomorrow, just like Cole's. Right after Mom and I clean the house and do the grocery shopping. Then we'll go to eat and to the movie. Sunday we go to church and read the newspaper and do the wash and ironing." He sighed again, as if he was already tired just from the thought of all that work. Then he started out, his shoulders slumped that much more. "See you Monday."

"See you, John." She pulled the letter opener from her middle drawer and sorted through the mail for anything that might be interesting or personal. She settled for the envelope from the American Nurses' Association. It turned out to be a dues notice.

"Hey!"

She recognized that "hey" without looking up. "Hey yourself, Cole."

"A hero's welcome if I ever heard one," he said as he hobbled toward her desk. In his caneless hand, he had the Greek mythology book she'd been reading aloud to him while he was in traction. He tossed the book into her out file and sat in her spare chair. "Need to catch my breath."

"You're doing great, Cole."

He tapped the cane to his cast. "Yeah? You should be on this side."

"For being stampeded by a bull, you look great. Believe me, I saw you just afterwards."

He laughed. There wasn't anything funny about it. She had been scared spitless that he'd die. Just the thought of losing him sent terror to her very soul. It had been a long time, but she'd never gotten over him the way he had her.

"John was just here. I can't tell you how thankful I am that you taught him that endearing 'hey' of yours," she added sarcastically.

"You're welcome." He brought out a pack of chewing gum and offered her a piece. She declined. He unwrapped a stick and stuck it in his mouth and started working on it. "Think I should teach him to bull ride next?" He shot the crumpled wrap toward her trash can. She'd have to remember to look for it under her desk. Hard to believe he used to throw fifty-yard passes. That's how he came to have the two front caps he was showing. He always smiled when he was embarrassed.

"How 'bout teaching him 'no, sir,' and 'yes, ma'am'?"

"Would, but I think he's mad at me. He left the ER mail in the hall outside the door."

"That's not like him, is it?"

He shrugged and pointed to the book. "Found it in my official personal-belongings bag when I got home. Right there with my very own water pitcher. Drained, of course. And my very own thermometer y'all got such a kick out of sticking up my rectum."

"Well, I make home visits if you ever need your temperature taken again."

"One of life's little pleasures." He smiled but she didn't.

"That reminds me, Cole, the charge nurse wants to know if you want your bedpan."

He pretended to think about it. "No, I guess not. My house is small, I don't know where I'd put it."

"Under the bed is always a good spot."

"I keep multiplying dust bunnies under my bed."

"You were always so self-sacrificing." She sighed. "All right, I'll let them know you're donating it to the hospital." She waited for him to make a move toward leaving. He didn't. "Anything else?"

"Can't I just sit and visit with an old friend?"

"Sure." She threw the pile of mail into her in box. "Your daughter's working here now?"

Sophie nodded. "Volunteering, anyway. Now that she's sixteen she'd like to have a paying job so she could buy a car, but we struck a compromise. I paid for her driver's license, upped the insurance and let her drive my car. Sometimes."

"Sixteen. Has it really been sixteen years?"

Terror tore through her like a speeding train through a tunnel. "What do you mean?" she asked guardedly.

He lifted his shoulders. "Nothing. It just seemed like yesterday when I called your mom looking for you after the school dorm said you'd moved out." He shook his head. "I couldn't believe it when she told me you'd gotten married."

She swallowed a lump that had risen in her throat. Neither of them said anything. But she was pretty certain they were both thinking the same thing. The page broke the choking silence.

"Dr. Morgan, report to the emergency room. Dr. Morgan, report to the emergency room."

"It's nice to know someone missed me," he uttered as he struggled out of the chair. "Pam's the greatest. I can't believe she's fresh out of school. She knows what I want before I do."

Sophie nodded. "She put herself through nursing school working as a nurse's aide. We're lucky to have her, all right. She is the greatest."

"I almost hate to see the week end. And speaking of Dennis's return, did you see him and Betty Sue when they were here with the baby yesterday?"

She put on a bright smile. There was nothing she liked more than new babies and proud parents. "No, but I saw the little fellow in the nursery. Gawd, he looks like his dad!"

"Dennis is the father, no denying that."

Sophie nodded weakly and pulled her mail out of the wire basket as he started out.

Chapter 7

Ellis

Big "X"s ran down the columns of Ellis's scheduling book except between two-thirty and five-thirty where the names of his patients were crammed. Today his patients would be packed into his office's waiting room, not because surgery ran overtime, but because he had to make a command appearance in the administrator's office. The missive didn't say what it was about; only that he was to be there at three o'clock sharp. It was the perfect way to end the week.

He had managed to see Mrs. Wright, reassure her that the mole he'd burned off her beautiful back was not malignant, and sent her on her way. He had even lifted Mr. Becker's chart out of the slot by the door, but Hillary's appearance quashed any notion of going into the examining room.

Hillary was out of sorts again. It was obvious from the way she bolted up the hall, if not the anger on her face.

"What's wrong, Hillary?" he asked as she got closer.

"Don't 'what's wrong, Hillary,' me!" She shifted her feet angrily, her face crimson with accusation. "What about lunch? You were supposed to stop by the book store and pick me up!"

"Hillary!" He grabbed her flailing arm, and then shielded himself behind Mr. Becker's chart as her other hand lashed out. She missed him as he stepped to the side, but caught the corner of the seascape on the wall behind him. A reverberating crash brought Patrick, a nurse, and his half-dressed patient from one of the examining rooms. They watched the performance only long enough for Patrick to herd them back inside and close the door.

"You goddamn bastard!" she yelled as she struggled out of Ellis's hold.

"Calm down, Hillary." She wasn't the only one on edge, but he hoped his voice was calmer than he felt. He knelt down and gathered up the papers from Mr. Becker's chart and put them back in the folder. There wasn't any point in surveying the damage to the picture. By the time he'd straightened up, the storm cloud had passed from her face. Thank God. He didn't have time for this shit today. "We didn't get out of surgery until two. Lunch completely slipped my mind."

"You could have called," she said, more hurt than angry.

He kissed her cheek. "I'm sorry, sweetheart, I completely forgot until now."

She fingered his tie. "You didn't eat at all?"

"No." He glanced at his watch. It was almost three. He'd have to give Mr. Becker a quick once-over and hightail it to the hospital.

"Neither have I. You can take me to lunch now."

He looked at her incredulously. "Hillary, didn't you see the waiting room? I have patients to see."

"And what about me?" she screamed.

"I think a less open forum is in order." Ellis took her arm and by no means gently dragged her into his office. "Look, Hillary. In less than"—he glanced at his ticking watch—"three minutes I'm expected to attend a meeting at the hospital. I have a patient stripped to his undershorts in an examining room and half a dozen more in the waiting room. I'll take you to dinner."

She pursed her lips and looked at him from under hooded lashes. "And you've also forgotten we're going next-door to the VanFleet's for dinner!" He hated going over there and watching the whole family shovel down food like pigs at the trough. Bad enough he had to see Ty VanFleet at the hospital.

He could hear the seconds ticking away. "I'll make it up to you later." He gave her a peck on the cheek and raced out, closing the door behind him. He heard the door open about the time he had his hand on the examining room's doorknob, and slam shut as he slipped into the room Mr. Becker was occupying.

His watch had ticked away another twenty minutes before he reached Marc's office. He was out of breath from running across the parking lot, but that was nothing compared to the stampeding horse stomping across his chest when he saw the elite gathering.

The hospital's attorney, Harry Wilder, rose and extended his hand. Emma Chandler inclined her head nobly, her back as rigid as a hickory tree. Marcus motioned him to the straight chair that had been brought in from somewhere to accompany the two blue-fabric easy chairs that somewhat matched the larger chair Marcus was settling back into behind his desk. The conclave reeked of disaster.

Harry gripped his hand reassuringly. What Harry was reassuring him about, Ellis had no idea, but feared he was about to find out. Find out in spades, he soon learned.

Finally, the news was out. "Let me get this straight." Ellis looked directly at Harry since he was the bearer of the bad tidings. "Mrs. McQuade is suing the Chandler Medical Center and me for introducing the gram-negative bacterial infection that killed her husband via an incision on the dorsum of the foot during the lymphangiogram which *Bill Martin* preformed? This is utterly preposterous."

Marcus held up the X-ray report gingerly and read. "An incision was made on the dorsum of the foot by Dr. Johnston, who then injected ten milliliters of radiopaque dye."

"I made that incision superior on the dorsum to the one Martin had botched." It was all Ellis could do to keep his temper. "Martin's was a sloppy mess and I'm not at all surprised to hear that it became infected. He had no business doing the lymphangiogram in the first place, and especially under such filthy conditions. The room was under construction and there was plaster everywhere."

Marcus read through the rest of the report. "There is no mention of any other incision on the report."

"Legally, Ellis," Harry counseled, "you are the physician of record." Harry gave him a look of compassion, which Ellis suspected was more for show than an indication of his true feelings.

"Look, Bill called me in. I got up out of my sick bed to come in and help him out. If it had somehow slipped your minds, I too was gored by Cole's bull. Believe me, I was Jacob's saving grace. Bill is responsible for this debacle, not yours truly."

"Not according to the X-ray report," Marcus pointed out yet another time, lest Ellis forget.

"The X-ray report which Bill dictated!" Ellis slumped back in the chair. Jesus Christ, he was talking himself blue in the face and they still looked at him as if they didn't get it. "I can't believe this."

"What difference does it make who's responsible?" Emma offered authoritatively. "Let's stop beating around the bramble bush. We have decided to settle quietly out of court. That'll be the end of all this ugliness."

Marcus leaned back in his chair and turned away as if to tell Ellis that the unilateral decision to settle out of court was not of his doing.

Settling out of court was the same as admitting he was guilty. Even if they kept it quiet so as not to undermine the faith his patients had in him, he wasn't going to take the blame for something he didn't do. He had performed successful bypass surgery on Jacob, he had come in and cleaned up the mess Bill had made, he had driven out to Jacob's ranch to check on him, at Rosa's insistence, after Jacob had checked himself out of the hospital against medical advice. That was beyond the call of duty. He had given Jacob his best, and he wasn't about to let someone say he didn't!

"That's not the way I see it," Ellis said with as much restraint as he could manage. "It makes one hell of a difference to me, not to mention my insurance carrier. I'm not guilty of malpractice and I refuse to say I am."

"Don't buck me on this, Ellis!"

He had never heard Emma so much as raise her voice before. From the looks she garnered, Ellis suspected he was not the only one. "Or what?" he asked in a civil tone. "You'll close down the surgical wing?"

Emma regained her composure and gave him a viper's smile.

Chapter 8

Allison

The sound of shattering glass stopped Allison in midsentence. She left the moronic carpenters in the reception area and hunted for the source of the crash. Why couldn't the carpenters understand that the wood for the reception counter needed to match the door frame and window molding?

Allison didn't have time to bother with any of these stupid Houston workmen. She had job applicants stretching to kingdom come lined up around the entire block. Her ad in the paper had brought a hundred applicants for every job. How was she going to interview that many? But what could she do? The Houstonian Health Retreat couldn't run itself. It was hardly a self-service spa.

The source of the crash was in the aerobics room, Allison soon discovered. "Look what you've done!" she screamed at the two delivery men who had tried to carry one of the new machines right through the looking glass. Only this time, she was madder than the Hatter. Huge glass shards, like uplifted swords, replaced the middle section of floor-to-ceiling mirrors along the north wall. "Are you two stupid or something? Couldn't you tell that—"

"Calm down, lady." The huskier of the two movers whipped off his bandanna headband as he started toward her. "It's an accident. The insurance company will cover it." With one hand he wrapped the bandanna around his bulging biceps. Droplets of blood dripped onto the hardwood floor. He gave her a disarming smile as he held out his injured arm. "Can you tie it for me? Or is that asking too much?"

Taken back by his arrogance, the only thing she could do was to grab hold of the bandanna's ends like he demanded. She tied the makeshift bandage around the rock-hard muscle, a little too tight just to watch him squirm. Ballooning veins like tight piano wire threatened to burst out of his deeply tanned flesh. His shoulders! Never in her life had she seen such broad shoulders. He was a handsome specimen. "Does that hurt?"

He shook his head, a golden lock tumbled arrogantly over his forehead. His sexual attractiveness was not lost on either of them.

"You need stitches."

He gave the cut a perfunctory glance. "I'll put a couple of butterfly strips over it. That should hold it."

"There's a hospital right across the street." She hoped her grandmother would never get wind of her suggestion to send business to Chandler Medical Center's competitor.

He gave her a look that said she was being silly. He didn't know the half of it.

"You don't like doctors?" she asked with enough haughtiness to rival his own.

"It's not a matter of liking. Doctors don't know the first thing about holistic care of the body. No one messes with this body." His pecs undulated hypnotically under his sweat-slicked T-shirt. It was not altogether an unpleasant sight. "Each man's body is his temple and should be treated with respect." He gave a tiny pat to his tight tummy.

"And each woman's?"

"With even greater respect." Their eyes held long enough to read the other's thoughts. "Though no one can respect someone else's body unless that person respects it first," he went on, priest to acolyte. "Exercise, proper diet, no drugs, no smoking. All parts to make a perfect whole."

Allison nodded. She liked a man with strong convictions. She liked this one a great deal. "And what of my body?" She twirled around. "What would you change?"

From head to toe, she felt his admiring eyes burning through her like an all-consuming fire. "You need more sleep. Your eyes are tired. Your left shoulder is a fraction higher than the right. Carry your shoulder bag on the right side for a while."

Allison was truly amazed. Her purse did have a shoulder strap, which was always slung over her left shoulder. She was at a loss to know what to say, so instead of saying anything, she simply watched his chest rise and fall as he breathed. The spell was broken when the other delivery man stepped close enough for Allison to smell his sour sweat.

"Allison Chandler," she said, extending her hand in the hunk's direction before the smaller mover could interrupt.

Sparks flew as he touched the tips of her fingers. He took her hand stalwartly and pressed it into his. "Chandler? Of the Circle C?"

"And Rocking M." But what of this charismatic man? "And you are?"

His smile widened. "Sorry, ma'am. Jinx. Bobtail for Tom Jenkins. It's a pleasure to make your acquaintance, Allison Chandler."

It was not lost on her that his good-ol'-boy drawl appeared from out of left field about the time he found out who she was. "If you think I'm a country hick, Tom, guess again."

He cleared his throat and tested the kind of smile an embarrassed person might try. "It really is Jinx, if you don't mind," he said in a much more urbane tone that told her that he realized they had sized each other up and were finished playing games.

"Tell me, Jinx, how would you like a job working here for me?"

Chapter 9

Pam

Pam could tell that she wouldn't be making any more notations on Mrs. Willows's out-patient evaluation form—at least, not until she was finished watching Lisa Drummond steal Meredith Fischer's prescription pad. Meredith had left her white lab coat on the doorknob to the ER's waiting area while she decided whether the failed suicide should be admitted to the medicine floor or sent into Houston to the psychiatric hospital.

The young guy had borrowed a buddy's pickup and drove it into Buffalo Bayou, but jumped clear at the last moment. He had had only scratches until the buddy beat him to a bloody pulp for wrecking his truck.

Pam was more interested in whether Meredith would notice the missing pad and what Lisa was planning to do with it, than the well-being of the stupid guy who couldn't even do a decent job of killing himself. Pam had little patience for wimps. Besides, the boy's verbal abuse of both Cole and her when they were trying to treat him fell far short of good manners. She hoped they did send him to Houston.

Lisa slipped the purloined pad between two magazines she'd picked up off the waiting room's coffee table and placed them on her cart and wheeled off around the corner without so much as looking back. The girl had guts, Pam would give her that. She hoped

the girl did get away with it. For a while. Long enough
to do some real damage. Pass some prescriptions, have
the authorities after her. Wouldn't that be a kick in the
ass to Sophie's reputation when it eventually came
out? That's the kind of gossip the CMC staff thrived
on. It wouldn't do Aunt Emma's reputation much good
either.

Pam turned back to the patient on the examining table. Mrs. Willow, a seventy-year-old woman complaining of a gastrointestinal bleed, was waiting for the
X-ray tech to come for her. She was clearly failing, not
that that nincompoop Dr. Tilton and his senile partner,
Dr. Bell, could tell. Tilton had seen her in the office
and pronounced her well, saying her diverticulosis
must be acting up again. People in their forties had diverticulosis; seventy-year-olds had colon cancer. Fortunately, Mrs. Willow had come into the ER where Cole
had the authority to order a barium enema.

It had turned out to be one hell of a Friday afternoon
in the emergency room and they labored as hard as the
humming air-conditioning unit. What a way to end the
week! Oh, well, Pam's day shift would be over soon
and then she'd move on to Three North Monday evening. Until then, she was free. And Bill and she were
going to make the most of it.

Bill had an East Texas radiologists' meeting in
Houston Saturday and made some excuse to Karen
about a pre-meeting Friday night and a post-meeting
Saturday night. Whatever. Pam would get him for two
solid nights.

"Still here, Mrs. Willow?" The curtains parted and
Cole lumbered between the two examining tables to
have a look at the evaluation form. The robust voice
was pure bravado and it certainly didn't fool Pam.
Cole was in obvious pain. "Pam, why don't you give
X-ray a quick call to see what's holding up the show.
We need some eight-by-ten glossies of our star. And
call upstairs and tell them we've got one for them."

So the suicide wouldn't go to Houston after all. Pam

was at the nurses' station placing the first call when
Meredith retrieved her jacket. She didn't seem to notice her missing pad.

"Thanks," Cole bellowed after her.

Meredith gave a little wave and took off.

Pam watched and waited for Meredith to return.
After the second call, telling Three North to send an
orderly after the suicide and Meredith still hadn't returned searching for the pad, Pam was fairly certain
Lisa had gotten away with the theft.

So far.

The dome light broke the darkness. Neighborhood
kids loved shooting out the lights in the parking lot
with pellet guns. "What's in the box?" Pam asked as
she climbed into Bill's BMW.

Bill tossed her overnight case in the back next to a
huge box.

"Some sample drugs Karen and her wives' group
gathered from the doctors' offices. It's one of their
charity projects. She wants me to drop them by the
East Side clinic tomorrow. Nothing like driving a
BMW out to the docks. I'd be lucky if it isn't
stripped."

"I could run them out while you're in the meeting
tomorrow morning," she said, wanting to please. After
all, it was only a matter of time before she replaced
Karen as the head of the Medical Wives' Auxiliary. "I
could take a taxi."

He patted her knee, then ran his hand up under her
skirt. "No, no. Take the car. I trust you with it."

She snuggled into him, despite the console that
twisted her left ankle.

"Be sure you get the BNDD number of whatever
doctor accepts them. None of the do-gooders stopped
to consider that they're dealing with controlled sub-
stances. They forget that the reason they have samples
of drugs around their houses is because their husbands
are doctors."

Pam was certain none of the medical wives ever forgot they were married to doctors. Bureau of Narcotics and Dangerous Drugs number. Every doctor was issued one. She looked over her shoulder. "What's all back there?"

Bill lifted his shoulders. "Don't know. No one took inventory. Whatever was lying around the offices getting ready to expire."

No one took inventory? She'd go through the box herself before she handed it over to the clinic. "I heard something just awful, sweetie." She threw his arm over her shoulder and snuggled into him as much as she was able. He veered over into the next lane on Interstate 10, before correcting.

"What's that?"

"Oh, it's just so awful. Maybe it isn't true."

"What?" He flashed his bright lights at the slow-moving car in front of him.

"That Mrs. McQuade is suing the hospital."

"What's with this guy?" He pulled back his arm and put it on the steering wheel as he changed lanes. When he was ahead of the turkey, and back in the right lane, he said: "It's true, all right. Rosa and Ellis mismanaged the McQuade case and now the hospital will have to pay for their mistakes."

"Dr. Rosa Sanchez? She's involved? And Dr. Johnston?" she added as an after thought. Coral May hadn't said anything about suing Rosa, and she hadn't noticed anything in the chart to indicate Rosa had mismanaged Jacob. Pam liked Rosa a great deal. She was kind, considerate, helpful, and stuck up for her when Ellis had made such a big deal about the tape.

"Jacob McQuade had a lymphoma, which Rosa refused to identify or treat."

Pam righted herself in her seat and worked a kink out of her neck. From what she could gather from Jacob's records, there was a question early on about a spot on the lung, but all tests came back negative. "I thought he died of septic shock due to an infected incision."

"That might have been the immediate cause, but had she diagnosed his lymphoma properly and turned him over to me for radiation therapy, I assure you, I would have done something about his infection. Mismanagement, pure and simple."

Everyone certainly had a selective memory when it came to Jacob McQuade. She let it go, wondering what he'd say if he knew how close he had come to being named in the suit. "Think the hospital will settle out of court?"

"I certainly hope so. CMC doesn't need the kind of bad publicity malpractice lawsuits are noted for. We don't need the townsfolk driving into Houston for their health care. Business is bad enough as it is."

No, we wouldn't want poor Aunt Emma to get any bad publicity out of this. Pam wondered how well Aunt Emma was sleeping these nights.

Chapter 10

Ellis

Ellis found no quarrel with Ty's work as a pathologist, but otherwise he was a total jerk. And he wasn't at all happy about spending Friday evening with him. He needed to talk to Hillary about the lawsuit.

Hillary and he sat around the end of the dining room table nearest the kitchen with Tyler and his wife, Beth. Ellis's children, Amy and Will, were at the foot with the VanFleet's four little kids. The oldest piglet must have been in school, but the other three were surely too young. All four of the kids were good eaters and had the family roundness.

He shouldn't be so smug. His twelve-year-old Will was far from stocky, but like Hillary, Amy was on the high end of her desired weight and would probably fight it all her life.

"Ellis, you hardly touched your plate."

He glanced across the table and gave Beth a grim smile. She was big-boned and could tip the scales, but she didn't have a bad case of the fats like her husband. Her features were strong and harsh and she looked centuries younger than Ty, though he wasn't nearly as old as he seemed. Thin hair and stooped shoulders contributed to the notion that he was middle-aged, when in fact he was in his mid-thirties.

"It couldn't have been the meal, honey bunch," Tyler VanFleet said as he reached in front of Ellis for another high-calorie popover. "The standing rib roast was perfection."

Beth thumbed at her husband. "He should know. There isn't another gourmet of his caliber within a thousand miles."

Gourmand was the word she was looking for. Eating was one of life's *big* pleasures for Ty.

"Everything was absolutely wonderful, Beth," Hillary stated like a practiced dinner guest. "Ellis just isn't feeling well." Her motivation for that must have been their little conversation about canceling dinner. Tell them he came home from work sick, Ellis had begged.

Ty motioned for the butter. "Shoulder still bothering you?" Ty was referring to the bull horn Ellis caught while trying to free Cole from the bull. Being a rodeo clown had cost Ellis plenty.

"No, I'm being sued." Ellis grabbed for the butter as it plummeted out of Hillary's hand. Hillary was speechless for once, but shot him a look of reproach.

Ty's knife and popover had gotten to his plate without Ellis noticing. He shook his head when Ellis offered the butter. Ty had lost his appetite, too. The fear of malpractice hangs over every doctor's head. "Sued? What did you do?"

"It's what Bill did." He told them the whole sad story.

"When we were at Ty's ten-year reunion," Beth broke the unhealthy silence, "we sat at a table with six other couples from medical school. Ty was the only doctor at the table who hadn't been sued." If the little anecdote was meant to cheer Ellis, it failed miserably.

"Well, Ty, guess you can say the same about this table," Ellis's tone killed the joke.

"What are you going to do?" Ty asked empathetically.

"Fight. Have my day in court."

"But you said Emma wants it settled quietly out of court."

"This is my reputation we're talking about. I'm not going to sit back and let them do this to me."

Amy and Will looked at him as if their whole worlds had fallen apart. He gave them a reassuring smile. What he was reassuring them for, he had no idea. The little kids were getting restless. They couldn't have cared less about Ellis's plight if the knife fencing and cup banging were indications.

Ty pushed back from the table. "Let see if I still have a therapeutic drop of something or other in my study."

Beth raised a disapproving eyebrow and started gathering up dishes, spilling an ample portion of freckled cleavage. "Why don't you kids put on the *Beauty and the Beast* video. We'll bring you the dessert Mrs. Johnston brought over as soon as we clean up."

"Devil's food cupcakes," Hillary said too brightly as she and Amy pitched in.

"Hooray," three of the four trilled in soprano voices. The other was busy sucking his thumb.

Will played Pied Piper to the family room. Ellis followed Ty to the study.

Ty tripped the light switch, then dimmed it. It took a moment for Ellis's aching pupils to dilate, more so than normal because the room was designed to be dark. The windowless study was paneled in a dark wood on three sides with built-in bookcases on the fourth. His medical books and journals were meticulously stacked on the dusty shelves. A printed area rug, predominantly brown, covered most of the parquet floor. The wastebasket hadn't been emptied for some time. Ellis assumed the study was Ty's private domain.

"It's like a celebrity suing *The Enquirer,* Ellis—no one remembers whether he won or lost, just what he was accused of." Ty rounded the portable bar. "Better to settle quietly out of court and have it over with." He blew dust out of two shot glasses and arranged them on the bar. Ellis took a stool.

"Is that the prevailing wisdom?" Ellis asked with the bite of a scorpion.

"Snap all you want, Ellis. I know how you must be feeling." He stuck his right hand deep into his pocket and dug out a ring of keys.

"No, every doctor at the table of your ten-year reunion knows how I feel. Not you," Ellis answered.

Ty gave him a Cheshire Cat grin as he searched his ring for the dinkiest key, which unlocked the liquor cabinet. "And how thankful I am. But it's all luck. Medicine is not a science. It is the most scientific of the arts. We can't be right every time. You just hope you bury your mistakes deep. Say, six feet under."

"Tyler, I did nothing wrong. I got out of my sick bed to help Bill. He had already done the damage. Hard telling what would have happened to Jacob if I hadn't gone in."

"Jacob died. It doesn't get worse than that." Ty started to laugh, but stopped short. He sighed, wiped his brow, and bent down to look through his liquor cache.

"You're pretty cavalier about my problem, Ty."

"No more than you would be if it were my problem." He brought out a bottle of brandy, shook his head, and exchanged it for Black Velvet. "Smooth-blended Canadian whisky," the purveyor of fine spirits read from the label before pouring. "We'll get rip-roaring drunk and it won't seem half as bad."

"Until tomorrow," Ellis said as they clicked glasses.

It was as he topped their glasses a second time that Ty asked: "Who's your insurance carrier?"

Ellis told him.

"Thank goodness."

"Why?"

"They're not mine." Ty wanted him to laugh, but Ellis wasn't drunk enough.

"How come? Thought everyone switched over when they gave the County Medical Society a twenty-percent group discount."

"Too much trouble to switch over."

They concentrated on their drinks.

"You think I'm going to lose?"

"I posted Jacob. He had an overwhelming gram-negative bacterial infection originating in the subcutaneous tissue of the right lower extremity. If you can prove the infection occurred after he left the hospital, you're off the hook. If not . . ." he put the rim to his lips and sucked in.

"It didn't. Billy boy did it while he was in the hospital. But forgot to mention his botched attempt when he dictated the reports."

"Sounds like something Bill would do. See, he knows about burying his mistakes deep." Tyler topped off their drinks. "By the way, I was mightily impressed with the blind stitching you whipped into Jacob's chest incision," he added in booze-supplied sensibility.

"You be sure to mention it to the jury."

"The trial won't be for months. Lots of things can happen in the meantime."

"Like what?" Ellis asked, more thick-tongued than he cared to admit.

"Mrs. McQuade might change her mind. You might change yours. Tort reform might put caps on malpractice, making it less lucrative for scum-of-the-earth lawyers. A nuclear bomb might destroy the judicial system as we know it. Lots of things."

"Mighty few mights. If that isn't an oxymoron in itself." Ellis poured this time. "My favorite is the nuclear bomb."

"I'm partial to that one, also."

It was as good an excuse as any to drink to each other's health. They finally ran out of excuses about the time they ran out of Black Velvet, and called it a night.

Though they lived but a few acres apart, Ty gave Ellis a ride home. And it was a good thing, neither of them was in any shape to walk. Ty wasn't the best driver in the world, but Ellis was home safe and sound and he wasn't hearing any big bangs behind him. The lights were out, giving Ellis an excuse for tripping up the stairs and falling on his face. It didn't hurt—his whole body was numb.

What hurt was the reverberation of Hillary's voice when he made it to the bedroom. Somehow he'd expected consoling words, or applause for maneuvering the swaying staircase.

"Why didn't you tell me earlier? Do you know how humiliating it was to hear in front of the neighbors?"

The neighbors most likely heard all of their conversations first hand if the windows were open. Maybe even closed.

"I'm sorry, Hillary," he said as he flopped facedown on his side of the bed.

"You're drunk!"

He hoped it was a rhetorical remark. His mouth was pressing against the suffocating sheets and he didn't have the strength to save himself, let alone reply.

"How could you do this to me?"

A rhetorical question.

"Can you hear me?"

Of course he could hear her. He had cotton in his mouth, not in his ears. And she wasn't exactly whispering.

"Ellis, talk to me!"

He turned over and stared at the ceiling fan. He wasn't sure whether it was working or not. "What do you want me to say?"

"I want you to tell me what you plan to do about this lawsuit. I want you to explain why you would make us the scandal of C Springs. Why can't you settle quietly out of court like Emma wants?"

He heaved his shoulders as he thought. "In the morning, Hillary. In the morning." Ellis had a new appreciation for Tyler and was going to make room for him at the Maverick table come Monday morning Morbidity and Mortality conference. "Tyler's all right. You know that, Hillary?"

"Oh, go to sleep."

With pleasure.

Chapter 11

Lisa

"Where are they?" Ray asked as he parked his 1960 Plymouth at the curb around the corner from the Medicine Mart. It was the third Medicine Mart they'd been to tonight and the fifth Houston pharmacy.

Lisa handed Ray the Demerol and Preludin scripts without raising her head off the pillow on the front seat. Her mom was working an evening shift for somebody and wouldn't be home until eleven-thirty or so. Ray had promised to get her back to C Springs before then. She wasn't worried: Ray could drive stoned.

"Move over behind the steering wheel just in case we have to take off in a hurry." He yanked the pillow out from under her and stuck it in his jacket. Preludin was an amphetamine prescribed for weight loss and Ray wanted to look as fat as possible.

Lisa giggled at how funny he looked. "Be sure to cough for them."

"I'll have a regular coughing fit." He got out and slammed the door with a thick metallic thud.

All of her senses were incredibly alive. Pleasure, power. Everything was crystal clear despite her blurred vision, ringing ears, and racing pulse. She wanted to soar like this forever. Speedballing was the ultimate, nothing could come close to it. Fifteen-hundred-milligram injection of Preludin followed by a five-hundred-milligram injection of Demerol. Sometimes coke followed by heroin, depending on what was available. The ultimate high, ultimate chill-out.

Troubles with her mother, school friends, everything fell away with speedballing. She hovered over her body. Floating. Light as a feather. Floating.

She wished he'd left on the radio. She reached out for the knob, but the knob went right through her hand as if she were in another dimension. It was so mind-boggling, so enlightening. She tried it with the steering wheel. But instead of her hand floating through it, the horn honked. She yanked it away.

"What did you do that for?" Ray asked as he knocked her head to get her to scoot over.

"I didn't do it. It honked by itself."

"Didn't I tell you to sit behind the wheel just in case we had to take off in a hurry?" He squashed her into a two-dimensional being as he reached over and threw the white sack into the glove compartment. "You're so trashed you don't know what you're doing."

She smiled and recaptured the moving sensation as he sped down the street. She was the ruler of her mortality. She was powerful and could do anything she wanted.

Colors, more intense than ever before, flooded over her like a warm bath as they passed one neon sign after another. She liked the smell of green best. And blue. Blue smelled so heavenly. And banana. The stereo boomed red. Ray and she loved red. It was so earthquaking loud. Waves of music roared over her like a Galveston tide.

Neon strobing.

Strobe, strobe, strobe, strobe, strobe. Five-sense strobe. No, four senses. She couldn't taste the colors. Only cotton.

"Give me the next two," he commanded as he pulled into the drugstore parking lot. Six. Six bags full.

"The colors hurt, Ray."

"The floodlight, you mean? Close your eyes." He ripped the crinkled scripts out of her hand. "You can't shoot LSD and speedball at the same time. What do you expect?" His voice boomed out of hidden stereo speakers. The door opened, the bench seat whispered her name as it rose around her, leveling her head. The door slammed with an air-sucking bang. She could hear the clomping of Ray's elephant feet even as he stepped into the shadow of the store.

Yes, she could. She could shoot LSD, amphetamines, narcotics, anything she wanted. She loved the magic Ray's needle could work. Why did he worry about overdosing? Wasn't death the ultimate high?

"You still up?" Lisa's mother asked as she turned on the kitchen light.

Lisa shook her head, and then nodded. "Yes," she said instead, drumming a tattoo on the edge of the kitchen table.

Sophie came closer. Stood accusingly over her. "Why are you so jumpy?"

Because she was wired. What did the witch think?

Her mother put a hot hand on her forehead, the downy golden hair on her thick-boned arm swayed like a field of wheat on a breezy day. "You don't feel feverish." Her blue eyes glistened with motherly concern. "Your eyes look glassy." Her full lips pursed as she tried to diagnose. "You sure you're all right, baby?" she asked, as if to a tiny child.

Lisa didn't need her concern. "It's hot, Mom. Stifling. Why can't we have air-conditioning like everybody else?"

"And how do you expect me to pay for it?" Sophie unbuttoned her uniform to the waist, displaying wide swells over the tops of her bra and slip. "Get to bed."

Lisa didn't need to go to bed, she needed to shoot up again. "Installments. How much could it be for a dinky house like ours?"

"Too much, that's how much." Sophie took a glass out of one cabinet and the bottle of aspirin out of another. "John McNamara said you look pretty in your pink coat," she conveyed in a cheery voice, as if changing the subject would make the heat go away. "Said he's happy you're going to be around after school this year. That you'd miss us if you weren't. He's so sweet."

"He's a retardo."

"Don't say that, young lady!"

"Or what?"

She took her aspirin with a sigh and started out. "Do you want this light on, or do you want to sit in the dark some more?"

"Suit yourself, Mom."

She turned off the light. "Cooler," she said as she walked out.

It seemed only seconds later that the toilet flushed. Lisa waited until she heard her mother's bed creak, and then she went to her own bedroom. She closed the door loud enough for her mother to hear. She threw her spare sneakers at the closet door, and settled down on the bed with a long sigh. She waited, not daring to stir, listening to every peep the old house and darkness offered up.

When she heard her mother's even breathing, Lisa crept to the window and shimmied out. She raced like the wind down the dark alley, stumbling on an aluminum garbage can. A dog barked. She was five houses away, her mother wouldn't hear. She righted the container. A gummy paper bag ripped apart as she tried to throw it back in. Smelly cartons and cans crashed around her. The dog barked louder. A light came on over a back porch.

She hurried out of there at a crouch, and was out of breath by time she got to Ray's back door. She rang the bell forever. Finally, she went around to his window and pounded. What was he doing in bed at this hour? It couldn't be much after one. It took an eternity before he got to the window, and that much longer before he got the stuck window to raise up.

"What are you doing here? Want Frank to come looking for you again?"

Ray was maxing out in the paranoia department. Police Chief Frank Willis would be fast asleep. He and her mother saw each other Thursdays at choir practice, Saturday nights, and Sunday at church. "Mom's asleep, she doesn't know I'm here."

He gave her a stern look and motioned to the back door. She met him there. "What do you want?" he asked as he pulled her inside with a kiss.

Something better than sex. She pushed her sleeve above her elbow. She made a needle out of her forefinger and indented the skin around the tracks.

"You don't need another hit. Go home and sleep it off."

"No! I'm the one who got the prescription.pad. I'm entitled."

Ray gave in. She went into the bedroom and waited. It took forever before he came back with the needle. He tied the rubber thong tightly around her upper arm. She felt her veins pulsate. He set the point of the needle against the bulging blue vein and broke through the flesh.

She watched her blood seep into the syringe as he pulled back on the plunger. Then he slowly injected the liquid power into her vein. He untied the thong and the power was off like a racing thoroughbred out the starting gate.

The top of her head shot right through the ceiling. Every pore in her body tingled with delight. She flopped back on his pillow, oblivious to everything around her except the power skating through her veins.

"You all right?" echoed through her. "Speak to me!" screeched out at her. She felt someone shaking her. She ignored it. She wanted to be left alone to soar.

Chapter 12

Josh

Saturday night formal dinner parties at the Circle C were almost common as Emma's Thursday board meetings at the hospital. And Josh was becoming a regular. Being Allison's escort seemed to be an ancillary service of the very junior radiologist, and his title was always punctuated during introductions. In this company, it was considered his best feature.

Each of Emma's guest lists had a theme. Tonight's was Houston's media kingpins. The topic of conversation would turn to the grand opening of the Houstonian Health Retreat during dessert. Spectacular media coverage wouldn't hurt the new Chandler enterprise.

At Emma's right sat Senator Gabe Livingston, the drawing card. When not in Washington, the Chandler's lifelong friend was invariably up for one of Emma's dinner parties. He was a hearty eater and, on him, a white dinner jacket looked like a worn-out T-shirt found at the bottom of the laundry basket, but he was the senator. His meaty index finger was permanently stained yellow from years of cigar smoking. His one pretense at culture sat to his right.

Bea Livingston, heir to Denton Oil and sister to Lady Chatham of England, fancied herself a pianist. Though even with Josh's eyes closed, her music was overshadowed by the image of the thin woman's horse face. She was so thin that, seated between her husband and the heavy-set David Kurtz, kingpin of the radio waves, Bea looked like a wilted flower pressed between two unabridged dictionaries.

Like many silent-film actors whose voices couldn't make the transition to talkies, the inverse applied to David Kurtz. A melodious baritone bellowed between thick lips on a face that looked as if it had gone ten rounds with the heavyweight champ. His wife's banal appearance, by contrast, transformed into resplendence as she hung on his every word.

Houston's most popular TV news anchorman sat at Emma's left. Closing in on sixty, Roger Stiles showed signs of wear around his handsome face and his metallic dark hair didn't quite look natural. His neck had aged years ahead of the rest of him and hung loose above the tight collar. He tugged at his French cuffs as he laughed at whatever Emma had whispered in his ear. Josh sat at the foot of the table and, except for nuances, missed most of the conversation at the other end.

Seated next to the very stylish Mrs. Stiles, who was centuries younger than her husband, was John Gilmore, the editor of the newspaper's Sunday's *About-Town* magazine insert. A nice feature about the spa surely would be forthcoming. His date was the society-page editor, Robin something-or-other. Her healthy-looking glow made her appear as if she would be more comfortable writing the sports section.

Robin and Allison, seated next to her, were engaged in an animated discussion of current fashion. On Monday, they were going to do lunch at the Galleria, after a quick tour of Allison's drawing studio in the back of her boutique. If Robin were feigning interest in the newly designed, ivory-lace number Allison was wearing, it was an Academy Award performance.

Allison was beautiful and could get away with wearing Gabe's dinner jacket, but this design was as backward as a picture negative. It had a high priest collar and chastely covered her exquisite bodice and arms to the wrists, yet the shoulders were missing and cut out so deeply that the swells of her young breasts were exposed above each armpit.

"What's your opinion of the president's health-care program, Senator? Or should I say the Mrs. President's?" David Kurtz leaned over and pinned Bea to the back of her chair in order to eye Gabe.

Gabe flapped his lips in frustration. A flicker of contempt appeared on Emma's countenance before she was able to control it.

Posturing, Gabe said, "It's not an easy question as everyone on the Hill has concluded. There are so many factors to take into account." He cleared his throat. "I'm always interested in hearing from my constituents. What do *you* think of their plan, Josh? You're a doctor."

Wasn't he the crafty devil? Let the guy at the foot of the table squirm. That's how he had managed to stay senator all these years. Everyone stared as if Josh's pedigree papers were branded on his forehead. "I agree with you, Senator, it's a very complex problem. While everyone should be entitled to adequate health care, I'm not certain any national health care plan can provide it."

"Why do you say that, Doctor?" David Kurtz's ugliness spread into his voice.

"If you look at the history of price control, you'll see a mismatching of needs and resources. I am very unhappy with the restrictions the insurance companies place on us as for which tests and procedures can be ordered. Traditionally, doctors decided if a patient was ill enough to be hospitalized and how long the patient would stay. Now, Medicare, Medicaid, and other insurance companies make the decision. I hate to be a nitpicker, and don't know how long the insurance companies' training programs are, but I trained twelve years. Eight years, if you don't count college. I truly believe doctors are more qualified to determine the needs of their patients."

"But so many doctors do unnecessary testing," Mrs. Stiles offered, simplistically.

"That's a judgment call on your part, Mrs. Stiles," Josh said as friendly as he would have been had she complimented him on his choice of black ties, and with the smile he reserved for the most unpleasant. "What defense does a doctor have in a malpractice case if he or she didn't order a test that could have diagnosed the ailment? And given the prevailing attitude toward suing, a doctor needs to practice defensive medicine. Perhaps tort reform is the answer. Put a cap on some of these outrageous jury awards."

"You don't believe a person seriously injured through misdeeds of his physician is entitled to fair compensation, Doctor?" Kurtz challenged.

"*Fair* is the operative word. Lawyers go into court, spinning and weaving pitiful tales, working juries into an emotional state. And yet, they have little compunction against taking a hefty chunk of the settlement for services rendered."

"Senator?" Kurtz hammered.

"Lawyers! A whole different can of worms. Most of us politicians are lawyers." The senator laughed. "You know why lawyers should be used in laboratory experiments instead of white mice don't you, Allison?"

Allison shrugged her bare shoulders.

"Because there are just some things mice won't do." He laughed again. Everyone else laughed politely except Bea.

Bea slapped his thick wrist. "Oh, Gabe, you're such a kidder?" Bea, like many Texas women of her age and social class, habitually turned every statement into a question as though she needed someone to validate her opinion.

"The government is looking at the health crisis backward." Allison stepped up to the plate. "Throwing the burden of cost onto the employers' shoulders doesn't solve anything. The real culprit is the insurance industry and their failure to institute voluntary reforms in their practices. If the president wants to do something constructive, tell him to take on the insurance companies like he promised. Stop them from cherry picking, insuring only the healthiest people."

Like the oil companies, which in Texas were off-limits as dinner conversation, insurance companies were substantial campaign contributors. No president wanted to bite the hands that fed him.

Dessert was served and the debate about health insurance raged on. Emma was not altogether happy to have lost control, but rose in defense of privately owned hospitals as opposed to nonprofit hospitals belonging to religious institutions or government.

Josh watched the ice cream sundae sitting in front of Allison's empty place run down the sides of the crystal and puddle around the stem. She had left sometime ago, after one of the servants had whispered in her ear. Josh had heard a distant ringing moments before and deduced that she was called to the phone.

"Doctor," John Gilmore said, pulling Josh's eyes away from the melting ice cream, "would it not be safe to say that your profession could go a long way in correcting the problem if they would police themselves and control costs."

Josh nodded. "Absolutely. However, it's a thin line between not enough and too much. Should cost be more important than saving a life? Doesn't the answer depend on whether it's your life or the life of someone you love, or the life a stranger?"

Emma rose. "Well said. And with that, let us have our coffee in the parlor."

The press, Josh realized, played by different rules than most dinner guests. But the fact that Emma hadn't asked Bea to play for them must have meant that Emma intended to bring up the spa at coffee. If they would give her the chance.

Josh hung back as they all proceeded into the living room—"parlor," as Emma deemed it. Just as he was about to go in search of Allison, she came racing down the stairs. She had changed into jeans. "Josh," she said, pulling him toward the front door, "I have to go to the spa. There's a problem with some of the exercise machines."

"Do you want me to drive you?"

"No need." She planted a fleeting kiss on his cheek. "Don't know how long it'll take. I'll call you in the morning."

Josh grabbed hold of her before she got out the door. "Go in and announce it to your grandmother. They're not cutting her much slack and she needs an opening."

Allison looked at him as if she had no idea what he was talking about.

"Just be your charming self, say good night to everyone and mention you're going to the spa."

She hurried in ahead of him. "Nana, I have to drive into Houston. There's a problem at the health spa." Allison gave the judge her best smile. "Good night, everyone." With that she was gone.

Josh leaned against the door frame. "Hope it isn't much of a problem. The Houstonian Health Retreat's grand opening isn't far off, isn't that right, Mrs. Chandler?"

Emma smiled her thanks as Robin something-or-other asked about the spa.

Chapter 13

Margaret

Margaret had nearly worn out the satin edging around the summer-weight blanket, pleating and unpleating it. She scraped a fingernail over a crease as though to make it disappear.

If only she could make herself disappear. Even if her face could be restored, she wished she'd never agreed to the laser surgery. Her scar had been an excuse for not having a social life. She lied to herself, saying people couldn't get beyond her looks to see the real her. Now what kind of excuse could she use? Would she have the guts to admit, even if only to herself, that she was as scarred on the inside as out? She wasn't a nice person at all. A nice person didn't fall in love with her sister's lover.

She looked at the satin bundle in her hand, a folded fan Gothic heroines blushed behind. She held it over the raw-meat side of her face. A fan to blush behind. She flung it out, unraveling it like a runaway accordion. And gave way to her tears.

Margaret wasn't even into a full-blown cry-out when Nurse Suzette came briskly into the room carrying the sterile stock of her trade. She headed for the bed and then veered off at the last moment, dropping the supplies on the dresser with a decisive bang. Not everyone was overwhelmed by over-priced furniture.

She clucked her tongue and hurried toward the French doors. Looking every inch of her six feet—

Victorian carriage, shoulders back, chin up, thick waist tightly cinched by the belt of her starched uniform— Suzette carried her large bulk imposingly. With one easy stroke, she pulled open the heavy celery-colored drapes, exposing pale peach sheers. Suzette became a commanding silhouette against the brightness as she pushed back the sheers.

Suzette threw open the doors and stepped out onto the private balcony, breathing in the morning freshness and planters of California flowers.

Redeeming her nursely wares, she crossed crisply to the bed, opened a sterile pack and wiped Margaret's face with the stinging throwaway towelette. Her lips turned up, but it was more like an inverted frown than a smile. She twisted the corner of the towelette into a Q-tip and dug sleep out of Margaret's eye over her surgery. The mucus pulled away in a long string.

"Breakfast?" Suzette went to the closet and rummaged through Margaret's things.

"No."

"No?" Another cluck. "Breakfast, yes!" She draped the gray shirtwaist across the foot of the bed.

Margaret had dreaded Sunday morning since Sterling had informed her it was the day she would take her meals in the dining room with the other patients again. She didn't want to see anyone and didn't want anyone to see her.

Apparently, it made no difference what Margaret wanted. Suzette helped her into the bathroom.

Margaret brushed her teeth awkwardly, commanding the tingling corner of her lip to stretch back. Suzette brushed her hair with vigorous strokes toward the new hair. There, she gathered the greasy strands into her big fist more gently than Margaret suspected the Amazon possible of. Suzette took a pink bow from her own hair and secured the fistful over the ear, veiling the red welts of hair plugs.

Their eyes met in the mirror. Margaret smiled her thanks.

Suzette all but pushed her out into the hall, pointed her in the right direction, and nudged her on her way like a kindergartener's first day.

Margaret had eaten in the dining room the evening of her arrival centuries ago. All that had changed were the faces on the patients at the eight tables, and a melting-ice swan on a long banquet table set up for Sunday brunch replaced the dolphin. She got in line behind a thin woman with shiny straight blond hair turned under at the shoulders.

"Cheese and ham, Enrique, please," the woman said in a sophisticated rasp to the graying man in a chef's toque making omelettes to order.

Margaret dabbled in the fruit, trying hard not to stare at the woman's profile. Her eyes were puffed to cartoonish proportions. Black stitches formed half moons over her upper eyelid creases. It looked very painful.

The chef was looking at Margaret, waiting. Margaret inspected the contents of the steel bowls around his flame. "Cheese, ham, tomatoes, and mushrooms." He went to work on hers, stopping long enough to flip the finished one onto the woman's plate.

"Thank you, Enrique." She slipped a bill into his hand.

Margaret hadn't thought to bring money. She busied herself with the crab salad until he drew the sauté pan away from the fire. She held out her plate. "Thank you." She didn't feel she'd earned the right to use his name.

"My pleasure." His smile warmed her to the core.

"Enrique?"

He gave a nod and a broader smile.

"I'm Margaret."

He picked a sprig of parsley and centered it on her omelette. "For Margaret."

She moved a bit lighter through the steam trays.

"Ham?" asked the meat carver.

"The beef, please."

He carved off a juicy red sliver, and then another. The *au jus* ran over the meat and was soaked up by the cherry blintz.

She looked around the room for a free table. The woman in front of her had taken the last. Two middle-aged women at a table under the windows looked to be finished. One wore mummy bandages past her neck, with black holes around her eyes, nose, and mouth. The other had a red raw-meat face, much like her own except covering the entire face. Before she'd decided what to do, the blond tipper caught Margaret's eye and motioned her over.

"I'm glad I won't have to eat alone. In these times, it's a bit of a silly rule." She held out her hand. "Katherine Little." Her middle initial was "A." Margaret knew from the monogrammed pocket.

"Margaret Chandler." Katherine's hand was soft and delicate, her smile, effortless. From the lines running across her neck and radiating from her lips, Katherine looked to be in her mid-fifties. "Silly rule?"

"No visitors. But I can appreciate the reason." She pointed to her eyes. "This is usually an out-patient procedure, but I didn't want my husband to see me like this." Her nails were long and pink and cut square at the ends. "I know I'm far too concerned about superficial things. But appearance is everything here where industry is spelled with a capital 'E.' "

Margaret must have looked confused.

"Entertainment. Make-believe." She smiled at the waiter as he filled their water glasses from an ornately flowered pitcher that matched the china. "Thank you, Carlos." She turned her attention back to Margaret. "But you're not from here. You're from the south."

"Texas."

"And your surgery was corrective, not cosmetic."

"How did you know that?"

"You're much too young to need a chemical peel, and it's limited to one area." She gave a self-effacing laugh as she tossed her glistening hair away from her face. It did no good, immediately falling back over her left eye. "I'm considering one myself. It's not easy when most of the wives of your husband's associates have no idea who JFK was. Let alone remember where they were and what they were doing when he was assassinated. Of course, you're from Texas."

Meaning she should know about John Kennedy since he was assassinated in Texas. "Your husband is in the entertainment industry?" Margaret asked mainly to show that she hadn't taken offense. And she hadn't. She liked Katherine. Not so much because of what she said, but the way she said everything without malice. Openly.

"Little? Nathan Little?"

Margaret shook her head apologetically. "But I know who Kennedy was."

Katherine laughed genuinely. "Well, then you're my new best friend." She took a bite of her omelette. "Nathan's head of Cinema Studios. The seat of power in the industry. But if you're not in the industry, why would you care? It's rather refreshing, if you want to know the truth."

They ate in silence until Katherine said: "I did my eyes for me, not for Nathan. I know he'd love me if I were fat, bald, and toothless." This Margaret believed with all her heart. She too had fallen under her spell. Katherine was one of those people who exuded kindness from every pore. "I'm the one who's not comfortable knowing most of my life is behind me. And the mirror is a constant reminder. I looked so tired, I was tired. Old and tired. A deadly combination. Once the idea was in my head, I couldn't shake it loose."

"Do your eyes hurt terribly?"

"They say blepharoplasty is the least painful of all cosmetic surgery. I'm having some sort of allergic reaction to the stitches, but I'm told not to worry. It's God's way of punishing me for my vanity." She picked at her food. "And yours? Is it painful?"

Margaret shrugged. "This was the least painful of

my many surgeries. Grafts are much worse. And I've had so many over the years that my body looks like a patchwork quilt."

"Does it bother you to talk about it?"

She had never talked about it, and had no idea why she was confiding in a stranger. Perhaps because she didn't share the loss. It was all Nana could do to look at her. She was a constant reminder of that tragic night. "My parents and I were in a car accident when I was nearly two. We were going to the hospital. My mother was in labor. I remember a man reaching in through the flames to pull me out of the backseat. I remember the sharp stick of a thistle while I was being rolled in the dirt. My parents died from their injuries. My father on the way to the hospital. But my mother lived long enough for my sister to be born."

Katherine reached across the table and took her hand.

Chapter 14

Rosa

The Monday morning seven o'clock Morbidity and Mortality meeting was in full swing by time Rosa got there. She hit the serving table and took a couple of slices of cantaloupe, pineapple, and honeydew. Red watermelon for breakfast left something to be desired. Ditto the dried-up eggs in the steam tray. She picked up a caramel roll and dropped it on her plate, hoping it wouldn't be stale for once. She had the makings of a true optimist.

Sean pulled out the chair to the left of Sarah that they'd saved for her. Of course, they were all such creatures of habit that there wouldn't have been any question of saving her the seat, even though it meant Sean had his back to the podium.

"Welcome back, stranger," Sarah said in her usual cheerful voice, betrayed by tired eyes and grayish skin.

Meredith leaned around Sarah to give Rosa a smile.

You'd think she'd been gone forever the way they carried on. She had left Wednesday afternoon and was back at work Saturday. The room was jammed. "Nice crowd today. Something happen while I was out of town?"

Sarah shook her head. "Not that I know of."

Meredith sighed. "Too hot to sleep. Might as well get a jump start on the week."

Per bylaws, the doctors could miss only one meeting a quarter without an excuse and no one seemed to be missing today. Rosa's coffee burned the roof of her mouth. She put a spoon in the cup to cool it down. She noticed Sean had ice in his.

"The way I heard it, there's something new at the McNamara residence." Sean pointed to the top of his head.

"How could I forget?" Sarah rolled her eyes. "John finally saved enough money to buy the Stetson he wanted. The one like Cole's. He's so proud of it I barely got it off of him when he went to bed." She knitted her brows.

"What's wrong?" Rosa asked.

Sarah shook her head. "Nothing, just trying to figure. He talked about showing it to Cole all weekend. Then when we got here this morning, I couldn't talk him into going into the ER to show it off. Wonder what got into him?"

Rosa shrugged.

"Afraid his was nicer than Cole's and he didn't want to hurt Cole's feelings?" Meredith speculated.

"Don't know," Sarah said. "They tease each other to death. And he was sure mighty anxious to show it off."

Meredith looked around at Cole and then back to Sarah. "Maybe he saw something in the ER that frightened him."

Sarah nodded. "That might be. A core, maybe."

"Cores can be pretty scary, especially your first." Rosa could remember the first one she attended. For months after, in her sleep, she saw the man's body convulse when he was shocked.

"I would be pleased to have a chat with the lad," Sean offered. "Man to man."

"Thanks." A tiny tear formed in Sarah's eye. John was her whole life and Rosa could only guess how much she worried about his welfare. Sarah had confided that she was concerned how he would manage if she died before he did.

Sean must have noticed, too. He discreetly chose

that moment to turn around in his chair to give the chief of staff his full attention.

Richard Bell read the usual announcements. Nothing pertained to Rosa except the Wednesday medicine committee meeting. His head twitched and the papers in his hand shook. "Richard looks bad. Someone needs to straighten out his levodopa meds."

"Don't think he's even admitted to himself that he has Parkinson's," Sarah whispered back, "let alone anyone else."

"Bob Tilton surely can do something about it. What are partners for?" Meredith added.

The man was an imcompetent fool. Rosa had saved his skin more than once. "Remind me never to have a fool for a partner." Rosa's coffee had cooled off enough to sip.

"I see you don't suffer fools lightly. You need to work on that little character flaw, Rosa," Meredith said, lacking conviction.

"He speaks kindly of you," Sarah said and laughed so loudly that Richard stopped in midsentence to look at her over the tops of his reading glasses. His head oscillated back and forth like a sail in a gentle breeze.

"The hyperkinetic manifestations of his disease are so pronounced," Rosa whispered. "I think we should get a brain scan. Take a close look at his Basal Ganklin."

"How do you suppose we do that? Get Bill to ask him to test his precious CAT-scan machine?" Sarah shook her head slowly. "The day I'm in cahoots with Bill is the day I want you to take me out and shoot me."

Rosa whispered back. "Maybe we can get Josh to do it."

"And maybe pigs fly. He's not allowed to wipe his butt unless Bill okays it."

Rosa glanced at Josh and Bill sitting at the front-and-center table they shared with Bob Tilton and the remains of Richard's breakfast. Tyler VanFleet usually sat there, but wasn't today. Bill and Josh were a handsome pair, both coat-and-tie men. She couldn't appreciate Bill's good looks because of her biased perceptions of his skulduggery and black soul. As far as she could tell, the man had absolutely no redeeming qualities. But the young stalwart New Yorker was her paradigm of Prince Charming. Average height, with a slim muscular build which filled out his Armani shirt. A crooked smile was his only flaw, and not much of one.

Josh was the second "partner" Bill had had since she moved to Chandler Springs and she never could get the number before her time straight. It was a standing joke. In Bill's dictionary, partner meant slave laborer. And after the year of indentured servitude, Bill found some excuse to fire the partner. There was always an eager kid, fresh out of residency to take his place. And it was always a he, never a she. Bill was the biggest chauvinist pig who ever walked the face of the earth.

Like Ellis and herself, Josh had been elected to AOA. Alpha Omega Alpha was the medical honor fraternity. But not only was he a bright student, he was a superlative radiologist. She'd like to see him stay.

Rosa spotted Tyler. "What's Ty doing over at the Maverick table?" Sarah had dubbed it that. Rosa thought of them more as swashbucklers, but she reminded herself that she was in Texas now.

Sarah shrugged.

"Ellis hollered at him to join them as he was carrying his leaning-tower-of-breakfast to his usual table." Meredith looked over her shoulder to the table of the doctors most likely to be contrary. Ellis, the thoracic surgeon; Patrick, the general surgeon; Ken, the obstetrician; and Leroy, the anesthesiologist, would just as soon fort up the surgical suites like the Alamo and hold off the rest of the hospital. Despite coming straight from the do-as-you're-told, spit-and-polish military, Cole male-bonded well with the very independent Texans. But Tyler was no Jim Bowie.

"Are there any further announcements?" Richard asked, bending over the microphone.

"Yeah." Ellis's chair grated as he pushed it back to rise. "Has anyone taken Jacob McQuade's hospital records?"

Ellis had performed Jacob McQuade's bypass surgery, but Jacob had been Rosa's patient during his stay in the hospital. She'd been fired from his case when he left the hospital (against medical advice) and replaced by Richard, who didn't last much longer. What in the world was Ellis wanting with his record? "Why, Ellis?" Rosa asked.

He turned to face her. "Did you check them out, Rosa?" An uneasy combativeness crept into his voice.

"No, but why do you want them?"

"Well, for your . . . and everyone else's information"—he stared accusingly—"I'm being sued by his widow and would like to review the case." Rage had darkened and swelled his face, his pulsating jugular threatened to burst.

"Sued? What for?"

He shot her a look of reproach. "For malpractice."

"Malpractice!" That was insane. Rosa had asked him to go out to the Rocking M to check on Jacob when she learned that Richard had been fired, but it was too late to help the man. The only thing Ellis could do was call an ambulance to bring him in. Jacob was DOA. She'd climbed into the ambulance and had a look at his body herself. Livor mortis was well established. He'd been dead a good two hours. There was nothing Ellis could have done. The postmortem study revealed an overwhelming gram-negative bacterial infection and attributed the death to gram-negative endotoxic shock. That would have taken days. "What did you do?"

"Nothing. I'm being accused of causing the septic shock"—Ellis pointed an accusing finger at Bill—"*he* introduced."

"How dare you!" Bill bolted up, knocking his chair over.

"You're the one who ordered a battery of unnecessary tests and the invasive lymphangiogram after Rosa refused. You're the one who put that poor man in a room that was being remodeled and had plaster dust everywhere instead of taking him down to one of the surgical suites. You're the one who made the sloppy incision on the dorsum of the foot and tried to get a thirty-gauge needle into it. I'm not at all surprised Mrs. McQuade's suing—she's just got the wrong man."

Bill had closed in on Ellis, fists balled. "Why, you lying bastard!" Josh tackled Bill just as he was about to lunge. "Let go of me!" Bill exclaimed as he tangled with Josh. He pulled free and took a swing at Ellis.

Ellis ducked and managed a glancing blow before Patrick and Leroy restrained him. Bill was left with a wide-open, breadbasket shot and got in a solid hit. Josh blocked Bill as he started to throw the second blow. Ellis staggered back and crumbled over in pain as the guys freed him to seize Bill.

Sarah blocked Rosa's view momentarily as she hurried to Ellis's side. Ken beat her to him.

Meredith and Rosa exchanged worried glances. Although M&M conferences occasionally went beyond cerebral finger pointing and into shouting matches, Rosa had never seen one turn into a punch-throwing fracas.

Richard tapped on the mike. "Gentlemen . . . gentlemen, please."

Sean shook his head. "The Vatican will not be canonizing those two any time soon."

Rosa and Meredith broke out in tense laughter.

"Dr. Johnston to surgery," came the operator over the public address system. "Dr. Johnston to surgery."

Meredith raised an eyebrow. "Her timing leaves something to be desired." She was referring to the weekly page. Every week the guys at the Maverick table were called one by one out of the M&M meeting.

No one was fooled. And Richard had cause to be insulted, but he was inclined to take the path of least resistance and believe that they were needed in surgery.

Bill straightened his collar and tugged at his sleeves as he left the room with thespian dignity. The creep.

Ellis retrieved a folder from his table and started out.

Rosa watched the door close behind Ellis and tried to take it all in as everyone settled down and returned to their seats with whispering commentary.

Richard took off his glasses and wiped them with his handkerchief. They didn't quite suit him. He huffed and puffed and wiped them down some more.

Rosa got to her feet. "Richard, I was Jacob McQuade's physician of record and now I'm asking the question. Who has the file?"

Chapter 15

Sophie

Most of the lunch crowd had returned to work by time Sophie and Carrie, the new licensed vocational nurse she was orientating, went through the cafeteria line. Sophie spotted Avon and Vesta and headed to their table.

She introduced the three nurses.

"Hot enough for you, Carrie?" Avon asked.

The new nurse didn't answer. Sophie assumed it was because Carrie was timid and not because Avon was black.

"If we'd married doctors like our mothers had hoped we would when we went into nursing school, we'd be whiling away the summer day at the country club sipping wine coolers." Avon picked up her tuna sandwich with sassy flair. "Instead, I have sick kids biting my ankles all day and all night." She took a big bite and eyed Carrie.

Avon had a way of making the dullest thing seem exciting. Now that Avon worked the night shift in Peds, Sophie didn't get to hear many of her stories. Mondays were about the only day Sophie saw her. Avon was always willing to give a hand Mondays after weekends off, for which Sophie was grateful. Avon would work until three today and then be back by eleven without complaint.

"Where'd we go wrong?" Sophie squeezed the wedge of lemon into her ice tea and scooted over to

make room at the round table for the two surgical
nurses, Jennifer and Vicki. From the looks of their
sweaty surgical scrubs, they'd had a tough morning.
"Howdy. Y'all look bushed."

Jennifer set down her tray and plopped in the chair,
while Vicki swiped a chair from the next table. "Ellis
was having one of his throwing-conniption days and
it's only Monday," Jennifer offered. Jennifer had been
an army nurse in Vietnam, and then worked years at
Ben Taub, the charity hospital in Houston. Jennifer
looked after Dr. Johnston's interests like a mother hen.
He had to have done something terrible to make her
gripe.

"Going to be a long week, girl. Need some vitamin
C. Catch." Vesta threw an orange at Jennifer. But it
was Vicki who instinctively reached out and caught it
on the fly.

"No wonder you're the star of the softball team with
a catch like that," Sophie told the thickset girl. She was
also the barrel-riding champ for two years in a row.
"All that practice in the operating room came in
handy."

"You think I'm crazy enough to catch a scalpel on
the fly? And look." Vicki leaned her chair back on its
hind legs and took off a shoe. The crepe sole had a
curved suture needle embedded in it. "Ellis was worse
than ever. Dr. Thompson and Dr. Carter weren't even
kidding around with him. Something's up."

"Jennifer, Vicki, you haven't met Carrie Harper.
Carrie's our new LVN. She going to be working weekends on Three North and doing a little floating."

They exchanged pleasantries.

Sophie had had uneasy vibes about hiring Carrie.
She reminded Sophie of a tiny frightened mouse
trapped in a corner. The sloppy handwriting and spell-
ing errors on her application made it look like it was
filled out by a third-grader. But her former employers
had found no fault with her work, and she did hold a
valid nursing license. LVN, the equivalent to a licensed

practical nurse in many other states, was a one-year training program. On the nursing hierarchy, LVNs were below registered nurses but above nursing aides. While aides were capable of little more than changing the sheets and cleaning bedpans, LVNs could take a lot of the load off RNs. RNs could depend on them to perform nursing skills, such as putting in intravenous lines. With the nursing shortage the way it was, she hoped Carrie would work out.

Vesta gathered up her trash. "I've got to get back. Ken has a mother coming in at one to be induced."

"Let us know when the baby arrives. Getting tired of having an empty nursery," Jennifer said in her gruff, drill-sergeant's voice.

"Me, too. Nothing like a baby to liven up things. See y'all later," Vesta said. "It was nice meeting you, Carrie. You'll like it here."

Carrie gave her a weak smile.

Sophie watched Vesta hobble off on swollen legs. She'd be retiring one of these days. Not too soon, Sophie hoped. Vesta was the last of the old guard left from when Sophie started working at CMC. Vesta always had time to listen to her troubles in the early days when Sophie came home with the baby after the divorce. Her parents didn't handle it at all well. Staunch Southern Baptists believed marriage is forever, no matter how bad things got.

Vesta was also thrilled when Sophie was promoted to nursing supervisor, even though she shouldn't have been happy. Vesta was passed over because she was a non-degree registered nurse. Nurses with baccalaureate degrees were scarce even today and practically nonexistent in Vesta's era.

Dennis's long arms placed two trays on the table as he hunkered down into the chair Vesta had warmed. He was joining them out of habit. Betty Sue usually ate with them, and he always tried to eat with his wife if he could manage to get away from the ER. The new administrative secretary who was replacing Betty Sue now that she was on maternity leave ate with the girls in the billing office.

"Dennis, this is Carrie Harper, our new LVN. Carrie, Dennis Green, RN in the ER."

"Nice to meet you," Dennis said as he stretched out a hand.

Carrie shook it timidly. "Nice to meet you."

"Hungry today, Dennis?" Avon challenged.

"It's for the gimp."

Sophie looked around for the gimp. Cole bent his bullneck low to watch where he was placing his walking cast as he threaded through the roomful of tables to join them. She was worried that he'd lost too much weight after his injury. His shirt clung to his broad shoulders as if on a wire hanger. And it looked like he hadn't had the energy to run a comb through his sandy hair for days.

"Enjoy your week off, Dennis?" Sophie asked.

Dennis smiled the way only a new father could. "Can I make 'em big or what?"

"Going to have a new baby today," Sophie told him. "Ken's inducing."

"Betcha it's not twenty-two inches long." Dennis flipped out his paper napkin to its full size and let it settle to his lap.

"Be a month of Sundays before we see a twenty-two-incher again." Avon spread her arms out to the sides as far as she could reach and shook her head.

"Hey," Cole said as he made his way around the table to the empty chair between Carrie and Dennis.

"Howdy, fellow. Ready for the Boston Marathon?" Sophie asked as he was easing into the chair.

"Next year." Cole looked at Carrie. "New?"

Sophie answered. "Cole, I'd like you to meet Carrie Harper, our new LVN. Carrie, this is Dr. Cole Morgan. He's in charge of the ER."

"More accurately, I hang out in the ER. You nurses run it."

"False modesty," Sophie whispered in a voice loud

enough for everyone to hear. "He's trying to make a good first impression."

The confused look of Carrie's face halted the laughter.

Cole gave her a kind smile that barely parted his lips. His genuinely happy smile showed off the tops of the capped front teeth he'd gotten quarterbacking the homecoming game his and Sophie's senior year. They'd broken at an angle that left an inverted V in the middle. Sophie and he had gone to the celebration dance after the game anyway, and he'd pretended breaking them hadn't mattered to him and showed them off like a badge of courage. "The ER nurses answer to Sophie. The two physician assistants who cover the ER nights and weekends answer to me."

Carrie nodded uncomfortably.

He showed Vicki the tops of his caps. "Never got a chance to tell you that that was a damned-exciting barrel race."

"Never got to tell you," Vicki countered, "that was the best damned bull goring I ever did see."

"We aim to please." He smiled big.

"You must be including Ellis in that *we*. After his morning performance as the circus knife thrower, we're pleased as punch," Jennifer added.

Vicki's kidding tone vanished. "You know what's bothering him?"

Cole's smile faded. "Probably the heat." He picked up his fork and started gobbling. He didn't fool any of them, except maybe Carrie. Something was up.

Chapter 16

Allison

Allison inspected the mural on the thirteen-foot ceiling of the vast entry gallery, which led to the check-in area and the spiral staircase to the suites. Soft music filtered through in jerky intervals as the electricians fine-tuned the system. She ran a finger over one of the newly installed, stained-glass, beveled doors. It had better be the last time she collected a coat of dust.

Three sophisticated-looking receptionists—could she choose them, or what?—stood in a knot around the desk, waiting for her. In the mauve-flowered smocks she had ordered from Neiman Marcus, the fortyish women would look more like guests than the hired help.

The spa had come a long way, but it wasn't nearly enough. The grand opening was only two weeks away. So much to do and so little time to do it.

Laughter from the exercise room gained her attention. Jinx pumped iron as he watched the new aerobic instructor perform donkey kicks, her tight butt wiggling at him invitingly. What gall! Allison expected every employee to be single-minded in their quest to help, entertain, and see to the needs of the patrons. In short, make certain their stays were enjoyable. Women who would pay good money to get away from the routine of their everyday life, forget everything in order to get back on the road to a healthy existence, deserved nothing less.

It was Jinx's philosophy as well. Stumbling across Jinx had been the most serendipitous discovery of her life. Hiring him, the most brilliant. Jinx had a way of inspiring everyone to work hard at getting their bodies back in shape, something like Tom Sawyer and white-washing fences. Heaven knew, Allison was doing far more strenuous exercising than normal. And the healthy food! He almost had her convinced that carrots tasted the same as potato chips. Their women guests would love him to pieces. There wasn't anyone Jinx couldn't charm.

Allison wished she could say the same for perky lit-tle Cindy. She had severely miscalculated. The well-scrubbed, fresh face of the aerobic instructor had thrown her off-guard. The girl was trouble. Allison could tell that a mile away. She'd have to go, there was no two ways about it.

Cindy kicked out one last time and then grabbed a towel and sauntered over to Jinx. If that wasn't the most obvious . . . why, it must have been all Jinx could do to keep from laughing. No, he must have felt sorry for the misguided creature. That was more Jinx's style. His heart was as big as the rest of him.

He was so big-hearted, he'd let Cindy fawn all over him, never saying anything to hurt the poor creature's feelings. She'd better go help him out.

Allison handed out the list of pleasantries the new receptionists were to commit to memory, health ques-tionnaires to be filled out by the guests, and the floor plan. Every member of the staff had to be able to give directions to inquiring guests in the most courteous manner. "Study these for a while. I'll be back in a min-ute."

Cindy's sweat-stained Spandex number looked like a six-year-old's dance leotard. The blue dime-a-dozen tights came from Kmart, to be sure. She was trim in them, but that wasn't enough. The women who would patronize the spa would expect those who served them to have some class.

"You can name all of them?" Jinx asked. From a sitting position on the stool of one of the Olympic weight machines, he was eye-to-eye with the girl. He took a deep breath, fanning out his impressive chest. And then he genuinely smiled at the waif!

Allison's spirits plunged to the depths of her being. She had been a complete fool not to realize that Jinx might fall prey to another woman. But Cindy! What in the world could he see in the likes of her? Allison was a woman of the world—rich, sophisticated, traveled in the best circles, was entertained in the best homes. She, along with Margaret, owned one of the largest ranches in the state of Texas and was heir to another. Jinx would jeopardize a chance to share all that she possessed for this no-account? No, she didn't think so.

Cindy ran a hand over his back. "The lats, latissima dorsae."

He flexed.

Cindy rolled her hand over his arm as if she were taking a leisurely Sunday stroll with a lover. "Triceps, deltoids, and . . ."—she spread out her hand to include his pulsating chest—"pectoralis major." A little more of this and the two would be rolling around on the fucking gym floor. Or rather, rolling around on the gym floor, fucking.

"Amazing," he said, hardening his Herculean muscles one last time before relaxing. Even at rest, his muscles looked like mighty mountains.

"Jinx," Allison said as she slipped up on them, "would you go check on the plumbers in the men's room? I don't think I should go in there."

He looked at her as if she were speaking a foreign language. Gratitude for giving him the position of fitness manager of the Houstonian Health Retreat was a word that seemed to be missing from his dictionary. Apparently, he was not as ambitious as he had seemed when they first met, nor as appreciative. She wouldn't lose heart, and she'd forgive him. He preformed strenuously in bed. She gave him her most alluring smile. "Please."

"Sure thing." He bounded up. "Be right back," he added for Cindy's benefit. He might be right back, but the little schemer wouldn't.

"Cindy, would you come with me?"

When the little designer had placed her sweaty bottom on the new print couch Allison had ordered from Ethan Allen to match the wallpaper and drapes, Allison delivered the bad news. "Cindy, you simply aren't fitting in with the rest of the staff, and I'm afraid I'm going to have to let you go."

The girl looked up at her with Bambi eyes. "What did I do?"

"It's not a matter of what you did, as much as what you haven't done. Our clientele will be from the finest families, and I'm afraid you'll not fit in. I don't want you being uncomfortable."

"No, I won't be. I know lots of rich people. Really, I do. I was the personal trainer to—"

"Oh, Cindy, Cindy, Cindy." Allison sighed, telling the girl that if it were only true. "It's my mistake, not yours. But Jinx *is* the fitness manager here. I have to respect his wishes."

Horror contorted the girl's fresh face like a fun-house mirror. Anger and rage set in. "Jinx said I didn't fit in? Jinx said that? Jinx said that!"

Allison gave the girl an understanding smile. She went over to the desk and pulled her check book from the drawer. What was the lowest amount she could make the check for and still satisfy the girl? A thousand should gratify the greediest. She made it for five hundred. She tore out the check and placed it in the sobbing girl's hand, making certain the amount was facing her.

Allison helped Cindy to her feet and walked her through the other employees and construction workers to the outside door. She didn't want Jinx, or anyone else, stopping Cindy to ask any embarrassing questions. "Be kind to yourself." Allison opened the stained-glass door for the girl.

Cindy managed a weak nod, her shoulders hunched. Allison watched her walk aimlessly down the sidewalk until she was out of sight.

Allison turned to find Jinx standing there, looking on.

"What's wrong with Cindy?"

Allison shook her head. She pointed to her office to tell him that they needn't talk about the poor creature in front of the other employees. When the door was secured behind them, Allison wrapped her arms around his thick neck. "It was awful. So terribly awful." Tears glazed her eyes. "I took the call from her father. Her mother has been in an awful accident."

He ripped her arms away from his neck with more force than was necessary. "And you let her go off alone." His hand flew to the door in a panic. "I'll catch her. Take her—"

"No!" Allison's fingernails bore into the back of his hand as she held the doorknob steady. "Her brother came for her," she said in a calm, authoritative voice.

He looked puzzled as he rubbed the nail marks out of his flesh. "She had a brother? She didn't tell me she had a brother." He gave the back of his hand a long look, and then frowned. He never complained about the marks she left on his back.

Allison shrugged. "Did I tell you I had a sister?"

"Yes?" He made it sound like a so-what's-your-point question.

"But then you and I are a lot closer." She ran her fingers through his tousled hair. "Cindy probably would have mentioned him in time." Allison led him to the couch.

"You make it sound like she's not coming back."

"I did?" She nipped at the pectoralis major good ol' Cindy did such a nice job naming earlier. "She's welcome. It's just that I got the idea she'd be needed to nurse her mother back to health."

His triceps and deltoids turned to warm steel as he wrapped his arms around her. They fell as one to the couch.

"How long do you think we should keep her job open?" she asked between tastes. "Can you lead the aerobic exercises until she's able to come back to work?"

He broke away momentarily to concentrate on the question. He worked it through his head a long time, scowling as he gave it additional thought. The muscle holding his brains in was as thick as any in his body. But once it was penetrated, the mind worked rationally. "If she isn't back by the grand opening, I think we should replace her. It wouldn't be fair to our ladies."

Allison shrugged. "Whatever you think." She gave him a hard and deep kiss.

Jinx didn't respond. He seemed wrought with guilt. "We should buy her mother flowers. I'll pass the hat."

"No ... I'll send them. From all of us."

She swept her hand across his groin. Now she had his full attention.

Chapter 17

Rosa

Rosa closed the manila folder and tossed it to her desk. She didn't know what to think now that she'd had another look at Jacob McQuade's hospital records, which she'd copied after he fired her and checked himself out of the hospital. She turned on her microcassette recorder. "After reviewing Mr. McQuade's hospital records, I do not believe the theory of the gram-negative bacterial infection introduced during the invasive lymphangiogram is substantiated. Nor is it discredited."

Jacob's hospital stay was the prime example of Murphy's Law: What could go wrong, would. Leroy's choice of Inovar had made Jacob act bizarre, Bill's over-reading a routine chest X ray to justify initiating a battery of unwarranted and dangerous diagnostic tests, her going out of town to speak at a convention in Colorado, which gave Bill the opportunity to do the battery of X-ray tests, and then her humoring Jacob, whom she knew was not in his right mind, by letting him wear his clothing and his *boots* while in the hospital, and then allowing him to leave the hospital AMA, again when she knew he wasn't in his right mind. The only person who hadn't let Jacob down was Ellis.

Rosa glanced at the folder. They were still screwing up. Who took the original records and didn't place a referral card in its stead? Emma Chandler or her administrative henchman would be a good guess.

She checked her Rolodex and dialed the Dallas number. She counted six rings. It was only four P.M., surely Robert's office was open. A woman came on the line after the eighth ring.

"This is Dr. Rosa Sanchez calling long distance. Is Mr. Copeland available?"

"He's in conference, Doctor." The woman's voice was hesitant with new-employee uncertainty. Being in conference could mean anything from being in a conference to being on the toilet.

"Do you think he'll be long?"

Pause. "I wouldn't know."

"Would you ask him to return my call?" Rosa gave the woman her number.

"Okay, I'll . . . wait, he's free." There was a click and then Rosa was listening to nerve-soothing music for a few bars until another click interrupted.

"Rosa?" He put enough into his voice to fill an interviewer's questionnaire. They'd met at the medical conference in Aspen, Colorado, last spring. He was a legal expert on tort reform, setting caps on jury awards in medical malpractice suits. They were thrust upon each other by well-meaning friends because they had so much in common. In actuality, the only thing they ended up having in common, other than both being single, was living in Texas. A mighty big state. "Hi, Robert. I'd like to say I called just to say hi, but I'm afraid it's business."

"Well, you said hi, and I'm happy to hear your voice. I've been meaning to call, but good intentions and all that. I did get to Houston a few weeks ago, but—"

"Good intentions. I know."

He sighed. "Okay, no more apologies."

"No more apologies."

"What's up?"

"I seem to be embroiled, at least on the fringes of an

impending debacle." Rosa gave a heavy sigh, though it didn't lift the lead weight from her chest. "The surgeon who performed a bypass on one of *my* patients and the hospital are being sued for wrongful death."

"And you're not?" he got in ahead of her.

"Not that I know of. And that's the thing. The patient left the hospital AMA—against medical advice—and came back six days later DOA from septic shock. The wife claims the sepsis—infection—was due to a radioscopic procedure performed by the surgeon four days before he left the hospital. The case was mismanaged badly, and it didn't help that I was up in Aspen when this all started."

"Our Aspen meeting?"

"The very same. Anyway, I worked up the patient and called in the surgeon to do a bypass, I continued to follow the patient after the surgery, but I didn't order the radioscopic procedure." She explained about the radiologist taking that upon himself and calling in Ellis to help after he botched it up. "Do you think I might still be sued?"

"There is always a chance. Though if you haven't been named by now, it's a good sign that you won't. If I were the plaintiff's attorney, I'd name everyone involved in his care. Including the janitor."

"So there's a chance? That I might be sued, I mean. Do you think I should hire a lawyer or contact my malpractice carrier?"

"Before I answer that ... Are you an employee of the hospital?"

"No, I'm in private practice with privileges at the hospital. But it's not the hospital I'm concerned about. They're settling out of court. It's the surgeon. I want to help him some way. I'm the reason he's in trouble. I brought him in, and I'm the one who was following the case. I should have noticed the infection." And she would have if Jacob hadn't been wearing his boots to bed. Again, her fault. She knew he was not in his right mind; she shouldn't have coddled him.

"He's not settling out of court?"

"It doesn't sound like it. Why?"

"Deep-pocket syndrome. You set your digging rig where you expect to find the biggest pocket of oil. Hospital's are real gushers, but if they put the oil in barrels for you, you're going to take the new-improved rig you bought with the seed money over to the second-best pocket and tear the ground to pieces."

"I can't let them do that. He's the last one who should have been blamed for the negative outcome. I'm the one who told the patient he could sleep with his boots on. Not that I expected him to."

"What?" He choked on laughter.

"The anesthesiologist gave him something during his bypass surgery that made him loony afterward. When the patient threatened to leave the first time, I cajoled him by saying I'd transfer him out of ICU and put him on one of the floors to recuperate. That he didn't have to take another test and that he could wear his clothes, even his boots. He did. And no one could get him out of them to look at the incision on his foot." She could hear him covering the phone to snicker, and knew that he'd be telling this one at his next speaking engagement, but she kept on with the sordid details. "And then the radiologist gave him another test after I gave him my word that there would be no more tests, so his wife fired me and checked him out."

"Don't tell me any more. I can't stand it. Sounds like something out of *National Lampoon*."

"Yes, Robert, we're laughing ourselves silly over it."

"Rosa," he said, his tone serious, "this is something I learned in the army, not in law school, but it's my best advice to you. Don't leave the trenches unless you're ordered to."

After promises of keeping in touch and good-byes, Rosa picked up her copy of Jacob's medical records and slipped out of her office and headed for Ellis's. She was having none of Copeland's advice. If she had to take it on the chin, so be it. Ellis was the one person who had done his job properly, and she would stand behind him.

She caught Ellis in his waiting room, seeing out a patient. The poor woman looked to be the worst specimen Rosa had ever seen. Bloated and slumped in a wheelchair, the elderly woman looked up and gave Rosa a thin smile. Except for scant patches of lank white hair, the woman was mostly bald. Her skin looked to be the texture and thickness of white tissue paper, ready to tear at the slightest touch. A huge ulcer covered the back of her hand, while another spread over a leg.

"Now you be good, Mrs. Hart," Ellis said as he winked at a middle-aged woman, who relieved him at the helm of the wheelchair, "and let's not be hearing about how you robbed Father Donahey out of the bingo grand prize two weeks in a row."

The old woman's eyes came alive. She tittered behind her afflicted hand, proud of her good luck, and prouder that her physician thought enough of her accomplishment to mention it.

Ellis greeted one of the patients in the waiting room, apologized for running late to two others, and opened the inner door and ushered Rosa into the examining room's hallway. He pointed to the file in her hand. "Got one for me?"

Patrick was haunting the coffeepot. "No." She skirted Ellis and led the way to his office. He closed the door behind them.

"What's up?"

"This is for you." Rosa handed him Jacob's hospital records.

Ellis sat in the chair behind his desk and scrutinized the file. He looked up. "You had his file?" A combination of annoyance and hurt crept into his expression, as if to say "You had his file all the time I've been looking for it. Why didn't you tell me?"

"No, that's a copy of his file. I'd wager Emma or

her administrator has the original under wraps." She sat in the chair across the desk from him. "Look, Ellis, you're getting a raw deal. However I can help, I will."

His smile was as warm as it had been while speaking to poor Mrs. Hart. "Thanks."

"Have you spoken to an attorney, yet?"

He shook his head. "Notified my insurance carrier. They're to set up a meeting with an attorney." He set his face hard, trying to deal with emotions Rosa could only imagine. "My whole life has been put on hold, and they'll get to it in due course."

"It's merely a job to them." She gave a macabre laugh. "You're getting a dose of your own medicine. How many patients have said the same thing? That their lives are on hold while we spend days, weeks trying to diagnose their ailments."

Rosa got up and started for the door. She turned back to him when she'd reached it. "Ellis, if things get too tough, you know where to come." She patted her shoulder. "It's had some practice. My ex went through this."

She started out.

"Rosa?"

She turned back.

"Did he win or lose?"

"More importantly, he survived it. And so will you."

Chapter 18

Pam

"How are you doing?" Pam asked Mr. Reese as she checked his vitals. He wasn't long for this world.

Mrs. Reese, returning from the bathroom with a wet washcloth for his perspiring forehead, answered. "He's in so much pain. Can't you give him more morphine?"

"If it were up to me, I surely would." She held the man's frail hand. From his large frame, she suspected he had once been a strapping individual. Lung cancer had reduced him to gray skin and brittle bones. "I'd be happy to relay your request to Dr. Bell, if you'd like. He should be here, after a bit."

"We'd appreciate that," Mrs. Reese said, wiping a vagrant tear from her eye.

Of course they would. Patients and their families were universally afraid to ask their doctors anything for fear of being bad patients. They weren't intimidated by the nurses who cared for them, and felt no compunction in using and abusing nurses. Patients tended to dehumanize their nurses. Pam reminded herself that it was only natural. How else could you cope with having another person clean up your vomit or wipe your bottom, treating you like a helpless baby?

Mr. Reese smiled up at her. "That would be so nice . . ." A knock at the door startled him.

"Come in," Pam called.

Dr. Sanchez walked in. "Mr. Reese, I'm Dr. Rosa

Sanchez. The cardiologist. Your doctor has asked me to have a listen at your chest. Would you mind?"

"No, not at all," Mrs. Reese answered for her husband.

Pam gathered up her things. "I'll relay that request to Dr. Bell. We'll see what we can do."

The patient looked at her with his sunken eyes. "You're so wonderful."

Pam squeezed his hand and went out, nearly bumping into a boy who couldn't possibly have been fourteen, the minimum age limit for visitors. "Where are you going?"

"To get a candy bar." He pointed to the staircase beyond Mr. Reese's private room. "Sophie told me where the machine is."

Pam stepped out of the way and gave the boy the be-my-guest signal. If Sophie said so, then it was law. She wondered where Sophie and the new LVN were. They were no longer behind the nursing station counter. It was too much to hope that they had left the floor. She expected them to stay until five, another half hour. Sophie was really scraping bottom with the likes of Carrie.

At least they'd moved out of her way so she could write her nursing notes. She'd gotten report and five minutes orientation on where supplies were kept from the day-shift RN, spent a grand total of ninety minutes on the floor so far, and felt like she was barely treading water. She had twenty patients she was responsible for, hardly knew the floor procedures, everyone and his uncle were visiting, even though visiting hours were restricted from one to three and seven to nine. She was looking forward to the day she'd be a doctor's wife instead of an overworked nurse. Working as hard as she was gave her little time to concentrate on Aunt Emma.

The phone started ringing. Another interruption. "Three North, Pam Rogers, RN, speaking."

"Well, you don't have to sound so happy about it." It was Billy's voice.

"Hi," she purred into the phone.

"That's my girl. Sitting in my office all alone with no one to talk to. Why don't you sneak away for a while?"

Pam gave a deep groan. "I can't," Pam whispered into the phone. "Dr. Sanchez is rounding. Sophie's on the floor orientating the new LVN."

"Just five minutes?" he pleaded.

She wanted to squeeze him just like a teddy bear when he was like this. She covered her mouth and the mouthpiece when she saw Dr. Sanchez come out of 310 and head toward the nursing station. "I've got to go. Meet me at my place at eleven-thirty."

Dr. Sanchez dropped into the chair at the table behind the nursing station and spread out Carl Reese's chart. "The Reeses think you're Florence Nightingale's granddaughter."

"Poor Mr. Reese. He's such a nice man. I wish there was something I could do to help him."

Dr. Sanchez nodded. "I know, we all do." She sighed. "I wish I'd been a pediatrician instead of a cardiologist. Kids usually get well no matter what you do for them."

Pam could not believe Dr. Bell had called in the cardiologist to have a look at Reese. She couldn't understand why everyone and his uncle was so all-fired concerned about the old guy. He had cancer and was going to die. Give the guy his ten milliliters of morphine every four hours and leave him alone to die. Or up the dosage. Up it enough to put him out of his misery permanently.

"Mrs. Reese said you said he could have more morphine—"

That didn't surprise her. Patients and their families heard only what they wanted to hear. "What I said was that I would relay the request to Dr. Bell."

"That's what I figured. He shouldn't have a problem with that. I'll note it on the chart so you won't have to chase him down."

She wished all doctors were as considerate. The elevator chimed. Pam looked down the hall to see a dietary worker push the cart of dinner trays off the elevator. One of the wheels was in dire need of oil.

Pam watched her carry only one tray into 302. Great! The dinner request for the new arrival didn't get processed in time. She hated screw-ups. As soon as the aide returned with the Seven-Up to restock the refrigerator, Pam would have her go down and get a tray for the new patient.

"Nurses are patients' advocates," Sophie said as she and the LVN emerged from 306. "Patients don't always understand the system. It's our job to get them through it and run interference for them if there's a problem."

"What kind of problem?" the LVN asked. Her stupidity was getting on Pam's nerves. She hoped she'd never have to work with her.

Like a protective mother, Sophie put her arm around the girl and headed her toward the tiny stockroom behind the nursing station. "Let's see, once I wouldn't let a plumber into a patient's bathroom to fix a leak. The patient was being discharged that morning. I told the plumber to come back when he was gone. Another time I refused to let a husband visit his wife because he was drunk. She was there in the first place because he'd beaten her in a drunken rage. Things like that. The hardest of all, however, is refusing a physician's order if you don't think it's in your patient's best interest."

"You can do that?"

"If you think there's a problem, talk it over with your RN," Sophie said, skirting the question.

Pam returned to her work. She didn't have time to waste on stupid people and do-gooders. She had to focus, prioritize, and budget her time if she was to be the best RN this hospital had ever seen. Being charge nurse on an unfamiliar floor was not the easiest of assignments, even if the hospital was small and in a no-account Texas town. Sophie would notice her good work and would, at last, give her Wendy's position in ICU. Pam couldn't believe Sophie allowed Wendy to continue caring for critically compromised patients when she couldn't focus on anything but her own problems. Granted, Wendy had been stuck with a needle she'd removed from an AIDS patient, but she'd tested negative each time they'd given her the HIV test. The girl obviously couldn't get beyond herself and needed a less stressful job. Pam was tired of filling in and wanted a permanent job in ICU. She was a good ICU nurse. She just wondered how long it would take for Sophie to realize she needed to transfer Wendy out.

"Pam, would you open the meds cabinet? We need the heparin."

Sure thing, Sophie. Don't let my work interfere with your training session. Pam struggled out of her chair, bumping Dr. Sanchez's. She scooted over apologetically.

Pam unlocked the cabinet and hunted for the heparin. Heparin was an anticoagulant used to keep IV lines from clotting with blood. Pam assumed Sophie had found one that needed her urgent attention. She handed Sophie the bottle, deciding to worry about her nursing notes later and prepared the meds cart now. She wanted to give out the meds in a timely manner, especially with the director of nursing here to watch her every move.

She searched for the two sedative drugs she needed, Dilantin and phenobarbital. Found an unopened 500-milliliter bottle of morphine sulfate for Mr. Reese. He'd finished the last bottle, she'd learned at shift change. She placed a container of Valium on the counter.

Sophie seethed as Carrie drew up the anticoagulant. "How much diluting solution did you calculate you'd need?" Sophie asked with the slightest edge of annoyance in her tone.

Pam looked at the amount of heparin in the syringe

with disbelief. Properly *diluted* solution wouldn't fill
the syringe as well. She had enough to make the patient bleed to death. Had the girl really gone to nursing
school?

"The usual dosage is one unit per cubic centimeter
of fluid," Sophie reminded her. "A scant one unit," she
added.

The girl turned to the scratch pad where she'd calcu-
lated her figures. She nodded, and then looked at the
syringe, completely oblivious to the obvious problem.
How hard was it to multiply by one? A kindergartener's multiplication table.

Without comment, Sophie took the syringe and re-
measured the heparin, and then prepared the solution.

"Oh!" Carrie exclaimed, as though learning the
meaning of the universe.

"It's for Mrs. Griffith's IV," Sophie explained to
Pam.

"Yes, ma'am. I'll make the notation in Mrs.
Griffith's chart."

"Do I put it directly in the line?" Carrie asked stu-
pidly.

Pam heard the wheels of Dr. Sanchez's chair move
across the floor. She was either finished, or unwilling
to listen further to the training session. The chart
slipped down into the carousel of medical charts with
a metallic clang. Dr. Sanchez stuck her head around
the corner. "Pam, give me a call if Mrs. Calloway's
blood sugar shoots up. See you later, Sophie. Nice
meeting you, Carrie." She gave the LVN a hang-in-
there smile before disappearing. Sophie and Carrie followed her out with their syringe of diluted heparin.
Pam picked up a stack of pleated-paper pill cups to
count out twenty.

"Nurse?"

Pam craned around to see the dietary worker at the
nursing station, leaning over the counter. "Yes?"

"I didn't have a dinner tray for the patient in"—she
consulted a slip of paper—"three-oh-two B."

"She's a new arrival. I'll send someone for a tray."

"Okay," the woman said, nodding her head like an emptyheaded sheep. She held out the slip of paper. "Will you initial it?"

She'd never done that before. A new directive to complicate things? Pam put down the cups, returned to the nursing station, and did the woman's bidding. "Thanks."

"Okay." She backed away to her squeaky cart. " 'Bye."

" 'Bye."

The dietary worker pushed her steel cart to the side of the hall, out of the way, and joined Dr. Sanchez at the elevator. The latter pushed the down button like she was sending Morse Code.

When the elevator opened, Drs. Bell and Tilton got off.

"I had a look at Mr. Reese and left a note for you in his chart," Dr. Sanchez told Dr. Bell as she and the woman got in.

"Don't let it close," came a frantic voice, which sounded a great deal like their little lost aide, "I have to get off here."

The door reopened and Bobbie Jo, the nurse's aide, stumbled out juggling two six-pack cartons of Seven-Up.

Pam pulled out the charts the two doctors would be needing and laid them on the counter. "Good evening, Dr. Tilton. Good evening, Dr. Bell."

"Good evening." Dr. Bell nudged Dr. Tilton. "Doesn't she have the face of an angel?"

"Oh, Dr. Bell, you make me blush."

"Blush on an angel is most becoming," he said as Dr. Tilton scanned Mr. Reese's chart. "And there's another one." Dr. Bell fluttered a chart in Bobbie Jo's direction. "The angel with soda pop from the elevator."

"Want one?" Bobbie Jo asked him.

"Oh, no, no, no. Gas, you know."

Dr. Tilton divvied up the charts. "Rosa found Carl

Reese's bradycardia unremarkable and doesn't believe we should concern ourselves with treatment." Dr. Tilton looked at his partner as if to say, "Didn't I tell you as much? Who cares that a dying man's heartbeat is slow?"

"Good, good, good. Yes, yes. Let's go see him."

Dr. Tilton didn't see Dr. Sanchez's medication request, or maybe she hadn't written it, Pam thought. "Doctors, Mr. Reese complains of pain and asks that his morphine dosage be increased."

Dr. Bell opened the chart and scribbled new orders. "Every three hours instead of four, if he requests it."

"Yes, Doctor." Pam returned to preparing meds when the two family practitioners disappeared into room 310. Despite Bobbie Jo clinging and clanking in the refrigerator, Pam heard the ding of a call light. The light was on over the door to Mrs. Griffith's room. Sophie was summoning her.

She raced around the counter of the nursing station and into the room to find Sophie cranking down the foot of Mrs. Diehl's bed. The curtain between Mrs. Griffith and Mrs. Diehl's beds had been pulled, but not so much that Mrs. Griffith couldn't peek around the end to see what was going on.

"Page Rosa," Sophie told her in a calm voice to ease the patient's anxiety. It didn't help much. Mrs. Diehl's eyes were wild as she labored to breathe. Huffing in and gurgling out. "And bring Lasix for an IV push." Carrie stood frozen at the foot of the bed behind Sophie. There was a phone at the woman's bedside, but Pam hurried back to the nursing station and called the operator from there.

Mrs. Diehl looked to be in frank pulmonary edema from her congestive heart failure. The left ventricle of her heart couldn't propel the blood from her lungs as fast as it was accumulating. It often happened to CHFs—congestive heart failures—in the horizontal position. Sophie was lowering her feet to pool some of the blood. The Lasix was a powerful diuretic to get rid of the fluid in her lungs.

As the page for Dr. Sanchez to call 3125, Three North's extension, came over the public address system, Pam pushed the syringe full of Lasix into the IV line. Usually only a physician could give such a directive, but she was following her supervisor's orders. Sophie would take the fall if Dr. Sanchez challenged the IV push of Lasix.

Bobbie Jo appeared at the door. "Dr. Sanchez phoned. She's on her way up."

Mrs. Diehl coughed profusely.

"Thanks," Sophie acknowledged as she wiped away the frothy blood-tinged sputum. "Your doctor's coming, Mrs. Diehl. You're going to be just fine."

The dietary worker, coming to collect the dinner trays, won the foot race a hair ahead of Drs. Tilton and Bell, Mrs. Griffith's doctors. They stopped at Mrs. Diehl's bed, instead.

With all the excitement Pam had forgotten to tell Bobbie Jo to fetch a dinner tray for the new patient. Pam nodded to the worker that it was all right to take Mrs. Diehl's dinner, even though it had hardly been touched.

"Pulmonary edema?" Dr. Bell asked Sophie.

Sophie didn't answer. And why should she? The symptoms were pretty obvious and it didn't take much of a clinician to diagnose the trouble as pulmonary edema.

Pam caught Carrie's eye and motioned her over. "Carrie, will you go tell Bobbie Jo to go down to the kitchen and pick up a dinner tray for 302B?"

Carrie hurried out of the room as if message carrier was her calling. Dr. Sanchez and the slime Dr. Ellis Johnston, rushed in. Bill had told Pam what the bastard did to him at M&M that morning. Pam hoped Coral May nailed him good. Pam was certainly going to help her in any way that she could. Emma would surely send the man packing before long.

The room was taking on the circus atmosphere of a code. Dr. Sanchez shoved her way to the head of the bed, her stethoscope in her ears. She listened to Mrs. Diehl's chest for an eternity. Her lungs must have been totally involved.

Lisa came into the room. "Mom, when are we going home?" Lisa asked with the arrogance only a teenager would.

Sophie was noticeably embarrassed by her daughter's lack of good sense. "Take a chair at the nursing station. I'll be with you in a minute."

Lisa stalked out.

Dr. Sanchez handed the stethoscope to Dr. Johnston. His hand brushed over hers as he took it. And Pam's impression of Rosa Sanchez made a hundred-and-eighty degree turn. Pam had known the woman was too good to be true. It was all an act so no one would find out about the two of them. What in the world did she see in the likes of him? Pam knew from the grapevine that Ellis's wife was even crazier than he was. Wouldn't she just love to find out about the two of them?

Chapter 19

Emma

"Pam Roberts . . . I don't believe I know her." Emma looked up and down the board-room table before settling her gaze on the hospital administrator.

"A new nurse. Came to us straight from nursing school." Marcus conferred with his notes. "Colorado."

Emma folded her arms and studied his reddish, mottled neck across the table. She wondered if he knew it gave him away. "How new?"

"She's been here almost four months. A floater. Sophie considers her quite capable." Marcus paused, waiting for everyone else to agree. "This is her first black mark."

"She's very nice." Richard Bell thought everyone was endowed with the quality of golden goodness. "She was responding to an emergency."

Excuses. It didn't matter if she were nice or new or the next Messiah. She should have locked up the morphine. Her negligence had caused all this trouble. The hospital didn't need something like this, not on top of Coral May's lawsuit. Bad enough they wouldn't be able to keep the lawsuit quiet, not unless that varmint Ellis gave up his insane conviction about going to court to prove his innocence. She could see the headline in the newspapers now: FAMILY OF FORMER BOARD MEMBER SUES CMC DOC. Revenues were down twenty percent from this quarter last year. Adverse publicity would drive prospective patients into the city. Stephen

F. Austin Hospital would be sending her an engraved thank-you note. Worrying about it got the acid juices in her stomach churning. She hadn't gotten a decent night's sleep since Coral May had slapped the document on this very table last Thursday. Now this! She was beginning to dread coming to town for Thursday morning board meetings.

"How many people know about this?"

"We interviewed"—caught off-guard but pretending otherwise, Marcus moved the eraser end of his pencil down the list—"five nurses, four doctors, a dietary worker, the security guard, and two maintenance staff workers."

His blasé attitude was beginning to do more than infuriate her. It was making her consider running an ad for a new hospital administrator. "Who?"

Her chilled tone caused the anxiety-drawn crinkles on Richard's forehead to deepen. It was a pity the hospital administrator couldn't read her black mood as well.

All ears, Allison leaned forward and planted her chin in her hands. She didn't have much use for the Yankee administrator and was enjoying watching him squirm. She was still young.

"The day-charge nurse who signed the pharmacy receipt, an LVN who was with Sophie on the floor during that time, a nursing assistant, Miss Roberts, and Sophie, of course." He pointed to Richard. "Dr. Bell, who was on the investigative committee with Sophie and myself, Dr. Tilton, Dr. Sanchez, and Dr. Johnston, were all on the floor during the time the medication cabinet was left unlocked." Marcus gave a nervous cough.

A cynical smile played around Allison's lips. Richard tidied papers, while Harry Wilder, the hospital's attorney, wore a judicial look. Yes, they were all of one mind. Major embarrassment to Chandler Medical Center. "What about the maintenance workers? They had access to the drugs?"

"No, they, along with the security guard, went through the trash looking for the missing bottle of morphine."

"Which, of course, was never recovered." It was a fool's mission to try to cover up something like this. Too many people knew about the theft. She looked at Harry. "If we call the police, the matter will no doubt become public. We simply can't afford to have Chandler Medical Center's name tarnished in any manner. Especially now, with the lawsuit."

"I don't see how we can avoid it. The chief of police is Sophie Drummond's boyfriend," Marcus explained, with an air of being rather pleased with himself. He didn't seem to understand that, as hospital administrator, he was the director of nursing's boss. He could order her to keep quiet. "He probably already knows," he added, as if reading Emma's mind.

"That's all we need, a little innocent pillow talk. . . . Nana, look at the time." Allison apparently couldn't appreciate the seriousness of the matter. But she was right, the board meeting had run far overtime, thanks to this calamity.

Allison and she had a one-thirty appointment with the media specialist in Houston, which meant they'd have to be out of here by twelve-thirty, even at the lofty speeds Allison drove. The brochure mock-up for the Houstonian Health Retreat was ready. They needed to be printed and in the mail as soon as possible. Except for the opening week, which was booked solid with a block reservation from a California party, bookings were practically nil. But even if they were forced to close it down and let the place go to seed, it would be worth whatever the financial loss to keep it out of Stephen F. Austin's hands. Emma considered it a major coup against their closest competitor.

Her one concern was for Allison. She was working much too hard, as the black circles under her eyes attested. Ordinarily Emma would have suspected she was out with Josh, but Emma knew better. Josh had called every evening this week looking for her. Emma wished Margaret would get home to take some of the pressure off her sister.

That was another thing keeping her up nights. Why was Margaret still off gallivanting around? Emma had asked Rosa as much, but the cold fish stared through her like she wasn't even there and mumbled that Margaret would be back soon. Who was Rosa to be so high and mighty? Wasn't Emma her benefactor, not to mention Margaret's grandmother and guardian? Well, former guardian. The girls had reached their majority in the eyes of the state of Texas. Still, the girls lived under her roof. And as long as they did, they had an obligation to respect her wishes. Margaret was so willful!

Emma took a deep breath to calm herself. She couldn't let her thoughts become muddled. She would worry about only one problem at a time. And this was a doozy. "What is your recommendation, Harry?"

"I see this as two problems. First, whether the authorities should be called in to investigate the theft of the narcotic. Are we certain a crime has taken place? Perhaps the bottle of morphine will turn up. Before calling the authorities, seemingly more prudent would be appointing an ad hoc committee for an in-house investigation and initiating any needed changes recommended by said committee. Second, what disciplinary measures should be taken against Miss Roberts for her negligence? In light of the fact that Nurse Roberts was a floater and had not been properly instructed on floor procedure and that the negligence occurred due to being summoned to an emergency situation by her superior, firing her would be an open invitation to a lawsuit."

They needed another lawsuit like a hole in the head.

"Marcus representing hospital administration, Richard representing the medical staff, and Sophie representing the nursing staff will make up the ad hoc committee," Emma informed them. "As for this nurse

. . . if it isn't prudent to let her go, find a place for her
where she can't get into trouble. Put her on the night
shift in pediatrics. How much trouble can she get into
with sleeping children?"

Chapter 20

Meredith

Meredith had made a grievous error. She would surely be drummed out of the American Psychiatric Association, the American Psychoanalytic Association, lose her BNDD number, as well as her Texas State medical license, if she were to own up. How had she been such a fool?

Simple enough. She thought she was covering for Sean. There wasn't a person on earth she loved more than that Irishman. How could she not protect him? But she had been so wrong. So terribly, terribly wrong.

When she received the query from the Bureau of Narcotics and Dangerous Drugs about the inordinate amount of Demerol and Preludin prescribed to Sean O'Neill within such a short span of time, Meredith jumped to the wild conclusion that Sean had a drug dependency problem and had forged the prescriptions. The irony of his supposed plight was not lost on her. Sean was a behavioral psychotherapist with his own addiction in a rehabilitation center. But he was not the first impaired professional, and the closest coworkers were usually the last to know.

She thought his recovery could best be handled in-house. Who was better qualified to help him than she? To the Bureau, she wrote affirming that she had written the prescriptions in question, and had justified her actions by stating that the Preludin was indicated in the management of the patient's exogenous obesity—they had no way of knowing Sean wasn't fat—and the Demerol was indicated for severe back pains due to his obesity. *What a tangled web* . . .

The corner of the white, business-size envelope protruded over the edge of her desk. She wanted to reach out, read the anonymous letter one more time, and make certain it wasn't a bad dream. She wanted to, but she wouldn't. This was Carolyn Wright's fifty-five minutes.

Carolyn Wright, a former model married to a wealthy oilman, required no more from Meredith than her chaise longue. But Carolyn Wright was paying for Meredith's time, and she would get the full fifty-five minutes of her undivided silence.

Meredith was resigned to Carolyn's daily fifty-five-minute-psychoanalysis-in-absentia sessions. Carolyn had been coming faithfully for two years. For a while, Meredith had tried to explain to the reluctant analysand that her silence was detrimental to successful therapy and that no progress could be achieved without Carolyn's full cooperation. Finally, in utter frustration, Meredith withdrew from the case, stating flatly that she could not treat her. Carolyn's reaction was pathological. She became hysterical, insisting that the sessions were doing her a world of good. It had been the only symptom of her undisclosed complaint.

What that complaint might be was a source of wild speculation on Meredith's part. Last week's scenario had Carolyn attending her grandfather's funeral at an early age and becoming frightened by seeing him in his coffin. Of watching the coffin inch into a freshly dug hole on a bitter cold day. This week's was uninspired. Carolyn was an obsessive-compulsive shopper. The drive from the ranch to Chandler Springs and back took such a big chunk out of her day that she didn't have a chance to shop. The flaw in this scenario was that Meredith had never seen Carolyn in the same outfit twice. She was finding enough time to shop. And

Bubba Wright had enough money to see that she did it in style.

"Carolyn?"

As if shaken from a forbidden sleep, Carolyn quickly sat up. "Is it time, already?" She whirled around to have a look at the clock.

"No, I was wondering about the outfit you have on. Is it new?"

Carolyn looked down at the peach, scoop-neck T-shirt and matching sarong skirt as if trying to place it. "It's one of Allison's. From her spring collection. It's Thursday. Thought I might run into her."

The weekly board meeting. "Do you buy a lot of her clothes?"

"Enough to remain on friendly terms." She slid back down on the chaise, one of her bare legs exposed where the sarong parted.

Maybe Bubba was a sex fiend and chased her around the house all day. She came here for an hour of rest. Meredith liked that one a great deal.

Lisa Drummond.

If Meredith could believe the anonymous letter writer, Lisa had stolen a pad of scripts.

What could Meredith do? Going to the authorities was out of the question, thanks to her inaccurate response to the Bureau of Narcotics and Dangerous Drugs query. Doing nothing wouldn't help Lisa. And might be an impossibility, considering the letter.

She'd seek Sean's advice. She closed her eyes and seethed, thinking about how she would put it to Sean.

"Dr. Fischer," Carolyn exclaimed as she jumped up and slipped bare feet into her sandals. "Look at the time!"

Today's was a sixty-minute session. "Sorry, I must not have been watching carefully enough."

Carolyn gave her a warm smile. "It's all right with me. But you know how Hillary is." She fluffed out long russet curls, picked up her ring of keys from the chrome coffee table, and hurried to the door. "See you Monday." She had canceled Friday's session.

Meredith got up and followed her to the door. She did know how Hillary was. It didn't suit her to wait.

Carolyn threw the door wide open then turned back. "Hillary's not here!"

Meredith followed her into the reception area. Hillary wasn't there. "How strange."

"I hope she hasn't been in an accident," Carolyn offered with more compassion than Hillary would have if their roles had been reversed.

"Surely it's nothing serious."

"You don't think she left because my session ran over, do you?"

Meredith shook her head.

Carolyn shrugged. "Well, see you Monday."

"Have a nice weekend, Carolyn."

"You, too, Dr. Fischer." Carolyn crossed the reception area the way she always did, like a ramp model. It would be easy to hate the beautiful woman if she weren't so nice.

Not that Meredith had anything to complain about. She was well-proportioned and had a nice face. She was no longer a blond towhead like when she was a child, but her hair was a nice "dirty-blonde" shade that hid the few gray hairs cropping up.

Meredith went down the hall to the restroom. Hillary wasn't there. She caught up with the clinic's receptionist in the occupational therapy center, making a ceramic pot. It was coming along about as well as any of the patients'. "Ruthanne, did Mrs. Johnston call?"

"No," Ruthanne said without looking up from her work.

Meredith admired a ceramic piece or two before going next-door to Sean's adolescent group therapy. Sean and a half dozen eating-disorder teens were sitting in a circle laughing about something or other when she slipped in. She waited by the door, hoping to get Sean's attention. Instead, one of the skeletal girls noticed her and got Sean's attention for her. Sean's grin was replaced by concern when he saw her. He hurried over.

"Sorry to interrupt. Will you come to my office when your session ends? I need to speak with you."

The dreaded knock on the door came a half hour later.

"Come in."

Instead of Sean, Ellis entered.

"Am I disturbing you?" It was more a reprieve than a disturbance.

"Not at all, Ellis. Have a chair. I was going to give you a call."

Ellis flopped in the chair on the other side of her desk. "About Hillary missing today's appointment?"

Meredith nodded, waiting to hear what he had to say.

"She's not coming back." Hillary wasn't coming back to therapy, or back to Ellis? She waited for him to tell her more. He didn't.

"And how are you doing?"

"My malpractice carrier is sending an attorney to see me next week. Maybe that will help. I want the wheels of justice to start turning."

"I'd like to be able to tell you not to think about it, but I know it would be impossible. It's a curious matter, that you were singled out."

He guffawed. "One nice side of this awful mess is that I've had my eyes opened to the doctors around me."

"What do you mean?"

"People I barely took the time to know have come out of the woodwork to rally behind me. Ty, for instance. I've lived next-door to him for almost two years and I really never understood him until now."

That explained what Ty was doing at the Maverick table last Monday. "What did he do?"

"Nothing really. Got me drunk and let me cry on his

shoulder. Rosa, too. She offered me a shoulder, and found a copy of Jacob's file for me."

"I'm a good listener, Ellis. Any time you need a shoulder, mine's available."

He nodded.

"Want to talk about Hillary?"

He nodded again.

She waited for him to start. A knock at the door came first.

"Am I—"

"You're fine." Meredith motioned him back into his chair as she got up and went to the door. Sean was standing there with a grin on his face. What she had to tell him would wipe it off fast enough. She stepped into the hall and closed the door behind her. "Sean, I need to speak to you about something important. But I'm tied up now and have to drive to Houston this afternoon for a behavioral symposium at the Texas Medical Center."

"How about dinner?" he suggested with mixture of boyish glee and manly insightfulness in his Celtic lilt.

"My place at seven?" No reason not to put off her execution.

"I'll be there with bells on." He did a little jig as he went off and she laughed, in spite of wanting to cry.

She would try to put her problem out of mind and concentrate on Ellis's. "Sorry," she said as she took her leather chair. "You were saying that Hillary isn't coming back."

"Hillary doesn't see the need. She thinks that her only problem is my obsession with being a surgeon to the point that I don't have time to be a husband and father. That she has to be both a mother and father to the kids."

That was a heavy trip to lay on him at a time like this. Of course, she was correct. All surgeons were obsessed with their work. That went without saying. The standing wisecrack among surgery residents was that the only thing wrong with taking call every other night was that they were missing half the cases.

"Ellis, you know she has a personality disorder exhibiting sociopathic and paranoid features. You have always taken her tirades in stride before. Can you think of a reason you aren't this time?"

He scrunched down in the chair, propped his head up with one hand, grimaced, and then shifted to the other.

"Your shoulder still bothering you?"

"No." He shifted back, leaning his injured side hard against the arm on the chair. It was pure bravado.

"Shall I tell you what I believe, Ellis?"

"Please." He could have exhibited a trifle more gratitude. Most people paid for her counsel.

"You're of the opinion that your life is unraveling. Your bull-goring injury, the lawsuit, Hillary's invidious behavior. You have feelings of inadequacy and incompetence. Everything seems to be stacking up against you."

He pondered her declaration. She knew imperfection was not an easy thing for a surgeon to admit. He rubbed his hands over his face. "All right, let's say you're right. What's the cure?"

"Cure? My field's psychiatry, we don't give cures. But the prognosis is good. You are a very strong and resourceful man, Ellis Johnston. Don't let the bastards get you down."

Chapter 21

Margaret

It was a fool's errand. But more fun than she'd ever had. Texans could paint the town red, and do so in the most ostentatious manner in the world. But to cast Margaret in the role of traffic controller in the middle of Rodeo (which Californians pronounced entirely wrong) Drive with two lines of luxury cars beeping up a storm while her partner in crime parked a Rolls-Royce at the curb between two meters was right out of science fiction. Katherine insisted it would be a hoot to see if she could still parallel park. What was the challenge of getting out of the car and having it magically disappear to a hidden valet-parking lot? Well, it was a horn-blowing hoot, all right, as Katherine met her challenge bumper to bumper.

Katherine told Margaret when she picked her up at the clinic that her regular car was a Range Rover, but that her son had taken it to Death Valley for a UCLA-class-something-or-other. She was reduced to taking the "old nag out of the stable." And so began Margaret's Rodeo Drive shopping folly.

The Mercedes in front of the vacant space inched up as Katherine tapped its bumper. She rolled down the smoke-tinted window to admonish Margaret for having her hand up to her face. The healing skin itched, but the hand was there out of habit, nothing more. Margaret quickly withdrew her hand so Katherine could turn her attention back to parking. The BMW behind gave even more after a persistent nudge. Katherine's Rolls-Royce was snuggled tightly between the cars. Margaret got out of the street, and the anxious blocked cars hurried on their disgruntled way.

"See, wasn't that fun?" Katherine's door slammed with the tightness of a vacuum-sealed coffee can. She fished through her Chanel purse for quarters to feed the meter. Margaret was holding an assortment of change, but only the quarter was acceptable meter food in Beverly Hills.

"It was a hoot," Margaret said with enough sarcasm to wilt a potted palm tree.

Katherine laughed genuinely, wrapping her arm around Margaret's. "Now, Margaret, cheer up. It's absolutely unnatural to be depressed on a shopping spree. Forget *him* for the next few hours. You can wallow in self-pity when you get back to the clinic." Margaret had confessed her foolish lovesickness to Katherine, but she'd refused to give him a name. She couldn't bring herself to tell anyone, not even Katherine.

"If I find lots of treasures, I might be so busy trying them on all night that I won't have time to think about *him* until tomorrow."

"I'll tell you this one last time, my dear, and then I'll never mention it again. You have your whole life ahead of you. If *he* isn't the one . . ." She shrugged her shoulders instead of finishing the sentence. She often didn't finish her sentences. And she was right. About Josh, that is. He wasn't the one for her. He was Allison's. "What's meant to be, will be. What's not meant to be. . . ."

They marched arm in arm down the street to their first stop. A yellow corner shop. "Try to think about his negative qualities instead of romanticizing."

"He doesn't have any."

"Everyone has them. You'll just have to search for his unattractive traits. Is he cheap, selfish, a wimp? Does he pick his nose in public? If he doesn't, pretend." Katherine took off her sunglasses and stuck them in her bag as they entered the store. Her eyes had healed nicely. The only tell-tale sign was a red line in each crease of the upper eyelids.

"Afternoon, Mrs. Little, so nice to see you!" The Oriental beauty rounded the cosmetic counter to greet Katherine. She was noticeably pregnant.

"And look at you." Katherine took both of the young woman's hands in hers and held her at arm's length. "Why, the last time I was in, you were telling me about your bridal shower." Katherine counted deliberately on her fingers. She stopped at eight. The salesgirl laughed. "I haven't been in since Christmas? My husband must have hypnotized me."

"Well, thank goodness you came out of it."

Margaret and Katherine turned in unison to see a—
"Fred!"
—Fred standing behind them.

"Katherine!" It was his turn to hold Katherine at arm's length. "You look absolutely marvelous, Katherine. Have you done something to your face?"

She swatted him. "Of course I have. And how very naughty of you to notice." Katherine batted her eyes, and then showed off the red scars.

"You look so rested."

"So do people in coffins. But enough about me." Katherine reined in Margaret. "This is my dear friend, Margaret Chandler. We have hair appointments down the street in forty-five minutes, so if you want to show her your fall line," she warned.

The warning was well-taken. Three outfits and fifty-five minutes later, Katherine and she had their heads in the beauty parlor's wash basins.

Over the spraying water, Katherine said, "Another twenty years and you'll appreciate a little help from color, Margaret." She looked up at Toby. "She's a gray, beige, and navy person."

Toby tsked. He turned to have a good look at Margaret. "Sky blue, that's your color."

Sky blue was close to the color the makeup artist at

the cosmetic shop, their third stop, was using on Margaret's eyelids. Though it wasn't the eyeshadow she was admiring in the mirror. She couldn't get over how full her hair looked, now that it was cut even with her jaw. It wasn't actually cut even. That was the trick, Tiffany had told her as she took a curling iron to the ends. Cut each layer on top of the last a tiny bit shorter so it fluffs out. Frosting, to highlight her mousy blond hair, helped to make it seem thicker, too. Maybe it was frosted a little heavy. It was so blond. At least, Allison would love it. Especially the Garbo-ish long blond streak that started at the side part, ran down the lock that half-hid her eye, like Katherine's, and curled around the cheek that used to be scarred. The cheek was a pale, pale pink now that the makeup artist had covered it with foundation.

Margaret put on her glasses and held the mirror up to watch how the lip liner should be drawn. "I don't think I can do this," she said, trying not to move her mouth.

"Yes, you can," Katherine admonished as she hovered over her like a mother hen. "A little practice is all it'll take."

After lunch and hopping in and out of one shop after another, Katherine promised that this store, her favorite, was to be their last.

"Mrs. Little, what a pleasant surprise." A young woman with long shiny brown hair greeted Katherine as they stepped into the store. There hadn't been one salesperson in any of the shops who wasn't young and stylishly beautiful. "I have something special for you, today."

They followed her to the scarf counter. She spread a black-and-white Art Deco scarf the size of a shawl across the glass. "Wouldn't this look lovely with your yellow suit?"

"Yes! You are such a clever girl to remember." She looked at the price tag. So did Margaret. "And such a bargain. Wrap it." Katherine pointed excitedly to a similar scarf in lavender and green. "And gift wrap that one." She whispered, "Now, that will make your beige outfit." With the eight-point-five sales tax, Katherine had dropped six hundred dollars in less than a minute. Allison would love this place.

Katherine took her arm and led her into the back room while their salesgirl wrapped the scarves. "Now, here's something with your name on it." Katherine held up a silver, silk-shantung, strapless evening gown. Pearl beads covered the bodice and rimmed the hem of the bell skirt. "If this doesn't make some wonderful man notice you, nothing will."

"I don't want anyone to notice me."

"Best way to turn off the love spigot is to turn on another." Katherine thrust it at her. "Try it on."

Margaret studied the handwritten label in the dressing room. It told her everything but the price. When she took it off the hanger she discovered a long chiffon scarf to drape around the neck. And a ten-thousand-dollar tag.

She had to hold the gown up it was so big, but the back was high enough to conceal an old skin graft and she really did look pretty in it. Katherine and the salesgirl embarrassed her to no end going on and on about how the man who was looking at the purses had popped his eyes clear out of their sockets when he saw her.

"It's so expensive," she whispered to Katherine.

Apparently, she didn't whisper soft enough. "It's forty percent off," the salesgirl announced.

Katherine threw up her hands. "Well, that does it. You *must* have it!"

Six thousand was much, much, much too expensive, but Katherine talked her into buying it for the opening of the Houstonian Health Retreat. It would be altered, and Katherine would personally bring it to her in Texas.

There was a parking ticket on the Rolls-Royce.

Katherine leaned over the hood and retrieved it. "Now, we have one last stop."

"Where to?"

"To my eye doctor's. We're getting you a pair of contacts."

"I can't wear contacts. They hurt my eyes."

"Everyone can wear *soft* lenses."

Chapter 22

Pam

Wasn't this turning into a red-letter day? Thirty minutes into her three-to-eleven shift and Pam had already changed Mr. Bowman's bandages and his puss-clogged draining tubes, and picked up stool from the floor so housekeeping could clean up. Heaven forbid one of them should have to clean a spot that hadn't been "prepared." And now as she was coming out of the Diehl/ Griffith room, she realized Sophie was sitting in her chair at the nursing station bigger than nobody's business. The queen Nightingale perched on the lowly worker bee's bench.

Sophie caught a glimpse of her, too. But then turned away uneasily, pretending otherwise. Pam didn't like the reproachful look on Sophie's face. She was here to fire her over the morphine.

It was all Lisa's fault. That little conniving thief had caused all this trouble for Pam. She had to be the one who stole the morphine. Wasn't she on the floor during Mrs. Diehl's crisis? Didn't she steal a pad of scripts out of Dr. Fischer's pocket? Didn't her charming mother tell her to sit at the nursing station until she was ready to go? Was she there when they disbanded? No, she'd gone to the public restroom on the first floor, she said. More likely she stashed the morphine somewhere where she could retrieve it later. Pam hoped she would overdose on it.

Lisa was going to get hers, all right. Pam had seen

to it. Dr. Fischer must have gotten the letter by now. Yesterday. Today at the very latest.

Sophie wouldn't be here if Dr. Fischer had already gone to the authorities. She'd be over at the jail, trying to bail out her precious daughter.

If that retarded mail boy hadn't been in the wrong place at the wrong time and heard too much, Pam would have made a point of looking in his mailbag. Make sure Meredith got the letter. A pity, all that. Now, he ran from her whenever their paths crossed. A good thing. He would wish he had never been born if he dared to open his stupid mouth.

How long would it take the authorities to apprehend the girl? Better be in time to find the bottle of morphine and clear Pam's good name.

Still. She had little defense about leaving the drugs out. That mistake would go into her permanent record and follow her the rest of her career. Maybe she could forget to list Chandler Medical Center on her application. Say that she'd taken a few months off after nursing school to see the world. That would work. Not that she wanted to be a nurse anywhere else. Her whole purpose in going into nursing was to pull the rug out from under Aunt Emma.

There was still Bill. Maybe he'd feel so sorry about her unfair treatment over this thing that he would get a faster divorce and marry her. They could set up the out-patient radiology clinic that much sooner. Bring Aunt Emma to her knees that much sooner. Maybe everything would work out after all. It was just one little mistake.

"How's it going?" Sophie asked too sweetly.

"I've never seen puss clogging drainage tubes like Mr. Bowman's."

Sophie shook her head, feigning sympathy. She was really good at pretending she cared about the patients. Too bad she couldn't pretend to be a better mother. Pretend enough to fool Lisa. "The poor man."

Pam assumed she meant the poor man to be Mr.

Bowman, but suspected Sophie was saving some of the unwanted sympathy for her.

"Do you have a minute, Pam?"

"Bobbie Jo, run this down to the lab. Please." Pam held out a throat culture. Bobbie Jo plucked it out of her hand, thankful to have a reason not to be on the floor while Sophie was there. Bobbie Jo had not been thrilled with the third degree she'd gotten about the missing morphine, either. Nor did Pam want Bobbie Jo spreading first-hand word of Pam's firing through the hospital grapevine. Speculation would be bad enough.

Pam slipped into the chair next to her.

"I've just come from Marcus Laurence's office. The board met this morning and our problem"—she threw her head toward the back room to indicate the meds cabinet, like Pam didn't know what problem she was talking about—"was discussed. He didn't say what decision was made about it"—she threw her head again—"but said to let you know they weren't blaming you."

Pam held back a sigh of relief. This was not at all what she expected. She couldn't believe that of Aunt Emma. She didn't have an ounce of kindness in her stout body. Sophie was just saying that. "I blame myself. It was my mistake," Pam said reverently. "I should have put the drugs back into the cabinet and locked up before answering your call." Pam hoped the woman had focused on *your*. It was *Sophie's* fault. If she hadn't been in the way while Pam was trying to orient herself to her new surrounds, none of this would have happened.

"Now don't be blaming yourself, sweetheart. It wasn't really your fault. We're very pleased with your work overall. Most nurses aren't worth their salt first year out of nursing school. You've been wonderful. Really."

Sophie moved in closer. "But here's a little tip. A veteran nurse told this to me when I was a rookie." Sophie took her hand and patted it. "Never take the bottles out of the cabinet. Take only the required dosage, fill a pill cup and put the cup on the appropriate square on the room chart right then. That way if you're needed somewhere, you can close the cabinet, turn the key, stick it in your pocket, and you're gone. You'll learn to do it in a flash." The High Priestess of CMC's nurses spouted out this esoteric bullshit like it was scripture.

"Oh, thank you, Sophie. I should have known that. Really, I should have."

"Don't worry, these are little tricks of the trade you'll learn along the way. It will all come in time."

"I hope so. I feel so awful about what's happened."

Sophie nodded, a big fat touching smile on her holier-than-thou face. "I know you do." She clapped her hands as if to magically bring them out of the black hole of despair they had been sucked into. "Now for the good news. Remember I told you I would give you the first permanent opening that came along? Well, Wendy wants to work part-time for awhile so she can get her strength back."

At last! She was getting Wendy's ICU assignment. Yes! The ICU was Pam's niche. She loved the adrenaline rush of codes. And the ICU was code heaven. Someone was always trying to die there. Nothing got her blood pumping like knowing she was the only thing standing between her patient and death. She'd sound the alarm, grab the crash cart, and start resuscitation. "Code blue to ICU. Code blue to ICU" would be heard over the public-address system throughout the hospital. Time both would stand still and fly while she worked to keep the patient alive, knowing help was on the way. And then they would be there. Circus performers, shouting orders, scurrying from bed to cart. And she was in center ring. All eyes on her. And then that one was over. Win or lose, a pat on the back and a quick "well done" was her reward.

"Poor Wendy." Sophie shook her head. "The AZT treatment just didn't agree with her."

"I know. It's all so sad. Imagine the anxiety. Waiting out one blood test after another. Afraid to believe that she wasn't infected by the needle stick from that AIDS patient."

"She'll be fine. Chances are, if she's gone this long without a seroconversion, she won't. It's the AZT that's making her so weak."

"Oh, I'm sure she will be fine." Wendy was in some experimental program to examine the possibility of avoiding infection even after exposure. Maybe it had worked. Maybe that's why she never converted. Or maybe she wasn't exposed to the virus after all.

"Nurses will always be at high risk for HIV infection. But it's our obligation to provide care for AIDS patients."

Pam wasn't about to disagree with Sophie about anything now. She'd gotten what she wanted. The evening shift in ICU. Things were coming up roses and she wasn't about to blow it. "Oh, don't get me wrong, Sophie. I wasn't saying that we shouldn't care for all our patients equally. I just meant that I sure can sympathize with Wendy."

"Can't we all." Another sigh. Then Sophie smiled. Apparently, Wendy's misfortune was forgotten. "So anyway, next week I'm transferring Avon to the ICU and giving you her night shift in Peds."

What! Night shift in Peds! Why wasn't she being given the ICU job? It was the first opening that came along. Not Peds! Who did the bitch think she was, giving that lazy, good-for-nothing colored girl *her* job? Sophie had promised it to her. It was to be hers. Pam was the best nurse for the ICU opening!

Bobbie Jo had gone in to see what Mr. Reese wanted. Everyone else was tucked in for the night and Pam was trying to finish up her nursing notes before the night-shift staff arrived and she had to give report on each of the patients.

Pam was still pissed. She didn't want to work nights

and she certainly didn't want to work in Peds with all those little bed-wetting monsters. She hated kids! She hated them almost as much as she hated Sophie for sending her there.

She wished she hadn't invited Billy over—she wanted to be alone tonight. She couldn't decided whether to tell Bill what had happened or not. She wanted to cry on his shoulder, but if she were smart, she'd say nothing and pretend she was enjoying his company.

"He wants his morphine," Bobby Jo informed her as she slumped into the other chair, one eye on the ticking clock.

So Mr. Reese was in pain again. What a surprise! She had half a mind to let him suffer. It was his fault all of this was happening to her. Wasn't it his morphine that Lisa stole?

Pam put down her pen and got to her feet. "It's been three hours since he had his last one. He's entitled." She drew up the injection and made the trek down the quiet hall.

"Can't sleep?" Pam asked as she shone her flashlight on his pain-contorted face.

He groaned. "It's the dark lonely nights that get to me most. Wondering if I'll see another sunrise."

She turned on the night light over his bed and moved around to his IV line. "You're a brave man, Mr. Reese."

"No, I'm not brave at all. What if they're wrong? What if there is no God? No heaven? No afterlife? What if this is it? I cease to exist?"

Why couldn't you have ceased to exist before you caused me all this grief? "There's a God and He'll receive you with open arms. Bright light all the time. No darkness or fear there." She stabbed the needle into the IV line.

"You have been so wonderful to me," he said in a choked voice. "All of you. Angels of mercy. Especially Sophie. She's the salt of the earth."

"Yes, Sophie's the salt of the earth," Pam said, pulling the tip of the needle out of the IV line before pushing in on the plunger. The morphine streamed to the floor. She obliterated the puddle with the sole of her shoe. She turned off the night light. "Get some sleep now, Mr. Reese. I'll see you tomorrow evening." She hoped he suffered quietly.

Chapter 23

Sean

Sean stared at the moonlit shadows playing on the ceiling as he held the exhausted woman in his arms. Meredith's even breathing told him she was finally asleep. This had unbalanced him so. What had they gotten themselves into?

If he didn't fear waking her, he would clean up the Chinese food Meredith had picked up in Houston on her way home. Dinner wouldn't be fit for swine by morning. He felt, more than heard, his stomach growl. Sean wished she had waited until after they'd eaten before telling him about the BNDD query and the anonymous letter about Sophie's young lass. Or wished he hadn't ruined their dinner by throwing such a fit.

How he wished he could have taken back his angry words that had led to the opening of Pandora's box. Until she confessed them, he had no sense that she had such strong feelings for him. Not the slightest inkling. He'd tried so hard to fend off advances from the wee lasses at the center, that he had not dreamed Meredith harbored any such notions about him.

It was only natural for him to pick her up and carry her into the bedroom after he had reduced her to tears. And only natural to comfort each other. Comfort that led to unbridled passion. His mother had been writing from Mullingar, hinting of her longing to see him settled. Saying a man of thirty-five needed a wife and children around him at the hearth. Perhaps it was time.

He tucked a lock of hair behind her ear to have a better look at his intended. She lay small and delicate against his big arm. Her pale hair, where it didn't glisten from rays of moonlight, blended into the white pillow. He traced a finger ever so lightly down the long line of her neck, remembering.

"You look out of sorts, Meredith. Surely this important news of yours could not be so beastly."

She gave the kitchen spoon a crashing fling to the sink, picked up her wine goblet and drank from it like she was looking for the bottom. She was as troubled as the Irish Sea.

"What is it? Tell me," he insisted as he tipped the goblet away from her wet lips.

"My career." She drained the goblet.

Thoughts whirled in his mind. " 'Tis the center? The new Waller County rehab center is forcing Miss Emma to close us down?"

Meredith gave a lachrymose laugh and turned her back on him and reached for the bottle. "I wish."

"You don't mean it!" He grasped her shoulders and spun her around. She needed no further sustenance. "What is it that lays so heavy on your soul?"

"I did a very stupid thing. I received a missive from the BNDD challenging the exorbitant amount of Preludin and Demerol I was prescribing for you."

He freed her. "For me? Prescribing Preludin and Demerol for me?"

"I assumed the worst. That you had a drug problem and were forging my signature."

"How could you believe me capable of such a thing? How could that have even crept into your mind?" He was angry, but more than that, hurt.

"I don't know. They were made out to you. I believed the worst because of the facts presented. What would you have thought given those facts?"

"That my name was counterfeited on bogus scripts."

She nodded. "Yes, I realize that now. Today I received an anonymous letter stating that Lisa Drummond, Sophie's daughter, was the one forging the scripts. Anyway, I answered the BNDD query by saying that I wrote the prescriptions."

"Why would you do such a thing? Why would you lie?"

"I wanted to protect you."

"Protect me from what? The truth is my protection. Did you have so little faith in my character?" His fierce anger backed her into the corner against the stove. "You have hurt me to my very soul." Her legs gave way and she slid down the wall. She buried her head between her legs and wept. " 'Tis my life I have dedicated to saving the troubled from their addictions. My mission in life. How could you believe *me* an addict?" he badgered on over her jagged sobs. "We have worked side by side all this time, and you thought me capable of such an insidious crime?"

She lifted her tear-streaked face to him like a defiant adversary bravely facing a firing squad. "I thought my love for you was blinding me to the truth about you. And I would have done anything to protect you."

And now, hours later, stripped naked and having bared both body and soul, they curved together in the unequivocal exhaustion of spent passion. He watched her chest rise and fall until his eyes became heavy. He brushed his lips across her cheek and surrendered to sleep.

Sean woke clutching a pillow in the empty unfamiliar bed. Early morning sun had crept into the room, but not with the kind of summer brightness he was used to waking to after his alarm rocketed him from slumber. He lay drowsily awaiting her return. When it became clear she wasn't coming back, he got out of bed, donned his pants and went searching.

He found her in the damp-smelling courtyard, huddled in a blue director's chair. She pulled her white terrycloth robe together when she saw him.

"What are you doing up so early?" He pulled the

other chair away from the wrought iron table and joined her.

"Watching the sun come up." She was embarrassed—it was obvious from her haughty tone. It was the self-protection mechanism she employed when she believed she was losing control. And it told him that she would undo last night, if she could.

He needed to validate last night, drive away her fears. Nurture the insecure child in her. He followed her gaze to the red easterly sky. " 'Tis beautiful here at this time of morning," he said, not knowing how else to begin. The sprinkler on the automatic watering system gave the hibiscus one last spray before disappearing into the clay. It was now the mighty plantain's turn.

"Tolerable still, almost cool," she allowed, swatting away a shrilling cicada. He reached out and took her hand before she had a chance to object. He pulled her out of her chair and settled her on his lap with only token resistance on her part. "You'll break my chair," she said, half-capriciously.

"We can buy a new one if it comes to that. A swing would suit our purposes better. I fancy the one Ellis has."

"We?" she challenged.

"You won't help me purchase it? Then I'll buy it alone, with part of your dowry."

"Dowry?"

"You don't intend to have me marry a lass without a dowry? Do you believe me a man without pride or principle?"

"No. But until this very moment, I had not realized you to be a silly man."

"What is so silly about a man wanting his lover to be his wife?"

She scrambled up in earnest and circled the patio until she focused on a weed growing between two flagstones. She stooped over and gave it a sharp tug. The damp soil yielded up her prize. She turned to him and held it up. "I don't understand weeds. They seem to spring up overnight." She pointed to the dripping plantain tree. "While my bananas never seem to grow."

He slipped from the chair, landing in front of her on one knee. He took her hand and parted it from the prize weed. "Meredith, will you consent to be my bride?"

"I'm forty-four years old, Sean. A good ten years older than you."

"Nine. But who's counting?"

"Everyone will."

He pulled her down and sat cross-legged on the damp patio so he could cradle her in his arms. "Would it bother you so much?"

A syllable rolled over her tongue, but she swallowed the rest. She took another stab, but sputtered to a stop. She was clearly frustrating herself in an attempt to be her own Devil's advocate. "I'm your boss," she said, giving another foolish excuse instead of owning up to her true feelings.

He crushed her tightly in the folds of his arms. Two could play at this game. "Ma will be so happy. She has always wanted a doctor in the family. She hoped desperately my sister Maureen would set her cap for the young country doctor. Instead, Maureen married a dairy farmer who gave her a baby each year for seven years in a row."

The tiniest snicker escaped her pursed lips. But soon enough, melancholy claimed her. She twisted around to look him in the eye. "I doubt I have another seven reproductive years left."

He kissed her cheek, ready with his counter-attack. "Ma will be happy about that, too. Her arthritis is bad these days. Suspect she has one, maybe two pairs of booties left in her crippled hands."

She collapsed against him in frustration, her resolve spent. They'd lost track of time as they sat silently in the garden, each thinking their own thoughts, until the sun was up fully and beating down upon them.

"You should go," she told him as she got to her feet, "or we'll be late for work."

"Not without my answer. Yes or no?"

Meredith turned to him and looked him square in the eyes. "No."

"Why not?"

"You are an honorable man and in your twisted nineteenth-century morality, you believe marrying me is the right thing to do. These are the nineties. People don't marry simply because they enjoy sex with each other."

" 'Tis reason enough."

"But you don't love me."

Sean had never been in love. It was an emotion so foreign to him as to be utterly unimportant. Why was it so important to her? "I enjoy being with you. Last night was important to me. We found that we . . . fit. There is no one with whom I'd rather share my bed and my hearth. Isn't that enough?"

"No."

Chapter 24

Ellis

" 'Nowhere to run, baby. Nowhere to hi—' "

"Ellis?" came Vicki's gruff voice over the OR intercom interrupting their music and Leroy. "Your office is calling. They want to know how much longer you think you'll be."

Was it too much to ask to change a pacemaker battery in peace? "Why?" he shouted back through his mask.

"Someone's waiting in your office."

"Who?"

"Gee, Ellis, you going to be finished changing batteries in forty-five minutes if it's a tax man, and thirty if it's the Queen of Sheba?"

"It's a good thing she can barrel race," Leroy disclosed to Jennifer as he pinched the patient's cheek to make sure blood was getting to his brain. "The girl's about to lose her day job. 'Nowhere to run, baby. Nowhere to hide,' " Leroy added without the least bit of help from Martha and the Vandella's.

"We're in the subcutaneous pocket now," he hollered for Vicki. Great! A bleeder. "Clamp," he held out his palm. "Tell them about forty-five. And find out who it is."

"Yes, Boss." The intercom clicked off and the last three bars of "Nowhere to Run" came on.

"Can you move the hemostat out of my way!" How did Jennifer expect him to see what he was doing?

" 'I got to find a place . . .' " Leroy's singing was beginning to grate on Ellis's nerves.

Vicki was back on the intercom and the deejay was off before Ellis had attached the transvenous electrode to the new Chardack-Greatbatch pacemaker unit. "The mystery man is none other than," she gave three trumpeter's toots, "Robert Copeland."

"Put the music back on," Leroy, the music critic, pleaded.

"Who the hell is Robert Copeland?" Ellis yelled for the intercom's sake. "The Silastic adhesive," he added for Jennifer's.

Jennifer handed over an adhesive strip to seal the connections. It stuck to and ripped his glove. Could anything else go wrong?

"How the hell do I know? He's visiting you, *Doctor* Johnston, not me."

"Do you want to be regloved?" Jennifer asked.

"No," he wadded up the bloody tape and tossed it to the floor. "I want another piece of tape. Well, find out, Vicki!" Warm blood was seeping through the hole in his glove.

" 'Come on, baby, . . .' "

"Is it functioning properly?" Ellis asked.

Leroy moved his eyes from the clock to give a be-patient look as he recounted the beats. "Steady seventy-two." Seventy to seventy-five beats per minute was optimum. Higher rates did not result in significant increases in cardiac output. On rare instances Ellis had set them higher to suppress attacks of ventricular fibrillation.

"Suture." He held out his hand to Jennifer.

The Hagedorn needle snapped on the curve. "Is it too much to ask to have some decent equipment?" He threw the tip behind him and dug the eye end out by one of its flattened edges, blood sloshing under the glove. Jennifer readied another.

" 'I feel good.' " James Brown and Leroy were the only ones feeling good.

The incision was nearly closed when the music quietened in favor of the static-charged intercom. "He's a gawd-damned lawyer from Dallas. And you're very welcome, *Doctor* Johnston."

Robert Copeland must have been his malpractice carrier's attorney. About time. So it was *Doctor* Johnston, now? She was apparently angry at him for something. "Thank—" The static clicked off before he had a chance to thank her. "What do you think riled Vicki like that?"

"One could merely speculate," Jennifer answered.

" 'Baby, please don't go. Baby, please don't go.' "

Robert Copeland from Dallas. Why not a Houston lawyer? Someone who knew the territory, and had contributed heavily to the local judges' campaigns. What good would a lawyer up in Dallas be? Everything in his life was falling apart.

Ellis clipped the silk thread, satisfied with the simple procedure. "Okay. He's all spiffed up and good for another three years or thirty thousand miles." Ellis ripped off his good-for-nothing gloves. "I'm out of here."

Jennifer would take the patient to recovery where they'd monitor the electrocardiogram to make certain the pacemaker continued to function properly and to detect ectopic rhythms. Rosa had been controlling the patient's ectopic rhythms with potassium. That was before the occurrence of the battery depletion, manifesting in the gradual slowing of the pacemaker discharge rate.

" 'What a wonderful world.' "

Ellis found this Robert Copeland in his office. Sitting behind *his* desk, papers sprawled. Papers from the folder Rosa had given him on Jacob McQuade, he noticed as he reached the desk.

"Have a seat. I'm almost finished." Robert Copeland motioned to the green leather chair Ellis customarily offered his patients. Patrick never needed an invitation and thought it was the most comfortable in the whole building. Ellis found it about as comfortable as sitting on cardboard.

Ellis drummed on the arm of the chair, scrutinizing his pseudo-host. If first impressions meant anything, this was not the man to win over a rural Texas jury. Full head of dark hair, handsome, bright blue eyes, a smallpox mark on the bridge of his nose to break up the monotony of perfect facial features. Clean-cut and urbane, he looked as if he'd be more at home in the Oval Office. He arched an eyebrow as he turned a page. Ellis felt like the dimwitted schoolboy, watching his teacher grade his homework, waiting to be found out.

Finished, Robert gathered up the papers, squared them and put them back in the folder. He laced his hands over the closed folder and leaned across the desk, a serious look on his face. "They sure gave you the shaft."

There was no question about it. This was his kind of lawyer! He masked his elation. "What happens now?"

"First, I'll have my medical experts look this over. Then I'll make my recommendation to your insurance carrier. The rest is up to them."

"The hospital is pressuring me to settle out of court. But I'm not guilty and want my day in court."

Robert Copeland inhaled long and slow. "It's not as easy as that. The bean counters have the final say. It all comes down to money. Pay up and cut their losses, or pay to fight. I'll tell you now, they aren't going to put up the eighty to a hundred thousand it'll take to put on a defense if there isn't a substantial chance of winning."

"But I did nothing wrong."

Robert Copeland leaned back in the chair as if he owned it. "Let me be perfectly frank with you." He snapped back in the upright position. "This is not an easy case. I agreed to fly down here to have this chat because of Rosa Sanchez."

"Rosa?"

"She's an acquaintance of mine. She spoke to me about her involvement before your insurance carrier called. After reading the file, I can appreciate her concern. As the primary physician, it could be said that she was negligent in not diagnosing the infection."

"Jacob was an uncooperative patient. His case was difficult to manage. I can't imagine a jury in the world placing the blame on her. But isn't this a conflict of interest? I thought you were supposed to be representing me."

He shook his head. "If I decide to take the case, I'll be looking after your interests and the carrier's. However, part of the decision will rest on who her insurance carrier is."

This was getting more bizarre by the minute. "You mean if we're insured by the same carrier, they'll settle out of court?"

The man gave him a no-hard-feelings smile. "There's that possibility."

Ellis could hardly believe his ears. He didn't know about Rosa, but he knew for a fact that Bill, the real culprit, and he were insured by the same folks. Fort Bend Medical Society got a twenty percent discount for a group deal. That was before Rosa came to town. "Even though I'm innocent."

Copeland held up his palms and shrugged. "This isn't about guilt or innocence, it's about winning or losing."

Ellis's spirits were shattered. They were going to force him to capitulate. Take the blame for Bill's blunder, to protect Rosa who just happened to be this guy's friend. Ellis needed his own lawyer, someone who cared about his interests, not the insurance company's.

"Is he in his office?" throbbed Hillary's angry voice through the wall. This was all he needed. Robert Copeland wore the look of a civilian caught up in a medical emergency.

"It's only my wife. She's a little high-strung." Rising to her defense.

Relief didn't exactly wash over the stranger.

"Mr. Copeland, I want my good name back. I pay good money for insurance—"

The door flew open. "How do you explain . . ." Hillary stopped as she got to the desk. "You're not . . ." She found Ellis, a big scowl on her face, and then looked back at Robert Copeland, ready with the answer to *Sesame Street's* "What's-wrong-with-this-picture?"

Ellis got up and gave Hillary his chair. "Hillary, this is Robert Copeland. The lawyer from the insurance company. Robert Copeland, my wife, Hillary."

Robert walked gallantly around the desk and extended his hand, a practiced smile on his face. "Bob. It's a pleasure, Mrs. Johnston."

She lifted a dainty hand. His charm wasn't lost on her. Fortunately. "Hillary, please." She was going to behave.

"I must be going." He picked up the folder. "I'll have your receptionist Xerox this for me, if that's all right?"

"Certainly."

He was at the door for a fast getaway. "I'll have our medical consultants look it over and I'll give you a call next week."

Ellis wasn't finished. He had a list of questions he wanted answered. He reached out for the records. "I'll Xerox—"

Robert pulled the folder away. "No, I can take care of it." He nodded to Hillary. "A pleasure, Hillary."

She gave him her warmest smile. That smile was gone before Ellis had closed the door behind the lawyer. "Make it quick, Hillary, before he slips away."

Hillary was rebuilding a full head of steam. "All right, I will." She jumped from the chair and waved a letter at Ellis. "Let's see you explain this away. You dirty bastard." She slapped it into his hand.

It was addressed to Hillary at the bookstore, with no

return address. A local postmark. Like the address on
the envelope, the letter inside was typed.

Dear Mrs. Johnston,
I believe it should be brought to your attention that
your husband is having an affair with Rosa Sanchez.
Sincerely,
A friend

Why would anyone say something like this? He
barely knew Rosa Sanchez and had never thought of
her as a woman—she was just one of the doctors. "It's
utter nonsense! I'm not having an affair with Rosa
Sanchez or with anyone else." He ripped both the letter
and envelope in two and threw them in the wastebasket.

"Then why did I get it? People don't go to the trouble of writing something like that for no reason."

"Maybe the person hates you." He went to the door.
"Now, if that's all you had on your mind, I have important things to do."

"Is that all you're going to say?" she screamed.

"What more is there? You get some crazy letter and
barge in here and interrupt a meeting and act like a
crazy person yourself. What do you want me to say?"

"I want you to tell me the truth. Admit that you're
having an affair with Rosa Sanchez," she screamed
loud enough for Rosa to hear in her suite of offices on
the next floor down.

"I've already told you I'm not." He opened the door
and went out. Hillary slammed it for him.

Patrick was in the hall pouring a cup of coffee for
Bob. He wore a why-you-sly-dog look. Ellis could
hear the Xerox machine humming around the corner.
Patrick held out a cup for him. An invitation to come
over and 'fess up. Comforting to know your partner
was willing to believe the worst. Ellis slunk over to
them. He didn't know what Rosa and the lawyer's relationship was. He was embarrassed and couldn't quite

meet Robert's stare. "I'm not, you know. I have never so much as seen Rosa outside of work."

Robert nodded like he didn't believe him.

Quick to realize he had missed something, Patrick glanced at Robert, and then Ellis. He put down the coffeepot and started off. Ellis knew Patrick well enough to know he would be back for an explanation as soon as the dust settled. "Hi, Hillary."

"Don't 'hi Hillary' me. Did you write this?"

Ellis turned around to see Hillary hand Patrick the pieces of the letter she must have dug out of the trash.

Patrick put the pieces together and read it. "Nope. If this is the kind of friends you have, Hillary, you don't need enemies."

She ripped it out of his hand and stormed out. Patrick stuck his hands deep into his pant pockets and rounded the corner into the reception area to answer the phone for Valerie, still busy photocopying Jacob's file.

"When are you flying back?" Ellis asked.

"Tonight. I was going to pay a call on Rosa." Meaning: But not if I'm stepping on your toes, Buddy.

"Believe me. I have all the trouble I need. Rosa is nothing more than a colleague. Could we forget Rosa for a few minutes and talk about my problem? I feel like you're hanging me out to dry and I want some straight answers now, not next week."

"For instance?"

"If there's a court case, when will it be? I need to schedule some vacation time for it."

He shrugged. "Next spring. Summer, maybe."

"What! I can't live with this thing over my head for six, nine months. I want to get it over with."

"The wheels of justice turn slowly, Ellis."

Valerie was back with his copies.

"Thank you." Copeland took the papers and watched her walk down the hall until she disappeared into the reception area in the front. He gave Ellis a patronizing pat on the back. "I won't have answers until the file has been reviewed by our medical experts. Just try to forget about it. Let your insurance company handle it. That's what you buy insurance for."

The man made it sound like Ellis had been in a minor car accident.

Chapter 25

Pam

Pam counted the houses as she drove down the street in case she didn't recognize Sophie's house from the back. She'd waited long enough for Meredith Fischer to do something about the stolen prescription pad. She would take matters into her own hands.

She would have preferred coming under the cloak of darkness, but the house was empty now. Pam would plant the drugs she'd laid aside from the batch she'd taken to the Houston clinic. She hadn't had a chance to follow up, or even know how to go about selling them, but she suspected the street value of her cache was more than she made in a month. Maybe the police would estimate it for her when they announced the seizure in the newspaper. Whatever it was, it would be worth it to get even with both Lisa and Sophie for what they'd done to her.

She went around the corner and up the alley. One, two, three—what an obnoxious dog—four, five, six, seven. Okay. She pulled to a stop and cut the engine. Sophie's house looked more shabby than the others on the block.

Pam put on her driving gloves and got out of the car, the sack secured under her arm. "Here, kitty-kitty. Here, kitty-kitty," she called, in case nosy neighbors with nothing better to do were peeking out their windows. The gate was off its hinges and she had to lift it up to swing it open. It gave a long rasp. She left it open far enough to squeeze soundlessly through when she was done.

"Here, kitty-kitty. Here, kitty-kitty." She started toward the house by way of the dry border bushes. She bent low, pretending to look under them for a cat.

There was no deadbolt on the back door, but it was locked. The house was old and the windows were the kind that slid up. Not that it mattered, she discovered. All the windows were open.

The screen on a dirt-spotted window half-hidden by a catalpa was raised far enough for a person to crawl in. Pam did.

From the heavy-metal posters on the walls and the stuffed animals on the floor around the unmade bed, Pam realized she had picked her window well. This hot and stuffy room was Lisa's.

A thick white coat of lacquer on the chest of drawers was chipped and showed a rainbow of previous layers down to its mahogany base. In the top left-hand drawer, Lisa kept the beauty supplies that made her look like a whore. The one next to it was cluttered with junk jewelry. She kept her shabby underwear in the drawer under the jewelry. There wasn't room for the drugs in that drawer or in the next one, which pulled out hard and yielded pounds of movie magazines. The remaining two were filled with like crap.

She opened the closet. It was an oven and smelled of years of sweat. The jeans over wire hangers and the crumpled pair on the floor looked as shabby here as they did when the girl wore them. The sweaters and blouses looked cheap, gaudy, and faddish. A couple of them were hung carelessly and gave off a peculiar scent—a mixture of cigarettes, body odor, and cheap perfume.

On the floor, back in the corner, was a Madame Alexander doll box. Pam opened it. Beneath the blue tissue paper, she found a queen doll dressed in gold broadcloth with a blue sash across the bodice, and blue matching gloves. The crown on her brown shiny hair was woven with gold elastic thread. Pam scooted the doll to the edge of the box and shook out the contents of her sack. She folded the tissue paper over the doll and put the lid back on.

Unlike Lisa's, Sophie's room was tidy. So was the living room. The kitchen had breakfast dishes in the sink. Pam went out the back door, making certain it locked behind her. She walked through the backyard in the shadows of the bushes. She closed the gate behind her, cringing at the noise, and got into her car.

She didn't see anyone and hoped no one saw her. She threw the empty bag on the seat beside her, started the engine and drove away. She would wait a couple of days to tip off the police so no one would connect her to it. Just in case someone noticed her. The one thing she could count on was that Lisa wouldn't be playing with her doll.

Chapter 26

Josh

"Hurry up, her plane's landed." Allison raced toward the escalator crowded with Friday-night travelers, leaving Josh tangled in a hot-pink, spiraling cord that bound a mother to a rambunctious child.

As the escalator moved her to greater heights, Allison gave him a must-you-be-such-a-slow-poke glare and waved frantically for him to catch up. He would like nothing better. But did she expect him to hurdle luggage and mow the masses down?

Seemed if she'd been ready to go a little sooner, they would have had plenty of time to meet Margaret's plane. He certainly did his part. He arrived at the spa ten minutes before the appointed hour, knocked on the locked front door until his hand gave out, then walked around the building twice looking for an open door. She came out thirty minutes later and expected him to make up the time by driving through rush-hour traffic like a New York cabby daredevil.

He was glad that the grand opening was only a week away and that Margaret was finally back to take some of the pressure off Allison. The spa was consuming her in its glorious conflagration. He hadn't seen her since Emma's last dinner party. And then, only at the party. Now she had disappeared again.

Josh stepped off the escalator and got a glimpse of the back of her raven hair as she bobbed toward the gate. Josh felt like a spawning fish fighting the current of disembarking L.A. passengers beating a path toward the baggage claims.

"Excuse me," he said, skirting a woman standing square in his way. He'd lost sight of Allison again.

"Josh!" The woman grabbed and held tightly to his arm. "It's me, Margaret."

"Margaret?" He wasn't entirely convinced. He took a closer look. Could this stunning creature be *their* Margaret? If so, she had had surgery to eradicate her scar. Though he had trouble seeing the involved area through the sheen of artfully applied makeup, he thought he distinguished a slight rawness. But her eyes! He would have remembered such beautiful blue eyes. The smile was wrong, too. He didn't have words to describe the subtle difference. It was just different, somehow. Not Margaret's kind smile, but a womanly smile.

"Is that all you can say, Joshua Allister?"

Margaret's voice. But where had this spunk come from? The new blond hairdo, the makeup, the absence of her unbecoming eyeglasses, and her sophisticated clothing were all superficial by-products of the remarkable results from the surgery. The monumental consequence was how it had improved her scarred self-esteem.

So totally surprised, he took several seconds to gather his wits about him. And that much longer to find his tongue. "I didn't recognize you," he said lamely. "You've done something to your . . ." Her smile fell away. Now he knew her. The air of assurance had slipped away, replaced by her usual insecurity. "Hair," he added, like a true Philistine.

Josh knew that self-image rarely changed. An obese child would see himself as an obese person all through life no matter what the mirror told him. He didn't want to say or do anything that might destroy Margaret's self-esteem.

"You look great!" He held her tight, smelling a trace of floral scent. He'd never inhaled a more delicious

fragrance. "I've missed you so." He gave her a big
bear hug, and then let her go when they were bumped
by stampeding hordes. "Come on, let's find your sister." He took her overstuffed tote bag with one hand,
and her arm with the other.

"See her?" He studied her profile in fascination as
they threaded through pedestrian traffic. Laser surgery.
Must have been. Amazing! He had never realized her
classic bone structure before. His eyes were always
drawn by professional curiosity to the scar.

"There!" She stretched out an arm and pointed.
"Allison," she called and waved, genuinely excited to
see her sister.

Josh couldn't help but grin when he saw Allison's
jaw drop almost to her chest. It must have been the
biggest surprise of her life. It was in his. She took a
couple of hesitant steps, but Margaret and he did most
of the traversing to reach her.

"Margaret?"

"Yes, it's really me." She giggled.

Josh delighted in her joy. He was so happy she was
back.

"What have you done to yourself?" Allison looked
stricken, not at all elated by the astonishing surprise.
She ran a hand over Margaret's newly smooth cheek.
"How come you didn't tell me you were going to do
this?" She pushed Margaret's hair back, grimacing.
"And what's this?"

"It's a hair transplant," Margaret said defensively.
"They took little plugs of hair from the back of my
head." Margaret turned and flipped her hair up in back
to show her. "See?"

"It looks awful!" Allison exclaimed, abusively.
"Look at it, Josh."

Josh was furious with Allison and ready to rise to
Margaret's defense without looking. He didn't know
what kind of magic Rosa had used to instigate this mi-
raculous metamorphosis, but he was not about to stand
idly by while Allison sabotaged her wonderful

achievement. Josh stepped in close for better viewing.
His comprehensive study revealed an area bulging with
red swollen knots. "Looks good to me. Just healing,"
he said, offering his professional opinion free of
charge. "And you look good to me, too, Margaret.
Wonderful! Fabulous!"

Margaret's neck blotched red in embarrassment. The
treated skin marbled slightly.

"What happened to your glasses? You have a
drawerful of contacts you wouldn't wear." Allison
gave her sister's eyes a myopic stare.

"They're soft lenses."

"Didn't *I* tell you about soft lenses?" Allison broke
the eye contact. "And look how you dressed! You
don't wear suits on planes."

Margaret looked devastated. It hurt Josh more than
he could bear. For the first time, he realized how much
he really despised Allison. Why couldn't she see that
Margaret needed her confidence bolstered? Her surface
scars had healed nicely, but it would take everyone's
help to heal the deeper ones. Allison's ragging was just
the tip of the iceberg, he feared. She would wear Margaret down until she was back in her shell, believing
she was ugly.

He suspected that Allison saw her for the first time
as a competitor, someone with whom she would be
forced to share the spotlight. What neither seemed to
realize was that Margaret generated her own light.
Allison glittered, but Margaret was gold. And Josh
wasn't about to fail her. "It's a beautiful outfit, Margaret."

Allison rolled her eyes.

"You like it?" Not quite hiding her self-
consciousness, she spun around to show off a sky-blue
power suit.

"Like it? I *love* it!"

Allison took a sleeve and inspected a giant, gold-
ball-shaped button. "This is a Chanel. Why would *you*
buy something like this?!"

Margaret lowered her eyes. "A friend," she said, her voice barely audible, "made me get it when we were shopping on Rodeo Drive yesterday."

"You went shopping on Rodeo Drive?" A hint of envy crept into Allison's voice. "What friend?" she challenged. "We don't have any friends in California."

He wanted to reach out and pull Margaret into his arms, and protect her from all this. Instead, he silently bled for her.

"Someone I met at the clinic." She motioned to her cheek, a picture being equal to a thousand words. "She was having her eyes done. Katherine Little. Nathan—"

"Katherine Little! That's the name on the block reservation." A spark of excitement enlivened Allison's eyes. "Oh, now I see. You're responsible for the spa's early success. Good girl." She gave Margaret a radiant smile and a big hug. Sisterly love was renewed now that business opportunity had entered the picture. "We'll see to it that your new friends have such a wonderful time they'll tout us to all their friends. We'll make millions." Allison took them both by the arm. "Now, let's get your luggage and get out of here before we get trampled to death."

They walked only a few feet in silent bliss before Allison broke it. "Nana is going to drop dead when she sees you."

"Your grandmother is not going to drop dead when she sees Margaret." Allison had learned the knack of cruelty from Emma. Josh would manage to be present at Margaret and Emma's reunion. He didn't want to give Emma the chance to make shambles out of the great strides Margaret had taken.

"Well, I didn't mean she was going to drop *dead,* Josh. I just meant she was going to drop dead. Margaret knew what I meant."

That was the terrible thing about it. Margaret probably *did* know what she meant. He wished Rosa had confided in him. He would have boned up. Gone to Sean or Meredith. Psychiatry had been his least favor-

ite rotation in his clinical years of medical school. And
now he felt like he was flying by the seat of his pants.
Was he trying too hard to give encouragement? Was he
being too much the great protector? Margaret deserved
his best effort.

Allison had pretty much heard all about Margaret's
trip to L.A. by time the luggage, which included a couple of new-looking suitcases, was in the trunk.

"Nana is just furious that you went off with that
Rosa Sanchez," Allison was saying when Josh got in
behind the wheel.

"Why? Because I didn't tell her why I was going? I
didn't want to build up anyone's hopes. Just in case,
you know, like the other times."

Margaret was showing a healthy backbone. His opti-
mism soared. Maybe it would see her through Emma's
welcome home. "Seat belts," Josh announced as she
started up the engine.

Allison struggled with hers. "It's not that. It's because of all the trouble Rosa's . . . Oh!" She let the seat
belt recoil and turned all the way around to face Margaret in the backseat. "You don't know about Coral
May. You aren't going to believe what she did!"

"What?!"

"She's suing CMC over Grandpa's death!"

"No!"

"Can you believe that? *Our* Grandpa!"

"No!"

"Grandpa's got to be turning over in his grave. And
Nana's just beside herself."

"What's she going to do?"

"What's she going to do?" Allison parroted. "She's
going to settle out of court to keep it out of the papers.
Wouldn't *inquiring minds* like to get their pea-brains
on something like this? But get this. Coral May's suing
Ellis Johnston, too and he isn't going to settle out of
court. He's bucking Nana. Wants his day in court.
Never mind what it'll do to Chandler Medical Center's
reputation."

"Allison," Josh interrupted, "CMC will weather the lawsuit far better than Ellis. Ellis's reputation is on the line. He's the accused. CMC, only by association. I, for one, can appreciate his concern."

"You think we like being sued any more than he does? We're just hanging on by the skin of our teeth. If this gets out, more people are going to take their business elsewhere. We'll be forced to shut our doors, and then Chandler Springs will no longer have a full-service medical center, and people will die."

"Allison, don't be so dramatic. The worst that could happen, and I'm not saying it will, is for CMC to become a triage center dealing with emergencies."

Her composure broke. "After all my family has sacrificed for Chandler Springs's welfare, you have the gall to say it wouldn't be all that bad if Chandler Springs didn't have the medical center to turn to?"

"He didn't mean it like that, Allison. He just meant, you know, that if worse came to worse, Chandler Medical Center might have to give up some of its services. It would still be there for emergencies."

"Granddaddy wanted it to be a full-service medical center and Nana has sacrificed a great deal to keep it a full-service medical center. Don't you have any family pride?"

"Of course, I do."

"Allison," Josh said, tiring quickly of this childish bickering. "No one wants to see Chandler Medical Center be anything less than what your granddaddy intended. And it's not going to crumble because of Coral May's lawsuit. So stop borrowing trouble." In a lighter vein, he asked, "Now, where do you two lovely ladies want to go for dinner?"

"You and Margaret go. Just take me back to the spa. I still have a pile of work to do."

Seeing what kind of mood she was in, Josh was inclined to oblige her. "We'll eat somewhere quick. Then I'll take you back."

"I'm not hungry, Josh. Just take me back to the spa. Please!" Allison's *please* was anything but pleasant.

"I'll go with you and help," Margaret offered.

"It would take me longer to explain to you what needs to be done than to do it myself," Allison said, swept up by self-pity. "You go on back to Chandler Springs with Josh."

Chapter 27

Margaret

Margaret stared unseeingly at Pappamia's menu. Not even her favorite Italian restaurant could lift her from this gloom. Allison had realized right away what Margaret hadn't. She was going to be the laughingstock of Chandler Springs. She looked stupid in her new suit. This was Texas, not Beverly Hills.

She'd made a mess of Allison and Josh's night out. Josh tried to make light of it, saying that she'd been so busy he hadn't seen her in a week. It only made her realize that she should have been here helping out. Especially with this lawsuit.

"What's good here?" Josh asked in a chipper tone. He was certainly trying to be a good sport.

"Everything. Why is Coral May suing Ellis? Did Ellis have something to do with my grandfather's death?"

Josh shook his head. "I'm not certain what this is all about." He scrutinized the menu to avoid looking her in the eye. He knew more than he was letting on. "What are you having?"

She closed the menu. "Fettucine. I shouldn't have left Allison alone."

He closed his with a long sigh. "Margaret, Allison is not your responsibility. If she wants to pout, let her. This is *your* time, and I want to celebrate. She'll be fine tomorrow."

"But she wouldn't even let me see what the spa looks like. Or even let you walk her in."

"The lights were on. Workers were there. She was safe."

But that wasn't the worst of it. Margaret had let everyone down. If she hadn't been so crazy with thoughts about Josh, she might have been able to see that Grandpa was dying. Maybe she could have done something to keep him from dying. She felt tears come to her eyes. She turned away as if looking for the waiter.

Josh reached across the table and took her hand from her face and pinned it to the table. Didn't he know what his touch was doing to her? "Margaret, there's nothing to hide." He squeezed assurance into her hand. "You're beautiful, you know." He grabbed the other hand as it found its way to her face. "Bad enough you had to choose a dark restaurant. Or was that your intent? Make me strain my eyes gawking at you."

Margaret slipped her hands out of his and held them in her lap. "You're making me uncomfortable."

It was his turn to look around for the waiter. He waved. Now he was standing and waving. "Over here, Rosa."

Rosa? Margaret turned to see Rosa Sanchez and a tall, elegant stranger at the entrance. Rosa waved back and started toward them, ducking around the hostess, her handsome escort in tow.

"Josh! What a pleasant surprise!" She reined in the man. "This is a friend from Dallas, Robert Copeland. Bob, this is my friend Josh Allister." She turned to Margaret, waiting for Josh make the introduction. Rosa stared at her as if she recognized her, but couldn't place her. It came to her like a bolt out of the sky just as Josh spoke.

"And this is my friend Margaret Chandler." Josh beamed.

So did Rosa as she all but pulled Margaret from the chair to give her a warm hug. "Margaret!" She stepped back for a better inspection. "My, have you had a busy week!"

All of this was lost on Robert Copeland.

"I met a woman at the clinic who showed me around," Margaret tried to explain. "She'll be here next week. I want you to meet her."

"And so do I." She turned to include her friend. "Margaret, Bob. Bob, Margaret."

Bob offered his hand to Margaret. "Chandler?"

"She's Emma Chandler's granddaughter," Rosa explained. To Margaret, she added, "Bob came down for the day to speak with Ellis. He's a malpractice attorney."

Margaret mumbled that she was happy to meet him and took back her hand. She didn't know how to feel about the man who was representing Ellis. Did Ellis cause Grandpa's death? You don't usually sue people unless they've done something wrong. But CMC was being sued, too. She didn't know what to think about his not settling out of court like they were. She wished Coral May hadn't done this. Maybe if she'd been nicer to her about the Rocking M. No, Grandpa wouldn't have wanted it sold and torn up as a housing development. Maybe that was it. Maybe Coral May was suing Ellis because it was his testimony in court that saved the ranch. What was she thinking of, blaming Ellis for her grandpa's death when she should have been thanking him for saving Grandpa's Rocking M?

Josh summoned the waiter and asked for a bigger table.

"You will join us, I hope."

"Of course, we will," Rosa answered for the both of them. "How are you feeling?" she asked Margaret as they followed the men to a table that two busboys were readying.

"Margaret, here," Josh said, pulling out a chair. "Rosa, there," nodding to the chair across from Margaret. "Bob," he indicated the chair at Rosa's right, saving the seat next to Margaret for himself. Margaret put little store in his attentiveness. He was merely being polite.

"Something from the bar?" The waiter shifted his head from Bob to Rosa and back to Bob like a tennis spectator. Margaret and Josh had already declined.

"A bottle of your finest champagne," Josh answered for the table.

"Yes," Rosa seconded, "we're celebrating."

The lawyer raised an eyebrow as his smile widened.

Margaret wanted to crawl into a hole and pull it in after her.

"Where's Allison?" Rosa asked as the waiter turned his back.

"We just now dropped her at the spa," Josh explained. "She had some work to finish. She wasn't hungry. We both had cars." The smile slipped from Rosa's face for only a split second as she listened to Josh's hollow excuse.

Rosa held Margaret's hand and turned to Bob. "You wouldn't know it to look at her now, but Margaret had a scar removed from her cheek not long ago." She looked across at Josh. "My ex-husband has many faults, but he is the best damned cosmetic surgeon in the world."

"We will toast him if our champagne ever comes." Josh looked around to check their waiter's progress.

Rosa gave Josh a smile and turned back to Bob. "Do you think Sterling—my ex—could sue Margaret for a positive outcome? The reverse of the patient suing for a negative outcome? Start a new trend."

Bob threw his head back royally and laughed. "Point well taken. And I'm certain there are enough hungry lawyers in the country to take up arms." He looked under the able. "What's that noise?"

Margaret could hear it now.

Rosa retrieved her purse and turned off the activated beeper. "No rest for the weary, I'm afraid. Be right back." She got up to go. "Feel free to toast Sterling in my absence."

"Does Sterling really have two heads?" Josh asked Margaret for Rosa's benefit.

"Two faces," Rosa answered as she walked away.

"And a great pair of hands," Josh added, smiling at Margaret.

Bob bemoaned having already given up his rental car, Josh assured him they'd give him a ride to the airport if Rosa had to dash away, and the champagne in their glasses no longer bubbled by time Rosa came back.

"Sorry," Rosa said as she slipped back into her chair.

"You don't have to rush off?" Bob asked.

"No as a matter of fact, I now have time to kill." She looked at Josh. "Ken delivered a bad one. Sarah called to ask if I'd take a look at the baby, but Ellis had one look and told her to call for the helicopter." She turned back to Bob. "Plenty of time to see your plane off before moseying over to St. Luke's Hospital to give Sarah a ride home."

Chapter 28

Ellis

"Look at the poor thing." Sarah shook her head as the three of them hovered over the incubator. The newborn had a hypoplastic heart, the left side underdeveloped. "Makes it hard to believe in a perfect God. Why does He fail so many children?"

Ellis couldn't help thinking she was talking about her own.

Ken kneaded her shoulders, which were stooped from years of caring for ailing children. "They're a nice young couple, too. Hate to see them go through this."

"What kind of insurance do they have?" Ellis asked.

"Blue Cross."

"They can be thankful for that." Ellis hoped he didn't sound flippant. He was only trying to be practical.

"Okay, Sarah, let's go." Ken took her elbow and led her away.

She stopped to look in the three Isolettes positioned in front of the window for easy viewing. "Why can't they all be like these?"

Ken and Ellis exchanged knowing looks. She was stalling for time. Ken and Sarah were faced with the unpleasant task of telling the parents. Tell them before the helicopter arrived.

Ken put his hand to the small of her back. "Shall we go, Sarah?"

She turned and took one last look at the newborn in the incubator and then left the nursery, a condemned prisoner to the gallows. Ellis turned back to see the nurses fill the void around the incubator. They would ready the tiny creature for transport.

Ken paused at the mother's door, mustering courage. He gave Sarah a weak smile. Ellis couldn't see whether she returned it or not.

The young mother supported herself on shaky elbows. Her wild eyes darted from one face to the next, settling on her ob-gyn. Her blondish hair was matted with sweat and grease, her tender face pale with apprehension. She didn't look much older than his daughter. Her scrawny husband rose like a long weed and tipped his sweat-stained Stetson.

"Let's make you more comfortable." Ken raised the head of the bed for her.

"Thank you, Doctor Stevens." Her voice quivered with fear.

"Julie, Todd," Ken said, "y'all remember Dr. McNamara from the delivery room."

They nodded as if to hurry him onto the ghastly pronouncement he was surely here to make. There were enough clues for even the youngest, newest, most naive couples. Friendly nurses who had popped in and out to check on Julie and Todd before delivery were now avoiding them. She was in a private room on the far side of the wing, away from the other happy new mothers. The grandparents had been asked to remain in the waiting room. And most of all, her baby had been whisked away and not returned.

"And this is Dr. Johnston. Mr. and Mrs. Kilpatrick. Dr. Johnston is our thoracic surgeon here at Chandler Medical Center."

"Surgeon?" Julie swallowed hard. "Does our baby need surgery?"

Sarah stepped forward. "Yes, he'll need surgery. But not the kind we can provide here. He'll need to go to St. Luke's Hospital in Houston."

The young father took his wife's hand. "What's wrong with him?"

Sarah looked at Ellis. It was his turn. He looked the young father in the eye. Lies only postponed the pain, and false hope only worsened it. "Your son was born with what's technically called a hypoplastic heart. The left side of his heart is underdeveloped."

"Heart surgery? My baby has to have heart surgery?" the mother asked in a frantic voice.

Ken put a supportive hand on her shoulder. Sarah looked at Ellis imploringly. Years of compassion lined her face.

"Your son's heart can't be repaired." Ellis could feel Sarah's begging eyes burning through him. All right. So maybe he would be the lucky one. "We'll have to change it. Hope another heart can be found to replace it." He wouldn't be any more optimistic than that.

"Another heart?" the father asked as the mother broke down in tears.

"A heart transplant. Houston Medical Center pioneered the transplant era in the late sixties. Great strides have been made in the nearly thirty years since. Heart transplants are practically routine," Sarah tried to assure them.

Ken's hand glided over the woman's shoulders. "A helicopter is coming for your baby. We're going to bring in a wheelchair for you in a few minutes. Take you into the nursery to see your son. Okay, kiddo?"

She nodded, tears and fright welling in her eyes.

Ken patted her shoulder. "That's my girl."

Neither parent looked to have more questions, which suited Ellis just fine. The three of them left the parents to have a moment alone.

Out in the hall, Ken sighed. "I hate this shit."

"I've got to call home. Tell John I'm going to Houston. What do I have that he can fix for dinner?" Sarah was talking to herself, clearly distraught. "We've got to hurry this along."

"Give them a couple more minutes," Ken said.

"What about the helicopter?" Sarah reminded. "It'll be here any minute now."

"I'll check the helicopter's progress."

They both headed toward the phone at the nursing station.

"I'll get the wheelchair," Ellis offered, not certain either of them heard.

Ken used the phone. Sarah disappeared into the nursery. Ellis went for the wheelchair. He might as well be an orderly for all the good he was doing.

A pall of sadness could be felt in the unit. The three occupied Isolettes were now abandoned, the babies having been taken into their mother's rooms. The double doors into the ob wing had been closed and the NO VISITOR sign hung out. Everything had been readied for the Kilpatricks.

The young father pushed his wife's wheelchair to the nursery door. The o.b. nurse took it from there. Wheeling through the aisle of empty Isolettes.

Numb and bewildered, the mother drew an overwhelmed breath as she saw the tiny baby, with tubes and lines radiating from his body, looking like an alien from outer space. Ellis, having the best hands, had started the IV line in the head. It was his bloody thumb print on the tape.

"Touch him." Sarah slid her hand through one of the side perforations to demonstrate, stroking the baby's chest with her index finger.

The mother looked first to the father. Both parents were so wracked with emotion that they couldn't speak. He nodded. She twisted a hand through the second opening. Her hand moved tentatively toward the baby, afraid of dislodging the cardiac leads and drips.

"It's okay, Julie," Ken assured her. "You won't hurt anything."

From inside the incubator, Sarah took Julie's hand and guided it under the wires and lines.

The mother stroked her baby cautiously at first. When she became secure, Sarah withdrew her hand and urged the father to take her place. He poked his hand through and touched the baby's leg and then replaced the mother's fingertip on the baby's chest as she coaxed the baby's fingers open. He did the same with the other hand. They settled into their son's unsteady breathing rhythm as though they were a trio band. Tears streamed down the mother's face. The father wiped a single tear with the back of his free hand.

Ellis heard the double doors down the hall crash open. He looked through the window to catch sight of an orderly pushing the transfer incubator down the corridor, followed by two haggard-looking flight nurses.

"Sarah." Ellis shifted his head toward the door to tell her it was time.

She gave a tiny nod. "Mr. and Mrs. Kilpatrick, the helicopter is here now." She nudged the father's hand as an added reminder that their time was up.

Mrs. Kilpatrick broke into wails. Her husband pulled both his hand and his wife's out of the incubator. "My parents . . . our parents . . ." his voice trailed off, replaced with broken sobs.

The nurse pressed a wad of tissues into Mrs. Kilpatrick's hand.

"They can see him in Houston," Sarah assured. "And when Mrs. Kilpatrick's discharged in a day or two, you can, too."

"Where will the new heart come from?" Mrs. Kilpatrick's choking question was directed to Ellis.

Out of the corner of his eye, he watched Sarah summon the flight nurses. "Your son will be put on a nationwide computerized list." He chose his words carefully to be as optimistic as Sarah wanted.

"When a donor is found, the heart will be brought to Texas and a team of surgeons will perform the transplant."

"How long will it take?"

Ellis assumed she meant finding the donor, not the transplant procedure. Most likely, not in time. "There's no way of knowing. Tomorrow, next week, a month." He shrugged.

She sought her husband's hand, clutching frantically for it. "What if it's tomorrow? I won't be there!"

Her priorities and expectations were so unrealistic. A blessing.

"I'll see that you get there if it's tomorrow," Ken promised. "Now let's get you back to your room and let these people do their work."

Ellis held back as they went off. Once the parents were gone, he and the nurses worked quickly. Detaching the cardiac leads, transferring the infant, hanging the drips. Both nurses were already wringing wet and they'd reached only the halfway mark in their journey.

Sarah returned and kept a careful eye on the newborn as the four of them hurried through the halls and out the hospital doors into the muggy evening.

The helicopter pilot opened the door for them. One nurse got in to help guide the incubator, and then the other nurse followed.

Sarah started in, and then turned back to Ellis. "I forgot to call John. Will you call him and explain? Tell him to open a can of soup." She looked old and tired and so terribly worried.

Ellis pulled Sarah back. "Sarah, go home to John. I'll fly to Houston."

"I couldn't—"

"Go home, Sarah." Ellis blocked her way and climbed in.

"Rosa's in Houston. She's to meet me at the hospital. Give me a ride back."

"Good. She can bring me home." He gave Sarah a tiny wave as the pilot closed the door.

He watched Sarah grow smaller and smaller as they lifted off. This little mercy trip of his was going to go over in a big way with Hillary.

Chapter 29

Pam

"What are you looking at?" Mr. Reese asked hoarsely of his wife.

"A helicopter." She came away from the window, but hesitated to come too close to the bed while Pam changed the drip. "They took away a tiny baby, I think. Makes a body forget their own troubles when they see someone else's."

"Come," he motioned with his fingers, "we'll say a prayer."

Finished, Pam tugged the sheet up to his neck, folded it over the blanket, and tucked it under the side. "There, all set. Be back in an hour or so. Call if you need anything."

Sweat-slick hands caught hold of her. "No, pray with us . . . For the baby."

Forget the other ten patients. Forget the medication cart outside the door she was pushing room to room, the blood sugars, the melting ice. Why should she take the time to change Mrs. Griffith's dressing when she could be praying?

Mrs. Reese fell to her knees beside the bed. Pam lifted the hem of her white uniform and got to her knees on the other side. She certainly hoped Mrs. Reese would remember to report this to her good friend Sophie. Mrs. Reese's good friend. Sophie and her despicable daughter could go straight to hell for all

Pam cared. Straight to Jail without passing Go, would be more appropriate.

They joined hands and Mrs. Reese bowed her long, thin head and closed her eyes tight. Mr. Reese closed his morphine-glazed eyes.

"Dear Heavenly Father," Mrs. Reese prayed, "Creator of all creatures here below. Watch over the little one in the helicopter and make the child whole. If it be Your will." She paused, eating a bigger bite out of Pam's precious time. "If You need her soul in Heaven now, comfort her parents. Give them the strength to understand Thy will. These things we ask in Jesus' name. Amen."

"Amen." Pam got to her feet, call lights dinging in her ears.

Mr. Reese choked on his "amen" and sent it down into his lungs. The coughing spell reddened his face and sent sputum spraying. Mrs. Reese poured some water, worry deep on her face. Pam patted his back, while he hacked up a string of greenish phlegm. He fell back on his pillow, exhausted. His dislodged catheter soaked the sheets with urine. The indignity of dying.

This was how God answers prayers.

Finished with Mr. Reese, Pam stepped out in the hall and was blinded by the call lights. Everyone and her daughter wanted something from her. Relatives were the worst. She could deal with the patients themselves, but why did the relatives think no one would care for their loved ones unless they were around to supervise?

She left the cart where it was and backtracked. It was the light over the end room that worried her. The room was supposed to be empty. Had she missed a new patient at report? Her crepe souls squeaked along the tile hallway as she dashed to the end room.

"Nurse," Mrs. Griffith called as she passed. Pam hesitated, then thought better of stopping. She had an unknown patient who hadn't been fed or treated in the four hours she'd been there. She didn't need this on top of the missing morphine.

She ran into the dark room and tapped the dimmer switch. The sheet between the beds was drawn. She moved steadily toward the far bed. There was someone in the bed. A man. The back of a man's head was all that wasn't concealed by the summer-weight blanket. Why hadn't she been told of the new arrival at report? She rounded the bed.

A hand jerked out and pulled her off-balance. She screamed before a hand covered her mouth. She was being smothered with kisses. It was Billy!

"Gawddamit, Billy," she said as she stiffened and tried to push him off. "You scared the wits out of me."

He pulled at her underpants.

"Billy, stop it."

Persistent hands pushed her skirt to her waist and pulled her pants to her knees. "Just a quicky." He pushed himself inside, catching the delicate skin askew and causing a moment of stabbing pain. "I've waited all day for this," he said when he was comfortable. He pushed in and out with a fury.

Pam turned her face to the door to make sure no one had come looking for her.

Chapter 30

Rosa

From the bank of pay phones Rosa watched the hospital telephone operator cup her hands around the public address microphone. "Dr. Sarah McNamara call the operator. Dr. Sarah McNamara call the operator." It was Sarah's second page. Rosa would ask for the emergency department when the operator came back on line. Surely Sarah had arrived. And knowing Rosa was coming for her, she certainly wouldn't have left without her. Rosa was absolutely positive Sarah had told her Saint Luke's.

The static clicked into silence. "Hello," came a male voice.

"Oh, I'm sorry, our lines must be—"

"Rosa?"

"Yes?"

"It's Ellis."

"Ellis? Where's Sarah?"

"I came in her place. Where are you?"

"In the lobby."

"Stay there. I'll be right down."

Rosa thanked the operator in the glassed-off cage and then smiled to the security guard at the automatic glass door as she walked by. She had already thanked him for unlocking the doors for her after she whined about being lost and not knowing how to get to the emergency department from the outside. After he opened up and scolded her, she promised faithful observance of the rule to come through the ER after ten P.M. from now on.

She had her choice of all of the seats in the lobby and chose one close to the walkway where she could see Ellis when he came down the hall.

And what a treat it was. He strutted down the empty hall like he owned it. That of course was the trick: Make them think you know what you're doing and no one will challenge you.

Sterling and she found the principle sound when her father was in Cedar Sinai Hospital. They marched in like they had done it a million times and went directly up to the records clerk in the radiology department and asked her to produce Mr. Sanchez's CAT scans. Sterling flipped on the fluorescent light box in the hall and clipped the films, one after another, along the edges. Neither of them got much out of the films themselves, but as he was putting on a grand show for everyone, she read the radiologist's report that was inside the X-ray jacket.

"Waiting long?" Ellis asked.

"No." She cocked her head to the guard. "We have to go through the emergency department."

"Then, let's do it." He put his hand to her back and pushed her along. The halls were mainly deserted, patients bedded down for the night, visitors kicked out and locked out. An inhalation therapist was pushing her machine onto the service elevator; a janitor was giving the corridor a good swiping with his mop. Rosa could hear faint music spilling out of his earphones as they tiptoed over his wet floor.

"Ken had a bad one?" Rosa asked as they turned down a desolate hallway that housed the administrative offices.

Ellis nodded. "Hypoplastic heart. Where are you parked?"

She didn't want to talk about it any more than he did now that she knew the circumstances. Stillbirth would have been more compassionate. The parents would cling to hope as long as the infant lingered, maybe a year at the most, instead of grieving, getting over the loss, and going on with their lives.

"To hell and gone."

"More specifically."

"On the Outer Belt."

He stopped in his tracks. "The Outer Belt!" He eyed her suspiciously. "What was wrong with the parking lot?"

"I overshot the lot and couldn't get back. I ended up at the zoo before I could get into a turning lane. I thought I was doing well to get to the Outer Belt."

Ellis listened impatiently. When she was finished babbling, he turned her around. "This way."

They retraced their steps almost back to the lobby, and then ducked down two flights of stairs into the subbasement, and went through a furnace room. But when Ellis opened a double-steel door onto a long tunnel that looked like it could be a sewer pipe, Rosa held the line. "Are you sure you know where you're going?"

"I did my residency here. Why wouldn't I?"

She'd buy that. Rosa gave him a go-ahead gesture. She'd follow him through the tunnel. He could rouse the rats.

They emerged onto the sprawling grounds between the giant medical buildings. The ambient air had cooled off to a tolerable level since her protracted trek to the hospital. They followed a path lighted by mercury vapor lamps.

"Tell me about Robert Copeland," he said, out of the blue.

"Not much to tell. I met him in Aspen at a convention *that* weekend. The weekend Martin did the sleight-of-hand trick on Jacob. The lymphangiogram."

"It keeps getting worse with this Copeland guy." He was talking more to himself than to her.

"Why do you say that?"

"No reason."

"I got to know him a little better tonight." She didn't add that she would have just as soon skipped the opportunity. She grabbed his hand excitedly. "We had dinner with Josh and Margaret. You wouldn't believe how beautiful she looked."

"She always looks beautiful."

"No, I mean Margaret. The other one."

"The one with the . . ." He motioned to his cheek. "I thought Josh went with the pretty one."

"Allison was with them earlier." Her desire had been to share her excitement with him—now it had gotten bogged down. And it was too late in the evening to explain in the epic detail that was required. He could wait and see for himself. "Never mind."

"Who's your insurance carrier?" he asked after they'd walked a distance equal to a football field.

She noticed he gave a deep sigh of regret when she told him. "Is that bad? The County Medical Society endorsed it. We get a twenty-percent discount."

"No, it's as good as any other. I was just wondering."

That was about as weak an answer as she'd ever heard. "You can do better than that."

They trudged along while he thrashed his head around like he was debating with himself about giving her a straight answer to her question.

"Out with it, Ellis." Her anger soared as she listened. And like Popeye, when she could "stands no more," she interrupted. "Look, Ellis. This whole thing has snowballed until it's out of control. Robert Copeland is a lawyer, which is synonymous with a species of the lowest order, but I can't believe that his medical experts will come back with any opinion other than to fight the lawsuit."

She waited until a couple of nurses passed before she continued and by then she was really enraged.

"I could understand if the ditzy widow sued me and included you and every other doctor who I consulted. But to sue you alone makes absolutely no sense.

You're the one who did the most for him. The bypass was successful, you were Bill's saving grace on the botched lymphangiogram—"

"Not to mention patsy." He was not without humor, albeit black.

"And you were the one who went out to the ranch to check on him. Mrs. McQuade's mindset is beyond my comprehension."

"Oh, the reason she's suing me is simple."

Rosa stopped him. "You know why?"

"Sure. She feels that my testimony in court cost her the ranch. And it probably did. She forged his signature to a bill of sale and had her Mexican cleaning girls sign off as witnesses. Supposedly that all happened minutes before I arrived."

"And, of course, he was comatose by then."

He nodded.

"Well, that makes perfect sense. What did Copeland say when you told him?"

"He didn't give me a chance to tell him." Ellis flapped his arms in pure frustration.

"When he learns that, I think everything will turn around for you. And if not, my shoulders are broad enough to carry my own responsibilities. If she wants to sue me, I can deal with it."

"I'm not so certain the insurance company sees it the same way."

"I'll call Bob on Monday, see if I can do something to straighten out this mess. Wonder what they'd say if the County Medical Society decided to change carriers over this?"

"Anyone ever tell you you have the makings of a real trouble rouser?"

"Well, sometimes you have to knock them over the head to get their attention. By the way, Ellis. It's politically correct to call us Latinos, not Mexicans."

A vermillion tint climbed his face. "I'm sorry, Rosa, I didn't mean . . . it was more a . . . Latino. I'll remember."

"Ellis, I was teasing you. Lighten up."

He pulled her under his arm, and then just as suddenly pulled back. "I deserved it." He guffawed.

An uncomfortable silence followed until she spotted her car. "There it is." She pointed. "You were probably starting to think I'd walked to the city."

His laugh was forced for some reason known only to him. "Too bad you've already eaten. I know this wonderful dive not far from here."

She hadn't thought about it before, but with all the excitement over the newborn, he probably hadn't eaten since lunch. "Now, do I look like the kind of woman who would deprive a person of the chance to eat at a wonderful dive?"

Ellis knew the meaning of dive. Barn was a very appropriate name. The dark Barn was filled to its rafters with young country dancers in cowboy hats and boots. Her high heels were as appropriate here as they had been on her round-trip jaunt across the Texas Medical Center campus. And she was getting happier and happier by the minute to be in them.

A blur of denim and coarse nylon-net petticoats fanned her face as someone on the edge of the crowded dance floor twirled under her partner's long arm. Ellis said something she couldn't hear over the band and stomping boots. He took her hand and led her through the crowd to the dining room behind the bar.

The dining room, for lack of a more appropriate name, was only slightly less noisy, owing to the attractive cowgirl riding the mechanical horse in the far corner. Well, that wasn't quite true, she realized as a couple of the cowboys stepped aside to reveal a saddled barrel suspended between four thick springs strung up to the rafter beams. A husky cowboy stood in back pulling ropes. The harder he pulled the higher the barrel bucked. The rider flew off, tumbling an admirer. They rolled across the hay-covered floor, enjoying themselves mightily.

Ellis bused their table as Rosa slid over the wooden-plank bench. She felt her nylons snag on a splinter and run down the back.

"What would you like?" Ellis asked, beer bottle teetering on top of the stack of red, burger baskets.

"I'm fine." She pulled a couple of napkins out of the dispenser and wiped up the rings of beer and crumbs.

Ellis piled the trash on the counter and placed his order with the girl half-hidden behind a display of chips. He moseyed on over to the riderless barrel.

It looked like Ellis was instigating betting from the money that was coming out everyone's pockets. A pat on the back from a lanky cowboy and Ellis was up in the saddle. He wound the rope halter around the back of his hand, and then gave the signal.

Unlike the gentle ride the cowgirl received, Ellis was treated to the ride of the century. Four men jerked the two ropes for all they were worth. He was tossed high in the air and landed hard when he came crashing down again.

Rosa jumped to her feet, banging her knee on the underside of the rustic table.

Undaunted, Ellis held his free hand high over his head, rode loose, and whooped it up. The cowboy with both eyes glued to a watch in his hand called out. The barrel slowed, then came to a stop. Ellis threw his foot over the saddle horn and hopped off. He collected his winnings and a round of appreciative claps on his back.

He affected a cowboy gait as he came strutting back, accepting a handshake here and there from other diners. He swooped a basket from the counter and tossed it on the table. It contained the greasiest hamburger she'd ever laid eyes on. The fries didn't look cholesterol free, either. "A beer?"

"Mineral water. I'm the designated driver."

He disappeared around the corner into the bar and reappeared chugging a bottle of beer. Without apology he handed her a sweaty bottle of Coke. He hunkered down on the bench across from her.

"Thirsty work riding a barrel," she teased.

"Yip." He got a good two-handed grip on the deluxe hamburger and took a hungry-man's bite. Juices ran down his chin. She popped a couple of napkins out of the dispenser and handed them over.

"Where'd you learn to ride a barrel like that?" she asked in what she hoped passed for cowboy talk.

"My parents have a ranch north of town." He slapped the bottom of the catsup bottle until the fries were swimming. "I could ride before I could walk. Horses, I mean. We put our oil barrels to better use."

That part about the oil barrels almost got by her. Almost. "Y'all Houston's equivalent of our very own Chandlers?"

He shrugged and crammed a fistful of fries into his mouth.

She sipped her Coke in total bewilderment. He was a boastfully conceited surgeon but kept his social status under wraps. Though maybe she was the only one who didn't know. "How come you weren't in the rodeo last spring?"

"Was. I was the clown."

"I know that." She nodded to his injured shoulder. "How come you didn't compete?"

"Want another Coke, pardner?" he teased as he scooted out. Careful not to graze the back of the cowboy behind him.

"I'll drink this one first."

When he was back and settled in with his new bottle of beer, he looked over at her. "You don't know much about rodeoing, do you?"

She put her hands on her hips. "I can cruise Rodeo Drive with the best of them." She worked hard to control her smile, but he didn't appreciate it.

"Since there seems to be a ripple in your general knowledge, let me inform you that the clown is the most important person in the rodeo. And the best athlete. The performers are at their most vulnerable when they dismount or are thrown ... *especially* when thrown. The clown's the only one standing between the rider and an angry beast."

He slid across the bench and stuck his head out in the aisle to see better whatever it was in the main room that had taken his interest. He got to his feet and held out his hand. "*Waltz Across Texas*. Let's dance."

"I can't dance like that."

He grabbed her hand and pulled her up. "I'll teach you."

Ellis found a weak chink in the human ring circling the dance floor. He took great pains to position her arms as if they were ice skaters about to perform in the Olympics. She kept her eyes trained on his feet and tried to follow. She looked up at him for a second and lost her footing.

"Now you're catching on," he said after they'd circled the floor twice. Inspired by the couple in front of them, Ellis pushed her out of line and twirled her around. The second time was a little more dignified.

By the end of the third rotation, she was a regular two-stepping clomper. Rosa couldn't remember when she'd had more fun.

Chapter 31

Sophie

Saturday was a good day to die. All of Carl Reese's loved ones had come. Sophie had been shuffling them back and forth from the waiting room so they could all have a chance to say good-bye. He was comatose, but Sophie had assured them that the sense of hearing was the last to go.

Carl's daughter sat on the edge of a straight chair by the bed and stroked her father's arm. His son stood beside her. Carl's mother sat in the lounge chair Sophie had the boiler room send up for his wife, Vivian, to sleep in before Carl insisted that she go home every night and sleep in her own bed. Pastor White knelt beside the chair on one side, and Vivian on the other. Together they held hands and prayed. Sophie couldn't think of anything worse than for a ninety-three-year-old mother to have to bury her son. Sophie hoped God would be kinder with her and take her before he took Lisa.

Sophie slipped around the other side of the bed and checked Carl's vital signs. She didn't know how he was managing to hold on. Everyone had had a chance to speak to him now. It was time for him to let go.

When Pastor White seemed to be winding down, Sophie joined them. She took hold of Vivian's shoulders firmly. Understanding the significance, Pastor White closed the prayer.

"He's suffered long enough. Go over and tell him

it's all right for him to go." Sophie helped her up. "He's waiting for you to release him."

The son and daughter made room for their mother.

Vivian turned to Sophie with pleading eyes.

Sophie nodded rigidly. "Go on, he can hear you."

Vivian pressed her lips together. She lifted his hand to her lips. "Carl, it's Vivian. We love you more than anything in life, but it's time to let you go." Tears rolled over her face unchecked. "It's time for you to be with our Heavenly Father. Time for you to prepare a place for us in Heaven. Watch over us . . . Carl." She broke into wracking sobs and threw herself over her husband.

Sophie pulled several tissues out of the box and pressed them into Vivian's palm. She gave some to the daughter. Carl's mother struggled to her feet, assisted by Pastor White. She took uneasy steps to the head of the bed.

"Son, you have always been a good boy." Her shaking hand touched his face. "God is calling you home."

Pastor White took his Bible and stepped to the foot of the bed. "Ecclesiastes three, verses one through eight. 'To every thing there is a season, and a time to every purpose under he heaven: A time to be born, and a time to die; a time to plant, and a time to pluck up that which is planted.' "

Sophie felt, more than saw, the door open. Wendy stuck her head around it and motioned to her. Sophie ducked under the drip line and tiptoed out.

" 'A time to kill, and a time to heal; a time to break down, and a time to build up; a time to weep—' "

Sophie waited until the door was completely closed. "What is it?"

"Frank's in the waiting room."

What was Frank doing here? He would be seeing her at seven, like every other Saturday night for the last eighteen months. She hurried down the hall. Frank was hugging Louise Miller, a cousin of Carl's and a fellow member of their congregation. Her bellowing soprano voice used to overpower everyone else in the choir, but the director had tactfully moved her over to the organ after Bertha's arthritis crippled her hands too badly for her to play.

"Cancer's an awful thing," Frank told Louise. Sophie's heart went out to him. This had to be a terrible reminder of his wife's torturously slow death to cancer. She had been one of Sophie's patients, and Sophie had gotten to know Frank so well because of her long stay in the hospital.

Sophie touched his sleeve. "Did you come to see Carl?"

He freed Louise, and took Sophie's arm at the fleshy part above the elbow and lead her to the far corner of the room. "No, I came to get you."

"Get me? What for?"

He decided they still didn't have the appropriate privacy. He took her out into the hall. Louise's husband passed them, carrying two cups of coffee. Frank pulled her into the stairwell. He looked over the rail to make sure they were alone.

"Here, sit down." He sat on the concrete landing.

"What's wrong?" she asked as she plopped down on the hard surface beside him.

"I need you to let me search your house."

"Why?"

"We received a call that it was Lisa who stole the drugs from the hospital and is hiding them in her closet."

"Who said this?" she demanded.

He shook his head. "We traced the call to the public phone next to the market, but no one remembered seeing anyone using it."

"It obviously a lie!"

Frank didn't rise to Lisa's defense like he should have. "Would you come with me, let me look around the house?"

"Now? With Carl dying?"

He took her hand. "I don't want to do this. But if I

don't check it out, people might accuse me of favoritism."

"Couldn't it wait until tonight?"

He shook his head. "Gretchen is already there, waiting."

So this wasn't "let's have a little look," but official business with the deputy staking out the house. She didn't know Frank at all. "Okay," she said formally like she would to any other official. Rising, she brushed off the seat of her skirt. "Let's go."

"Don't be like this, Sophie."

She pulled away when he tried to take her arm. She led the way down two flights of stairs. She sat quietly in the passenger's seat of the police chief's car, staring out the window.

"Sophie, look at me."

She obeyed, watching him run nervous fingers through his lank sandy hair, a habitual habit to cover the bald spot at the crown. His blue dress shirt was sweat drenched and the thick skin around the frayed collar glistened with water beads. He shifted nervously, bumping the tip of his .357 on the seat. She wondered what she had ever seen in him.

"Don't be like this, Sophie. It's not personal. I wouldn't be doing my job if I didn't check it out."

"So you said." Her tone spoke for itself. He concentrated on driving.

Gretchen was parked in the shade. She got out and ambled over to the car. The bean pole shoved her thumbs down inside her gun belt and nodded her tightly curled, blond head to the chief, her buck teeth protruding through thin lips.

They escorted Sophie to her door. "Lisa?" she called as she stepped in. The air in the living room was stuffy and not much cooler than the blazing heat outside. Though she had a pitcher of lemonade in the fridge, she didn't offer anyone a drink. "She must be in her bedroom."

Frank knew his way. Gretchen followed him down

the hall. He knocked at Lisa's door. After a moment, he called, "Lisa, are you there?"

Sophie brushed past them and opened the door. Lisa wasn't there. "Lisa? Lisa!" Sophie had given the girl explicit orders not to leave the house. She was a willful girl, but she had never stolen anything in her life, let alone that bottle of morphine. Sophie would have known if Lisa was a dope fiend. She turned to Frank. "Search." She sat on the bed, absolutely positive they would find nothing in the closet, and watched Gretchen go through Lisa's things from top to bottom.

"Chief?" Gretchen looked up at Frank. He squatted down on the floor next to her. There was something in her voice that made Sophie rise and start toward them, her feet moving of their own accord.

Frank pulled out the box of the Madam Alexander doll Sophie had given Lisa on her eleventh birthday. He laid the cover aside. Sophie looked over his shoulder as he brought out a handful of drug samples. Sophie took one out of his hand. It was Darvon, in the kind of package pharmaceutical representatives leave at doctors' offices and hospital pharmacies.

Chapter 32

Lisa

"Trash fever," Ray was telling her. "You got trash fever. Just have to ride it out."

Lisa puked into the toilet bowl, her head so heavy she could hardly keep it out of the water. Sweat dripped off her face and vomit rolled out her nose. She was sicker than a dog.

Ray must have drawn up a fiber from the cigarette filter he used to strain the liquid and shot it straight into her bloodstream. Why did this have to happen to her?

The chills started again. She rolled over onto the tile floor. She felt Ray pick her up and carry her to bed. He got an old blanket off the top shelf in the closet and spread it over her. If only she could stop shaking.

"It's going last eight to ten hours. You've got to get home."

Her mother was at the hospital, but was coming home for dinner. He was right about having to get home. Her mother would kill her if she knew she'd left the house. She'd taken the phone off the hook in case she called, but now what was she going to do? How was she going to get home?

When was the cocaine she snorted going to kick in? Mainlining took three to five minutes to peak. Snorting took twenty to sixty. Surely it had been twenty minutes.

Nothing was like how it used to be. Used to be she'd

get that pins-and-needles feeling in her fingers and toes. And electric current rushing through her as if she'd stuck a finger in a wall socket. Now it took more and more to get less and less. She wanted to recapture those feelings.

She turned on her side and rolled into a ball, but she was still so cold. She had to get to the bathroom before her stomach erupted. Her mouth was watering; she was going to throw up again.

Lisa threw back the covers and collapsed to the floor when she tried to get up, vomiting all over the side of the bed. Ray slapped her head to the floor, puke smearing her face. Everything went black.

She woke to find herself in the backseat of Ray's car. He said he was taking her home. Good. She wanted to be in her own bed. She wanted her mother to take care of her. She was so sick, she wanted to die.

"Lisa, can you hear me?"

She could hear him, she just didn't want to talk to him. She could only moan.

"Listen to me," he yelled. "There are two police cars at your house. You get out here and walk home." She couldn't walk home. She tried to lift her head to see where they were, but she couldn't. "Get out!" He was mad at her, but she couldn't help it, she was sick.

Something was wrong with her. Her heart was pounding. Her legs jerked out and a scream caught in the back of her throat. She saw circling stars, and then everything turned black. She woke up to find herself gasping for air. The car was moving. She was on the floor. She must have rolled off the backseat. Her head throbbed. Tires squealed to a halt. She felt him pull her out of the door, her bottom banging on the curb. She recognized the hospital. "You've got to go in alone. Just go around the corner and in through the doors."

There was something wrong with her. Everything around her was so dark and Ray seemed so far away. Her muscles were fighting each other, jerking her around.

He got her to her feet and leaned her against the scorching brick wall. "Just don't tell them who gave you the cocaine." He pushed her around the corner. Her head was swimming, she couldn't move her legs. She stumbled toward the door and fell over. Someone wearing white sleeves grabbed her. She couldn't catch her breath.

She came to on an examining table to find a mask over her mouth. People were crowding over her. Pushing and poking. Hooking up wires and tubes. She wanted her mother.

"One hundred and four and rising."

"Start a drip. I'll call Dr. Morgan's house. See which antiseizure meds he wants her to have."

Lisa tumbled down the bank of the bayou. Over and over. The sides were gone and she was falling. She splashed into the water. Sinking, sinking. The water was freezing. Steam blinded her.

Chapter 33

Cole

"Give her one hundred milliliters of fifty percent dextrose, one hundred milligrams of thiamine IV, as well as the Valium, and get her in an ice bath. I'll be right in." Cole hung up, found the keys to his pickup, and plodded to the door. His jeans were sprung out at the knee of the good leg and split to his thigh to accommodate his cast on the other. He was covered with corral dust from hat to boot, his cast so grimy, the autographs were unreadable. But he didn't have time to clean up.

They had Sophie's girl immersed in a tub of ice water by the time he arrived. Her temperature was down to normal after twenty minutes, but the rectal reading had gotten to 106 Fahrenheit. Cole figured, with all the metabolic activity taking place in the liver, it would likely reach 108, maybe 110. But possible liver damage was his second concern.

Cole lifted the girl's arm out of the frigid water to have a better look at the track marks. It was an addict's arm. And he'd seen its like hundreds of times, usually in charity hospitals bordering unsavory neighborhoods. He'd seen AIDS, serum hepatitis, bacterial and fungal contamination from needle sharing, which was an inevitable part of the drug culture. But to see it in his hometown, involving Sophie's young daughter, saddened him deeply.

The nurse had given the girl a nine on the Glasgow Coma Scale. Babbling, opening her eyes when a booming voice demanded it, and withdrawing from a painful stimulus rated a nine. Now the patient knew her name and was oriented to time and place. Cole upgraded the girl to a full fifteen, complete responsiveness. It was time to admit her and transfer her upstairs.

"Who's her attending?"

"Dr. McNamara," the parttime nurse answered. "We haven't been able to reach her, yet." Strange that the girl was still seeing a pediatrician: She was into big-league medical problems.

Her sweet face looked so much like Sophie's had all those years ago. So many emotions assaulted him. This girl was a bitter reminder of their failed relationship. How could Sophie have pledged her love to him and turned around and run off with another man in less than a month's time? She hadn't bothered to tell him, either. It was her mother, in her usual negative way, who broke the news to him. "Well, if she wanted you to have her new address, she would have given it to you. She's married now, you know." Of course he didn't know. Being told that four-headed creatures from outer space had landed would have been more believable.

But she had married. Here was the proof. He dropped Lisa's arm. "Admit her to ICU," he told the physician assistant, who covered the ER on weekends. "I'll go out and speak to the mother." The nurse and the physician assistant took in a communal breath, a sigh of relief in reverse. He had been told that Sophie had barged into the ER and tried to take over. But under the circumstances, the director of nursing had been treated like any other family member. She was ushered out and shown to the waiting room.

As soon as Cole pushed through the swing doors into the hall, Sophie was in front of him. One look at her and he wanted to grab her to him, hold her and comfort her. He wanted to be all those things to her they had planned when they were young and in love, before life had robbed them of their hopes and dreams.

"How is she?" Worry creased over her brow and bracketed her mouth. He wanted to be her knight in shining armor. He wanted to tell her that her daughter was safe now and everything would be hunky-dory. But the tracks told another story. The likelihood of the girl breaking loose of her addiction and leading a normal life was almost nonexistent. He felt so useless.

"Her temperature's normal."

She gave a sigh of gratitude. He only wished telling the rest would be as easy.

"Let's go into the waiting room." He hobbled across the hall, remembering all too well the extra care she had given him during his recovery. This was hardly fair reward.

The chief of police rose from the sofa when they walked in. Cole knew Sophie dated the man, but wasn't certain how freely he could speak in front of him.

"I wonder if I might speak with Mrs. Drummond alone?"

He started out. "I'll wait for you in—"

"No, Frank. Don't wait." Sophie was next-door to being rude. It was a side of her Cole had never seen. And a side Frank must not have, if Cole could go by the flabbergasted look on his face. "Or were you planning to keep her under guard? Being the desperate criminal you think her to be, maybe you could handcuff her to the bed so you won't have to sit outside her door."

Cole gathered from the remark that Sophie knew about her daughter's drug addiction. He was relieved he wouldn't have to be the one to tell her. He went over to the sofa and eased himself down, trying to extricate himself from the lovers' quarrel.

"I'll call you later, Sophie. When you're not so upset."

She neither answered, nor watched him leave. She headed straight for the sofa. "What happened to her, Cole?"

"Lisa overdosed on cocaine."

"Cocaine?" From her expression, he wasn't so certain Sophie knew of the girl's addiction after all. "That's impossible. I would have known if she was using drugs." Parents were always the last to know. Denial.

"Have you seen the tracks on your daughter's arm?"

"No, I haven't seen tracks on *my* daughter's arm. What's wrong with everyone?" She ran a dry tongue around her lips. "Okay, I'm not saying she's perfect, but she's not a drug fiend who goes around stealing medicine from the hospital. There's got to be some other explanation." She looked at him imploringly, with the same frightened eyes of the ten-year-old Sophie whose dog had been hit by the tractor. There wasn't much he could do for her then, either.

She retreated to the window and looked out so he wouldn't see her tears. Her quivering shoulders gave her away. He went to her and ran a hand over her back. He had so many things he wanted to say. But years of hurt kept him from uttering a word.

"What am I going to do with her?" She burst into a full-blown crying jag.

Cole pulled her into his arms, burying her wails into his chest. "Everything will work out, Sophie." He rocked her. "We'll make it work."

Chapter 34

Coral May

Saturday night at the Sundowner lounge in Richmond was always jumping. Coral May loved coming in now that she was a customer instead of one of the overworked cocktail waitresses.

"Keep the change," Coral May told Buster. He was the best bartender in the world.

Buster gave her a wink as he opened the cash register.

Coral May picked up her drink and moved to the empty chair at the piano bar. Troy gave her a warm smile. Just like when she used to serve him drinks. Buster always made them real weak on account of all the ones people bought for him.

"This next one's for you, honey." Troy cracked his knuckles and repositioned them over the ivory keys. He gave them a little running tickle to tease her. She knew what he was going to play, he always played it for her.

He placed his lips next to the mike and winked at her as he sang "*People.*" She loved that song. And loved the way his eyes were glued on her while he sang it just for her.

Her whole body was tingling, except her breasts, which had no feeling. She hoped everyone liked the way they looked on her because they'd cost her more than she thought she was paying. Not having feeling in her breasts was awful.

She sipped her scotch, never letting her eyes stray from Troy. He was probably sixty and looked Jewish with his long nose and fringe of dark hair in a horseshoe around his glistening scalp. She could forgive him those things. What she couldn't forgive him was that he liked boys. He never told her in so many words, but there were always younger boys hanging around until closing time whom he'd go off with.

Pam! Coral May caught sight of Pam passing behind Troy to go down the hall to the ladies' room. She'd catch up with her in a minute. But she didn't want to do anything until Troy finished her song. It wouldn't be polite, not with him singing to her and all.

She gave Troy a big hand. So did everyone else. She scooted around the piano bar and placed a kiss on the top of his sweat-polished head. "That was so sweet of you." She motioned to her drink. "Don't let anyone take my chair." She hurried down the hall.

"Pam," she called as she bent practically upside down to see which stall she was in. "It's Coral May, Pam, honey."

She might have acknowledged her. Coral May couldn't tell, on account of the flushing toilet. Pam came out pulling down her pink squaw skirt. It was real cute with the scooped-neck white blouse and ballerina shoes. She was just as cute as a button. "Hi, Coral May. What a surprise!" She fiddled with her concho belt, making sure the turquoise centers were all facing out. Then she gave her a big hug. "I'm glad to see you, Coral May."

"Whatcha doing in Richmond, for heaven's sake?"

"I, ah, I went to the movies."

"Me, too. And boy, am I mad. I saw Sarah and John McNamara in the lobby of the Twin Theatre, and you know what she said to me?"

Pam stooped over and tied the little tassel on one of her slippers. "What?"

"She tried to stick up for Ellis. Said Ellis gave Jacob the best care he could have gotten." Coral May was so mad. What business was it of Sarah's to lay into her like that. Ellis didn't give Jacob the best care he could have gotten. He killed Jacob! Jacob was dead. Dead from Ellis's surgery on his foot. His foot was real ugly. His heart was probably worse.

Coral May stepped aside so Pam could get to the sink. "Who does she think she is? How could she say that? Didn't Ellis lie about Jacob not being able to sign those papers? I sat right next to Jacob when he signed them—guess, I know better than he did. And Sarah sticking up for him!"

Pam dried her hands and tossed the paper towel in the wastebasket. "Don't let it get you down. Come on, I'll buy you a drink."

"I've already got one out by the piano." Coral May held the door open for Pam. "You know the song the piano player was just playing? He dedicated it to me. He always does. I used to work here, you know. Before Jacob and I were married, of course."

"I didn't know that."

Coral May nodded. "It's true."

"Where are you sitting?" Pam asked. "I just walked in the door. Should have used the restroom at the theater, but what a line."

"At the piano." That was a problem. There wasn't another seat for Pam. She looked around the crowded bar. "Over there." Coral May pointed to a free booth in the corner. It held six, but that was all right. And if two guys wanted to join them, Coral May wasn't about to put up a fuss. Coral May picked up her drink and gave up her spot at the piano bar while Pam hurried over to the booth before someone else came in and took it.

Gawd almighty! This town was just crawling with C Springs folks. Sarah and her son at the movies, Pam, and now she was seeing Billy. She wished she hadn't promised to have a drink with Pam now. She stopped to talk to him. "Billy Martin, I declare. I just can't believe how many people I know here." She gave him a speck of a kiss.

He got up and gave her a big hug. "I'm so glad to see you. Karen is supposed to be meeting me here. You haven't seen her have you?"

Like she wanted to see Karen so badly she could pop. "No, but Pam Roberts is here. You know her?"

He looked real strange, like he was really twisting out his brain to recollect.

"She's a nurse at the hospital. I know you do. She knows you. Speaks highly of you." She twirled around and pointed her out. Billy still didn't seem to recognize her. "Why don't you come over and join us for a drink? I'll introduce you."

"Karen should be along any minute. I better not."

She nodded that she understood. She sure didn't want Karen at their table.

"But I'll take a rain check."

She smiled. "Don't be a stranger, now. Come out to the ranch, sometime."

He gave her a little pat that she hoped no one saw. She worked her way over to Pam and slid across the leather cushions. "I just can't believe it, Pam. Billy Martin's over there. Three of us from C Springs. Is that the biggest coincidence or what?"

Pam shook her head. "That's amazing."

Susie must have taken Pam's order while she was visiting with Billy. She brought it back and put it on the napkin. She was having a Diet Coke. Coral May could tell from the red-and-white-striped straw.

"I asked him to join us, but he's waiting for his wife. I would have introduced you to him. I know you know who he is, but he didn't know you."

"Doctors are like that, Coral May. You can talk to them a hundred times about a patient, and they don't remember you the next time."

"That's terrible. They should treat nurses with more respect. Hospitals can be so awful. My poor Jacob sure found that out. But you were so nice to him. I'm much obliged." Coral May felt her bottom lip quiver as that terrible time Jacob spent at the medical center rushed back on her like a broken dam. She sipped her drink to calm herself. She just felt so sorry for Jacob. "But Billy's nice. You'd like him if you'd got to know him."

Pam shrugged.

Coral May had forgotten for a minute how young Pam was. She probably saw Billy as a father figure. "Really, it's his assistant you'd really like. Josh Allister. Know him?"

"Yes, I did meet him once. He goes with Allison Chandler."

"She's such a bitch. Believe me, he'll get tired of her soon enough." Coral May swirled her drink to keep the scotch from settling to the bottom. "Wonder what's keeping Billy's wife. He could have had that drink with us, after all." She sipped, feeling the scotch's smoothness coat her throat and warm her all the way down the pipes. "Now, he's a man I could go for. He's not too old for me by a long shot. Not after being married to Jacob and all."

"Too bad he already has a wife, Coral May." Pam eyed Billy. "You two would make a great couple. I can tell." She shook her head. "I heard from the hospital grapevine that he isn't at all happy with his wife."

He wasn't happy with Karen. Coral May sure knew that. Hadn't he turned to her for comfort? Poor Billy. He was so sweet. "Its so sad." She glanced over her shoulder. Karen was still keeping him waiting. "Look at him, all alone. She doesn't deserve him, keeping him waiting like that. Poor Billy."

"Maybe she's been in a car accident. Who knows? Maybe she fell off her horse and broke her neck." Pam shrugged and drew on her straw. "Maybe that wouldn't be so bad. Then he'd be all yours."

Coral May Martin had a nice ring to it.

About the time Pam said she had to go, Billy came over to say good night. He'd called home to find that Karen had come down with a bug and wasn't coming after all.

That's when it hit her. She kind of swooned into Billy's arms. "Guess I shouldn't have had that last drink," she told him. "Guess I shouldn't be driving home."

He didn't say anything, just eased her into a chair. He had always been such a gentleman, and he was so smart. Coral May didn't understand why he didn't offer to take her home. It was right on his way. She caught Pam's eye and blinked real fast for her to help out.

"Coral May, I'd be happy to give you a lift home, only I'm spending the night in Richmond." Pam was one sharp cookie. "Are you going back to town, Dr. Martin? The Rocking M is right on the way."

"Oh . . . ah, yes. I am." He sure had a good bedside manner and a smile to go along with it. "I could drop you by the ranch on the way to town."

"That would be so nice of you." She remembered the last time he took her home. The day Jacob had his heart attack. She tried to remember which sheets she had on the bed. He so liked the red satin ones.

Chapter 35

Ellis

"All available medical personnel to the emergency department. Multiple incoming. ETA eight minutes. All available medical personnel."

What a way to start off the week, Ellis thought to himself.

Everyone at the table started shoveling down Monday morning's breakfast. Cole took a last sip of coffee and maneuvered out of his chair and hobbled out to set up for the arrivals. The rest of them would be down by time the ambulances started arriving in eight minutes.

Rosa and Sarah trashed their plates and beat Cole to the door, Bill and Josh, right behind them. The orthopods and Tilton finished up. Meredith and Sean exchanged glances as if wondering if they should make an appearance, bag it and head back to the rehab building, or wait out the M&M meeting. It was a split decision. Sean got up and started out. There was something different about those two, but Ellis couldn't quite put his finger on it.

As if one, Ken, Patrick, Leroy, and Ellis headed for the door, leaving Ty as their representative. He knew he wouldn't be needed for a while. He would do the clean-up work on whatever bodies the rest of them couldn't salvage.

"Hope it's not too serious. These M and M meetings are bad enough on a slow week," Ken put in.

"Now, Ken, busy hands are happy hands," Patrick scolded.

"Busy those hands," Leroy chimed in, "praying it's not another school bus."

Today was the first day back to school. It could have been. Ellis looked at his watch. Seven-thirty. The bus was supposed to come for Amy and Will a few minutes before seven. Ellis remembered Hillary screaming it at Will when she was trying to get him moving this morning. A spasm seized Ellis. He saw Will's little frame caught under the overturned yellow bus, the "yellow zinger" as Amy liked to call it.

"You look green, my man. Anything I can do?" Sean asked as they passed at the ER entrance.

Ellis snapped out of his daymare. "I'm fine. You leaving so soon?"

"Merely had an academic interest in who would be here." He put his giant hands in his pockets and strolled off.

The place was swarming with nurses, inhalation therapist, X-ray and lab technicians. Dennis Green was racing around, pulling back the curtains between the examining tables and readying the work areas. Cole propped himself against the nursing station, the phone to his ear, motioning to the X-ray technician where he wanted the portable machine.

"Here." Rosa thrust bottles of Ringer's lactate into Ellis's arms. "Put your surgical talents to use."

Who better qualified to start an IV than a surgeon? "What are we expecting?"

"Thermal injuries. A fire at the old rice warehouse. The night watchman, and several of the volunteer fire fighters."

Ellis maneuvered around the busy beavers and out the automatic doors. A cloud of black smoke out by the interstate confirmed Rosa's information. So did the smell of the drifting smoke. A siren was nearing.

He looked at the salt solution in his arms and tried to remember his ancient lessons. The infusion-rate formula had to do with body weight and percentage of burn. The Rule of Nines determined the extent of injury. Head was nine percent, each arm received nine, the legs eighteen each, anterior trunk eighteen, and posterior trunk eighteen. Neck rated one. Though it would be of no real consequence. The initial fluid resuscitation therapy could be modified according to the patient's needs later in the morning. By tomorrow the electrolyte solution would be replaced with dextrose and salt-free water.

Ellis hung the solution on IV poles, and then found Cole to ask him the infusion-rate formula. Four milliliters times kilogram body weight times percentage of burn, Cole informed him.

He followed the commotion outdoors as a police car pulled in just ahead of the ambulance. He rounded the ambulance, catching a quick glance of a walking-wounded patient being helped out of the backseat of the car.

Ellis and Ken popped the ambulance's double doors open, careful not to hit the station wagon pulling in with more walking woundeds. Rosa jumped in ahead of them. She glanced at the patient on the right, then spoke to the screaming one.

"How are you feeling?" she asked the man on the left, looking to be in his late twenties. His face, neck, hands, and arms were blistered. Skin on the exposed chest was waxy white.

"You got to give me something for the pain." He was clearly in unrelenting agony.

"Do you know where you are?"

"Hospital," he said writhing. The ambulance driver squeezed in.

"Alert and oriented." Rosa motioned for them to take the young one on the left first. The attendant pulled the wire-net scoop stretcher toward him as the driver guided the top. "You're going to be just fine," Rosa assured the patient.

She motioned for Ellis and Ken to take the other stretcher. Ellis went around her to the head.

"How are you feeling?" Rosa asked.

"Puny," the man answered in an old voice. His skin was scorched black, his hair singed, and blackened fabric was melted and twisted into patches of translucent flesh and visibly thrombobesed veins. Vast flakes of crispy-burnt skin rimmed the stretcher. A sweet aroma like honey-baked ham hung over him.

"Do you have any pain?" she asked.

"No." His answer didn't surprise Ellis. A third-degree burn, like his, was full-thickness and involved the nerve endings. A burn from an iron or a stove could cause excruciating pain, but there was no pain with a burn of this magnitude. Pain was inversely related to the seriousness of the burn.

Ellis knew that the best thing that could happen to this man was to die now. Chances were good that he'd linger a week before his bodily systems shut down entirely. No one at CMC would know. A helicopter would come and whisk him away, and he would be out of their lives as quickly as he had come.

"Dr. Johnston." He looked up to see Sophie leaning into the ambulance. "Dr. Thompson needs you inside." Sophie climbed in and took over. She looked badly shaken.

Ellis waited beside the ambulance while the civilians Dennis had chased out of the ER moved the station wagon out of the way. Inside, Ellis caught a quick peek of the back of Patrick's head before he bent over and disappeared into the pack of medical personnel surrounding the far examining table.

So far there were six patients. The two burns from the ambulance, three men in sooty fireman garb being given oxygen, and the patient Patrick and his entourage were seeing to.

Ellis worked his way through.

The patient was receiving inhalation therapy, as well as an aminophylline IV to ease his breathing. The part of the grimy face Ellis could see looked familiar. "Who is this?"

"Police chief," Patrick answered. "Sophie's police chief." Reading between the lines, Ellis saw that Patrick had sent Sophie to fetch him to get rid of her.

Patrick was mopping up a long gash along the groin. "Bill has gone to set up for an arteriogram." To establish if the femoral artery had been perforated. An arteriogram should make Bill's day. One of his patients complained that she'd received a bill from Bill's office for over a thousand dollars for an arteriogram, a huge sum for a diagnostic test. Ellis looked around for Josh. He was clipping a portable chest X ray to the ER's fluorescent light box. Ellis hoped he'd be finished here in time to do the arteriogram instead of Bill.

Ellis moved to Patrick's side. "Think the bladder might be involved?" He ordered a Foley catheter. "What happened to him?"

"A metal beam fell on him."

"Chief, we're going to push a catheter up your urethra into the bladder to make certain there's no blood in your bladder and that urine isn't discharging into your abdomen. We're giving you a local anesthetic so you shouldn't feel it." The chief groaned his disapproval. Ellis suspected he would not be happier with the rectal exam.

Chapter 36

Sean

Sean stood over the bed. Lisa looked a great deal better than when Meredith and he visited her in ICU before she was transferred to the step-down ward. Meredith had had her turn at being the bad cop; now it was his turn to be the good cop.

The willful lass was awake, he could tell by how tightly she'd closed her eyes to pretend sleep. "Lisa, are you awake?"

After a moment, he picked up her arm and pushed up her sleeve to have a good look at the tracks. Embarrassment inspired her. She pulled her arm away. "What do you want?" she asked as she propped herself up on her arms.

"To talk."

She turned on the television set to the highest decibel.

He unplugged it and pulled up a chair.

She defiantly turned her face away. They were all hostile at first. He had seen tougher, more experienced addicts.

"I want to be your advocate, young woman." He slipped her chart and his assessment forms under his chair. "Do you know what that means?" She ignored him. "Tell me what it means so I know we are on the right track. Let it be our first step together on the road to achieving our goal."

"It's a friend."

"A friend, and more. I will stand up for your rights. I will defend you against your mother, against the hospital system, against the world."

"You sure did a fucking great job of that yesterday."

He laughed. "You Americans are so funny in your misuse of the English language. Do you know that your colorful adjective is mnemonic? Puritans wrote it on the punishment boards over the heads of the sinner on display in the township courtyard so everyone would be apprised of his crime. For Unlawful Carnal Knowledge. So you are saying to me, 'you sure did a for unlawful carnal knowledge great job of that yesterday.' You Americans."

Taken aback, she had no response. They never did.

Having chastised her enough, he turned his mind to the cache of stolen prescribed drugs found in her room. "We are alone now. Your mother shan't be creating a scene this time. Let us talk frankly about the drug cache."

"I don't know where that stuff came from. Honest." Lisa looked him straight in the eye. "I didn't have anything in my doll box. I didn't have anything in the house. How stupid do they think I am?"

"They do not think you stupid at all. You are *very* smart. You have turned your mother into an enabler. You fooled Dr. Fischer by putting my name on the scripts you forged. I believe from your conviction that you did not know those drugs were there." The expiration dates were near. She might have had them for a while and had forgotten. She admitted stealing the morphine; there seemed to be a pattern. Memory loss because of organic brain damage, he feared.

He saw a hint of appreciation in the troubled teenager's eyes.

"Let us not dwell on the past, instead, look ahead to the future. You have an addictive personality and must learn to conquer the problem instead of letting it conquer you. You and I, my dear, and the entire staff at the rehab center, have much work to do. The more you co-operate, the faster it will go."

"And what if I don't?"

"Then your twenty-nine-day program will be stretched out for as long as it takes."

"And I don't have any say in the matter?" Her hostility demanded a firmer hand.

"No, you don't. You see, we believe in what is referred to as 'hard love.' We love you enough to want you to live a productive, happy life. You have a terminal disease that can be controlled, but it will take a great deal of work on your part. We shall teach you."

"What do you mean a terminal disease?"

"People who crave chemicals are born with a genetic abnormality, a deficiency—a genetic predisposition, if you will. The liver, which normally breaks down most drugs, produces chemicals in these people and makes them respond in a much more favorable way to drugs. They crave drugs compulsively. It becomes the most important thing in their lives. The illness strips everything else away, and it makes no difference to these people."

He could see he'd stirred her craving.

"It is like a washing machine," he went on. "If you have never used one, you do not know what you are missing. Lose it and have to wash your clothing by hand in the washbasin, and you miss it terribly. That is what is happening to you. You have felt those feelings, enhanced by your body's chemistry. It's our job to teach you to deny those feelings. If we fail, you die. If—"

"What's so wrong with dying? Everyone has to do it. Might as well get it over with."

"You don't mean that. You think you do because the chemicals you have shot into your young body have scrambled your mind, confused your thinking."

He turned to his clipboard. "Might as well be starting. 'Tis a long haul." He showed her the forms. She gave a cursory glance and then returned to picking the tape around her IV. "I will be making an addictive disease assessment and taking a social history." He crossed his leg at the knee to better brace the clipboard. "You suffer from a polydrug addiction, this I know from the lab results. How long have you had a chemical dependency?" She remained silent. "A year? Two?" He went on after a moment of silence. "Your choice drug? Which do you favor above all others?" She was making good progress with the tape and he wondered what she planned to do once she had exposed the IV casing. "Do you have an alcohol dependency?" Still no answer.

He turned the page. "Now for the social history. Was the overdose which brought you here an accident or attempted suicide? Overdose, I'll be betting." He filled in the blank. "Overdose." He went on. "Do you feel a degree of embarrassment, shame or guilt?"

"No!"

He made the notation of "denies." "Do you have a group of friends?" No reply. "Are you a loner?" The usual response. He wrote a note at the bottom. "Emotionally underdeveloped."

He tucked the pen in his breast pocket and slipped the clipboard under his chair. "So, now we have started. It will be easier in time." He went to the window.

The mushroom cloud of black smoke was still in evidence.

Chapter 37

Emma

"Doesn't she look wonderful?" Katherine asked as she twisted a wisp of hair at the nape of Margaret's head to make a curl. The hairdresser the movie stars had brought along had already worked on Margaret's hair, piling it high on her head.

Emma gave Katherine a smile, and then both of them turned back to the full-length mirror to see Margaret's reflection. Margaret indeed looked wonderful in the silver ballgown Katherine had brought with her. Unbelievably wonderful. It was just something about the way this woman had come stampeding into the child's life, like an aggressive Jewish mother, that put Emma off. Margaret had had so many problems, she was so impressionable. Emma feared this woman would ruin the girl for life.

Why couldn't everyone stop paying so much attention to Margaret and let her have some time to get used to her new appearance? Josh had jumped all over her for no reason at all, and then this woman showed up. Emma guessed she knew what was best for her grandchild—she had raised the girl, nurtured her. What did those two know about any of this? Josh might have been a doctor, but he wasn't a shrink, simply a beginning radiologist who hadn't learned his place.

"Do you really think so, Nana? Maybe I should wear something shorter." Allison had told Emma that Margaret's dress retailed for ten thousand dollars. She had wasted too much money on it to let it sit in her closet. The social editor, or at least the fashion editor, would comment on it. News that some reigning princesses of Hollywood would be at the opening had been leaked to every newspaper and magazine worth reading, plus the trashy ones.

"Your sister will have on a long dress, to be sure. Wear it. You look lovely." Emma adjusted the chiffon flower at the hip of her crystal-beaded dress. She had paid a little over five hundred for hers. Margaret could have found something in that price range that looked every bit as good on her, if she hadn't been unduly influenced by this Hollywood woman.

Emma wondered what the pink suit Katherine was wearing had set her back. She supposed it depended on whether or not the ropes of pearls quilted into the front of the jacket were real or faux. The suit looked to be a size three. Why the woman and her movie-star entourage thought they needed to stay at a spa was beyond Emma. It would make wonderful publicity, however, Emma reminded herself. Emma was positive the enormous pearl droplets at her ears were the real McCoy.

A horn blast drove her out of her thoughts. "The limousine is back from the guest house. Let's go." She picked up her purse and silk scarf she'd laid on the chaise, while the other two scurried around like chickens with their heads cut off.

"Allison," she called in the hallway, "they're here."

"Be right there," she hollered through her bedroom door. "I'm going to the bathroom."

Emma had instilled that in the girls when they were preschoolers. The last thing they were to do before leaving the house was to go to the toilet. No matter where they were going, the car ride was long, and she didn't know how many times one or the other girl had made their grandfather stop the car before she'd wised up and taught them the bathroom ritual.

Margaret and her enthusiastic middle-aged cohort breezed past her and down the stairs, giggling like they were both teenagers. Emma steadied the Victorian stand and vase after Margaret's skirts brushed by.

"Allison?"

Zipping the side of what looked like some sort of Chinese coulee pants slit to the thigh, Allison came dashing out. She slipped a chunky satin robe belt down over the waist of the pants to reveal a bare midriff. The halter gaped about three inches in the middle and was held in place by three thin straps. Fortunately there was a Mandarin-style jacket over it.

"I certainly hope you're planning to fasten your jacket."

"Oh, Nana, you're so provincial." She bunched up her hair and stuck it under her Chinese coulee hat, revealing enameled chain-ladder earrings down to her shoulders. Her gold high heels looked like they were borrowed from Coral May's closet.

Josh approved. He practically bit his tongue off as he held the front door open for them.

The air conditioning in the limousine was noticeable after the few steps in the humid outdoors. Emma took a seat next to Margaret on the side, leaving Allison and Josh the jump seat facing back. She liked to see where she was going instead of where she'd been, but she had more manners than the big-hair, big-bosomed bombshells from La-la land who had claimed the backseat for themselves. These were the best of the lot, in Allison's opinion, and therefore were to arrive at the gala in the lead limousine.

Blinding sun was cut off abruptly as the chauffeur closed the door. Hard to believe it would be dark by the time they arrived.

She recognized one of the celebrities from television, now that they were all gussied up instead of the ragamuffins who clomped off Nathan Little's private jet. Her character on television was English. Emma hadn't heard this one utter a syllable. The tall skinny brunette was supposed to be a famous singer, who was married to a football player that Emma didn't know either. The other one, Carla no-last-name, was supposed to be the number-one box-office draw, and nominated for Oscars three years running. She had lost three years running.

The rest of their crowd of lesser celebrities would arrive separately in two other limousines with Judge and Mrs. Whitehouse, Senator and Bea Livingston, Bubba and Carolyn Wright.

The engine purred into action.

Allison, who had looked a bit miffed earlier, now seemed her old self as the singer raved about the disgusting Chinese outfit she was wearing. It sounded as if Allison was going to have her people whip up another for this woman. Emma wondered what kind of songs she sang. Tasteless ones, no doubt.

"I can't believe this place," Carla, the three-time-Oscar loser exclaimed. "You guys have your brand on everything. On the station wagons and pickups, on the windmills, on the oil-derrick signs, on the polo-grounds gate, over the ranch-house door, on the china, silver, and linen. I even saw it on the side of your plane when we landed at your airstrip."

"We put it on our cattle as well." Emma couldn't resist. The woman laughed. She was such a dope she didn't even know she'd been insulted.

"Ever go to the horse races in DelMar?" Allison asked the featherbrained girl. "Our jockeys wear the Circle C brand on their pink silk shirts."

"How many horses do you run?" the English actress asked in a charming accent.

Allison held up three fingers.

Carla ducked low, inadvertently freeing her breasts from the black skin-tight gown. She pointed a black-gloved hand toward the front window as they started through the gate. "Wow, that's the biggest brand yet." All of the guests turned to look out the back window as they passed under.

Emma didn't know what was wrong with her. Everyone else in the limo was happy and excited. She simply couldn't get enthused about anything these days. Nothing was like what it was in the old days. The Circle C and Rocking M threw such grand weekend parties. It was nothing to load up friends and neighbors and fly to a gala opening just like this. She'd looked forward to them for weeks; she had dreaded this one for as long. Caleb and Jacob were gone, as were most of the old guard. Nothing was the same.

The spotlights were clearly visible in the darkened sky from miles out of town. Featherbrain Carla squealed with delight seeing them. "I have that same feeling as that day they gave me a star on the Walk of Fame."

"They didn't give it to you, Carla, you earned it." Katherine leaned over and patted the girl's knee. She seemed to be everyone's mother hen.

The singer, Sandra, laughed mightily. "You may have earned the nomination, but Katherine's also right about them not giving it to you. What did you have to pay for it? Two thousand? Three thousand?"

Carla looked every bit the dumb blonde. "I paid for it? I didn't know that."

"That's beside the point, Carla," Katherine said. "You have to be a star of your caliber to be nominated. No tourist wants to take the time to read my name on one. And you can afford to pay the cost a sight more than the poor City of Hollywood."

The gala looked like Hollywood. Paparazzi everywhere. The Houston police had cordoned off the crowds and the impeccably dressed security men Allison had hired were taking invitations at the door. The band struck up "The Eyes of Texas Are Upon You" as the chauffeur opened the door. A thrill raced through Emma like electricity; it was just like the old days, hearing that tune.

Josh shot out of the chute first and helped Allison out, then Margaret and Emma. The crowd screamed as Carla stepped out. Clapped in wild delight as Sandra and the English actress emerged. Emma heard someone in the crowd ask, "Who's she?" as Katherine got out of the limo. Her sentiments entirely.

The inside was gorgeous. Emma didn't know how Allison was able to pull it together in such fine style in so little time, and without her sister's help. It looked as if the best of Houston had come. She spotted Ellis's parents and started toward them. She didn't know where he'd gone wrong—Claudia and Dwight were two of the nicest people in all of Texas. Dwight had taken over as president of the Cattle Growers Association after Caleb. His bust sat next to Caleb's at the Cowboy Hall of Fame in Oklahoma City.

"Miss Emma, it's been too long." Dwight threw his arms around her and squeezed the life out of her. She'd take it from Dwight.

"Much too long."

"Looks like you rounded up the usual gang."

"Fewer and fewer to round up these days. Just happy to wake up each morning and find my name's not in the obit column." Emma broke away and gave Claudia a kiss on each rouged cheek.

"Those girls of yours have outdone themselves," she said. "Just telling Dwight I'm thinking of spending a week here myself."

"And who'll tend the vegetable garden?" Dwight asked as serious as all get out.

"Don't pay him no mind. He watches the ticker tape all morning and then goes out and scrounges in the dirt like we were poor church mice."

"Do not."

"Do so."

"Well, even if I did, Miss Emma, taste better fresh out of the garden."

Emma hooked her arms through theirs. "Well, let's mosey over to the banquet table and see if they have anything fresh out of the garden."

The table was laid out with trays of hors d'oeuvres, caviar, shellfish, and loads of desserts. A fountain of champagne flowed freely and within easy reach.

Emma excused herself when she saw Ellis and that hideous wife of his heading toward his parents. She found Roger Stiles chatting with Katherine. Buttering up the number one television anchorman seemed the proper thing to do. Under the circumstances, she decided to join them.

"Katherine, you've met our Roger Stiles, I see. Roger is a nightly visitor in our home."

The television anchorman threw back his head and roared. "That was good, Mrs. Chandler."

"Emma, please." It wasn't that good. She suspected the champagne had something to do with it. She gave him a tiny pat and moved on. He wouldn't remember much in the morning. No sense wasting her time.

It was John Gilmore she was seeking. As editor of the *About-Town* magazine insert in the Sunday paper, he would make a prized ally.

She didn't see him anywhere and was afraid he hadn't come. Margaret was on the makeshift dance floor with Josh. Allison shouldn't be too far off, but she couldn't see her for all the folks milling around.

"There you are, Miss Emma." She turned to find Gabe with one of the California gang on his arm. Emma wondered what Bea thought about that.

"Ah, Senator, was wondering if you'd arrived safe and sound."

"Landsakes, yes. And in style." He smiled at the Hollywood beauty on his arm. Unlike the others in Katherine's party, this chunky woman could use a week's stay at a spa. "Why, Mrs. Ambrose and I have had so much to talk about. Did you know that her husband directed her in a Washington thriller?"

"That's how I met my husband. He said I was like clay, just waiting to be molded." She sighed. "I'm afraid those days are over. Once we married, he made me give up acting."

No doubt her director realized, as did Emma, the obvious. Her gluteus maximus was entirely too large for the camera and put it to better use in the bedroom.

Gabe patted her hand solicitously as if he had heard the worst war story ever.

Emma had had enough of the old codger's foolishness. "Shall we head over to the podium and get the opening ceremony underway? Allison must be around somewhere. Do you see David Kurtz?" David Kurtz was king of the radio airwaves and had promised to introduce the senator, who would give the opening remarks and help Allison and Margaret cut the ribbon.

David was found and brought to the microphone, a big social grin on his boxer's face. His booming voice earned the attention of the guests. They drifted over like cattle to a watering hole. "I don't know about y'all, but after partaking of the spread laid out yonder, I'll be spending a month of Sundays here. Might take up full-time residence."

The crowd laughed.

Margaret took her place next to the senator on the platform.

"I trust y'all took out the calories in those petits fours, Margaret."

Margaret shook her head. "Out of the celery."

Emma slipped up beside Josh as the guests laughed. "Where's Allison?"

He looked around. "Haven't seen her for a while. I'll look for her."

Emma pushed to the front.

"It is my pleasure to introduce Senator Gabe Livingston who needs no introduction ... Senator," David announced. He motioned for the senator to come front and center and take the mike. Gabe rose and walked distinguishedly to the podium.

Gabe tried in vain to quiet the crowd. "Thank you. Thank you, so much ... Thank you."

What in the world was keeping Allison?

"Thank you." Gabe cleared his throat. It came out of the public address system as a grating noise. The clapping petered out. Gabe postured. "Ladies and gentleman of the great and glorious state of Texas. We have

gathered this evening to pay tribute to this beautiful
building and to the two young women who made this
evening possible. I have known Margaret and Allison
Chandler since they were knee-high to a grasshopper.
We share so many happy memories. The Chandler sisters and I."

Emma saw Josh hurrying back into the room, but
without Allison. She should have gone herself instead
of sending him. He'd obviously failed his task. Relief
overtook her as she saw Allison appear. What was
wrong with that girl? Instead of hustling to the platform, she caught up with Josh. He brushed her aside. It
looked like another one of their lovers' quarrels.

She tried to catch Allison's attention without drawing any to herself. Emma was glad Gabe had everyone
listening. Allison was making a fool out of herself,
pulling on Josh's arm trying to keep him from leaving. In the end, he left and she remembered her
purpose. She fluffed her hair and started toward the
platform. Relieved, Emma turned her eyes to Gabe as
he droned on.

"Despite their tender ages, the Chandler sisters have
worked hard to reach their goals, always striving toward new ones. Their grandfathers built a dynasty with
cattle and oil, in true Texas tradition. Margaret and
Allison are cutting their dynasty from a different cloth.
A pattern for a modern Texas. Like their grandfathers
before them, they have devoted their resources to this
great State of Texas and to a dynasty that will reach
into the ages."

He held his arm out to the girls. Margaret blushed a
bright red at all the attention, but it was Allison's attitude that bothered Emma. She seemed nervous. "Margaret and Allison, the eyes of Texas are upon you."

The band struck up, the audience clapped and sang
as Allison and Margaret joined Gabe at the podium,
where he would present them with the giant scissors to
cut the red ribbon strung across the staircase leading to
the rooms.

Serenaded by the band and crowd, the three of them moved to the ribbon. The music died down and the clapping stopped as they and the press were in place.

At the big moment, Roger Stiles stepped in next to them, a mike under his nose, his cameraman illuminating them. He wasn't supposed to do that. "We're coming to you live, opening night at the Houstonian Health Retreat," he said directly into the camera. He turned to Margaret. "Is it true, Miss Chandler, that the only reason you renovated this dilapidated motel was to keep the Steven F. Austin Hospital from turning it into a guest house for relatives of their patients?" He shoved a mike under Margaret's nose.

Margaret brought her hand to her face.

Allison took the mike. "Of course, it isn't true!"

"Oh?" Roger Stiles took a sheet of paper out of his pocket, but before he could unfold it, a man stepped out of the crowd and punched him in the stomach. When Roger doubled over, the stranger coldcocked him.

Roger Stiles fell flat on his pretty face in front of all of Emma's guests, and his television viewers.

Chapter 38

Margaret

Margaret circled the Rocking M chuck wagon. The cook came out from under the canopy and waved his wooden spoon. Noon meal behind him, he was preparing supper. Fall roundup was a busy time for everyone. Just as well, she had a lot she wanted to forget. And keeping busy was the trick.

The helicopter had been Katherine's idea. She was right. Margaret was wasting too much time driving back and forth between the two ranches. Either run the cattle together or invest in a helicopter, Katherine had said. The Circle C was run by cowboys, while Jacob had always employed *vaqueros*. The helicopter would cause less problems.

She put down behind the corral, as far out of Coral May's path as she could get. Coral May had called the ranch last night screaming that the helicopter had gotten dust all over her car—the red sports car she bought with her settlement from the Chandler Medical Center. She might not have gotten it had they known in time that Ellis Johnston's insurance company would challenge the lawsuit in court. Nana was unreasonably upset that he would make Grandpa's death a public matter after she had paid Coral May to keep it quiet. But Margaret couldn't fault Dr. Johnston for wanting to clear his name.

The remuda—the herd of work horses—was depleted by this time, *vaqueros* being capable of working

twice as long as their horses. And during fall roundup
for beef to send to market, like the spring roundup for
branding, everyone toiled from sunup to sundown. She
picked out an Appaloosa and saddled up.

This was the first day her legs hadn't ached when
she mounted. Her seat smarted, though, as she came
down on the saddle. The insides of her knees were raw
from the friction of her jeans against leather. Being out
of the saddle all summer hadn't helped.

Going to the clinic was something she wished she
could undo. What difference did her appearance make?
Who saw her really? It hadn't changed her life, just
stacked up her work. She thought at first she would be
a new person, but once she'd gotten back to the daily
routine of running the ranches, everything was the
same.

Except Josh didn't come around anymore. Allison
didn't know what had gotten into him, and said she
didn't care. Allison always landed on her feet. She was
dating Jinx, the manager of the spa's training center.
And was so busy at the spa that she rented a condo in
Houston. Jinx had answered the phone last time Margaret called.

Nana had feared the worst over the adverse publicity
from the grand opening. But instead, the spa was
booked solid a year in advance. Affiliate stations
around the country ran the footage of Jinx punching
out Roger Stiles and women all over the country fell
head-over-heels in love with the trainer. The spa
couldn't have bought better advertising. Unfortunately,
neither could Steven F. Austin. Chandler Springs residents, for the most part, had been boycotting Chandler
Medical Center.

She should have known that Allison was the only
reason Josh paid any attention to her. She had to stop
eating her heart out over him. He didn't care for her.
He had been kind and supportive when she got back
only because he was a doctor and that's what they were

supposed to do. Rosa probably talked him into paying all that attention to her. What a fool she was!

Margaret whipped the horse into a canter despite the heat beating down on them. She was in a hurry. Raul, the foreman, was little more than a speck on the horizon. The westerly sun was working its way under her hat. Soon she wouldn't be able to make Raul out at all.

The ground came alive with the vibration of pounding hooves like the low rumble of thunder. She rode with a sense of abandonment. Faster and faster. She wanted to be free. Free of the heartache she felt every waking moment. Josh had even crept into her dreams. She whipped faster.

Suddenly, the horse planted his feet and braked to a sudden halt, flipping Margaret over its head and slamming her to the hard dirt, cushioned only slightly by a tuft of tumbleweed. She lay flat on her back, looking unfocused into the bright blue sky, and struggling to catch her breath. Pain clutched her chest like a steel vise as her crushed, empty lungs tried to fill.

Her breath came in uneven, jagged gasps. Her ears buzzed with a whirring sound. No, the noise wasn't from the fall. She was hearing it. She propped herself up on her elbows to find herself staring at the enormous head of a coiled snake, its fist-size head stood a good foot off the ground. The elliptical pupils that stared back at her told her what instinct had already guessed: A rattler. Harmless snakes had round pupils; this was a pit viper. Its forked tongue flicked in and out faster than the rhythm of its shaking tail.

It struck like a lightning bolt, sinking its long white fangs into her calf. It withdrew as quickly into a coil, readying to strike again. A strange metallic taste tingled on the tip of her tongue. Fright paralyzed her. She was helpless to scream, to run, to do anything but feel bile rise in her throat.

As if in slow motion, Raul swept out over the side of his horse and grabbed the snake by its neck. He whirled it overhead and flung it away.

Another *vaquero* jumped from his horse and ran to her side. He pulled the boot off her swelling foot and took a knife to the pant leg. The area around the calf was inflamed. Her leg looked like an inflating balloon.

Raul picked her up and carried her to a nearby tree and settled her against the bole. He unbuckled her belt and pulled it from the loops and wrapped it around her thigh, pulling it tight to keep the venom from getting into her bloodstream. The other cut an "X" with his knife. He sucked hard against the wound and spat a stream of bloody liquid. He did it several times before his face reeled. Everything around her faded away. Stars moved in dizzy circles.

Chapter 39

Rosa

Rosa was crossing the parking lot toward the ER doors
to begin evening rounds when the broken-down pickup
streaked up the ambulance entrance, leaving a vapor of
smoke in its wake. She waited until it had come to a
complete stop, and then raced to the back, where a second man was unloading the injured party.

It was Margaret, writhing in pain, saying a rattler bit
her.

The two men spoke simultaneously in rapid Spanish, telling her how they had killed the snake and how
they had already suctioned the wound. Which was
good. The value of suctioning was lost after half an
hour. Treatment in the first five minutes is most important.

The driver carried her inside, Rosa one step behind.
Inside, Cole and Dennis were busy readying an elderly
woman complaining of hip injury, for transport to the
radiology department.

Rosa directed the driver to the far examining table.
The left side of Margaret's body from the breastbone
down was swollen triple in size. Coupled with the
greenish hue of her skin, she looked like Incredible
Hulk before and after photos.

Dennis and an X-ray tech whooshed by with a gurney carrying the other patient. Cole limped over. His
cast was gone, but he was slowed by the atrophy of his
leg muscles. "How long ago did this happen?"

"Little over an hour, I gather."

"Impressive edema, Margaret. Ditto the erythema."
He ran a finger over the swollen, red inflamed skin.
"You do this all by yourself?"

"Horse threw me." Sweat rolled off her contorted
face in heavy sheets. Cole and Rosa glanced at each
other. Wrong answer.

"Do you know where you are, Margaret?" Cole
asked.

"Here."

"Where is here?"

She moaned something that sounded like Josh.

"What day is it?"

She didn't answer. Rosa and Cole exchanged knowing looks. She'd missed all the questions. Not being
orientated to time and place was a bad sign.

"Looks like Grade II, maybe III." Moderate to severe venenation. "Take off that tourniquet while I find
some antivenin ampules. She isn't allergic to horse serum, is she?"

Rosa shrugged. The massive edema nearly obliterated any trace of the tourniquet belt. She fought with
the knot and finally gave over the task to the driver,
while she looked through a drawer for scissors. She explained to him that if this should happen again, the
tourniquet should be applied loosely. The snake injected venom into the subcutaneous tissue, which was
absorbed by the lymphatics. The tourniquet needed to
obstruct only venous and lymphatic flow, not the
bloodstream.

"Dennis, two hundred fifty millilter five percent glucose solution," Cole bellowed from the nursing station
when Dennis returned.

It wasn't long before she could hear Cole on the
phone talking to Emma. She was happy to be struggling with the belt instead of seeking allergy information. The knot loosened enough for her to get a scalpel
in. She sawed through the leather belt until it gave
enough to pull free.

Cole's next call was to Richard Bell's office asking them to find Margaret's chart and let him know if she had any allergies. Apparently Richard got on the phone, for she heard Cole tell him that he was admitting Margaret.

Dennis ushered out the driver, assuring him in broken Spanish that they'd take care of her now. Dennis came back and started an intravenous line. Margaret kept calling Josh's name over and over. Rosa had a fairly good idea why. She'd watched them at dinner that night in Houston. They shared a genuine admiration for each other. The hospital grapevine had it that Allison had dumped Josh for that muscleman who punched the news anchorman's lights out. She hated all news anchorpeople now that Sterling was married to one, and had enjoyed the TV footage immensely. What Josh ever saw in shallow Allison was a mystery to her. Josh had been moping around the hospital long enough.

Cole returned with five ampules of antivenin Crotalidea polyvalent. It was a rather large dose of antivenin, but Margaret didn't weigh much. The smaller the patient, the larger the percentage of venom, and thus, a larger requirement of antivenin.

Dennis drew blood for typing and cross-matching, a precautionary measure. He started to recap the used needle, and then remembering the new AIDS preventive directive, tossed it uncapped into the red, heavy plastic container. Rosa suspected it had more used needles in it than the red disposal container in her office. She sent most of her patients to the medical center's lab for their blood work.

"You're giving it IV?" Rosa asked when he added it to the drip.

"Radioisotopes studies show that antivenin accumulates more rapidly at the bite site intravenously, rather than intramuscularly."

It didn't seem logical, but Cole was the emergency medicine expert, Dr. Bell was the girl's physician, and she was in interloper. "Well, guys, guess I'll round. See you later."

They both gave halfhearted farewells. "Dennis, push a tetanus toxoid." Rosa tried to remember back to when she had had a tetanus booster. Maybe not since she was an intern. She'd have to drop by Sarah's office one of these days and get one.

She crossed the hall to Radiology and found Bill in the reading room, looking at a dozen CAT scan films strung top to bottom across the light box. "Josh around?"

"In with a hip." Bill pointed at the wall as if he could see through it. Maybe he did have X-ray vision.

She went in the general direction he pointed out and haunted the closed door marked ROOM 1. She could hear Josh cajoling the elderly woman who had been in the ER earlier.

The door opened, but it was the X-ray tech who came out with two black film plates in hand.

Rosa stuck her head around the door. "Josh?"

He gave her a quick smile, and turned back to the woman on the X-ray table and backstepped toward the door. "I'll be right back, Mrs. Burns, don't you go away."

The woman giggled.

Josh gave Rosa his divided attention. She suspected he was afraid Mrs. Burns would roll off the table and break her other hip.

"Margaret Chandler is over in the ER. Rattlesnake bite." His hand flew to her shoulder as if through tactile osmosis he would learn all that she knew about it. The frightened look on his face told her all she wanted to know. Rosa, for one, was delighted. "She's been asking for you."

"Asking for me?"

Men were so slow about matters of the heart. "How many 'Josh's' could she know?"

He turned to his patient. "Mrs. Burns—"

Rosa was losing patience with the silly man. "Go on. I'll stay with her."

He raced down the hall. Rosa gave a long, relieved sigh. Water always finds its own level.

Chapter 40

Lisa

How much longer were they going to keep her in this dump? Locked up like a criminal. Sean had said twenty-nine days. It had been that and more. It was Dr. Fischer who wouldn't let her go. Lisa was positive. She played the good little girl for Sean and could twist him around her little finger. That was what Dr. Fischer couldn't stand. It was the doctor who needed an attitude adjustment, not her.

Lisa sat on her bed waiting for the five o'clock dinner bell. Her roommate, DeDe, had been called to the phone ages ago, leaving Lisa with no one to talk to and nothing to do. Lisa looked through the windows at the blue sky above the honeysuckles. She had to be standing at the window to see down to the bayou. And she couldn't think of a reason in the world why she would bother to do that. She looked for signs in the sky that it was cooling off. Her mother always made such a big deal over the weather when she visited. DeDe and Lisa would laugh themselves silly after her mother left.

Things had improved a lot once DeDe got here. This was DeDe's second stay at the clinic, so Lisa didn't have to teach her anything, she knew all the angles. She'd even been in the state mental hospital, misdiagnosed as paranoid schizophrenic. A common mistake to make with speed addicts, DeDe explained.

At seventeen, DeDe was the next youngest in the chemical dependency program, which was why they

were paired up. DeDe was a walking encyclopedia
when it came to drugs and had taught her more about
them than Ray ever had. And Lisa planned to show
Ray a trick or two when she got out.

DeDe hailed from Dallas and was here because her
family didn't want anyone to find out about her drug
problem. Tall, and so thin her hipbones stood out,
DeDe looked like one of the eating disorder girls down
the hall. It was because she'd been doing speed for so
long. Pardon her street language—not "speed"—rather
amphetamines or diet pills. She sure wouldn't want Dr.
Fischer going into one of her lectures again. The doctor was such a drag.

Now, ages after detoxification, the only pills they
were given were the kind to control them. DeDe taught
her how to cheek the pills so they could save up for a
blast out.

When was the dinner bell going to ring? It was a
hoot watching the anorexic girls forcing themselves to
eat the cafeteria slop. Poetic justice, DeDe called it.
Brenda and she had a pact. Lisa would clean up
Brenda's plate for her, and Brenda would cheek pills
for Lisa. Though that was just a drop in the bucket. If
it weren't for Henry, the orderly on night shift, Lisa
would be climbing the walls. He supplied DeDe and
her with drugs in exchange for a little night action.

Lisa inspected her fingernails for signs of paint.
There were a few gold flakes, not as bad as usual. She
had made her mother just about as many ceramic vases
and figurines as they had room for in their crackerbox
house. A gold Venus de Milo was her current project.
The lady didn't have arms and she was naked to her
waist. Lisa could hardly wait to see the look on her
mother's face. She wouldn't display it, that's for sure.
DeDe bet her a dollar her mother would accidentally
drop it. Didn't matter one way or the other to Lisa. It
was the thought that counted. And she thought no one
deserved a half-naked statue more than her mother.

DeDe came in and threw herself across her bed.

"What's wrong?"

DeDe opened one eye. "My father's coming down tomorrow for a visit." She groaned. "You don't know how lucky you are that you don't have one to deal with."

Lisa slid down until her head found the pillow. "I wonder sometimes what it would be like if I did. If I knew him, I mean."

"Did he die, or just doesn't care?"

"Doesn't care. Once, when I was real young, I asked Mom if we could go visit him. Or write to him. But she didn't have his address."

"She didn't know where his parents lived? Nothing?"

Lisa shrugged. "Guess not."

"They must really hate each other."

"Well, you know my mom. Who *doesn't* hate her?"

"Yeah, bet she tried cramming the Bible down his throat, like she does yours." She sat up and pulled a crushed joint out of her belt, and then rummaged through her underwear drawer for the aluminum ashtray and lighter. Lisa moved over to her bed. It took three sputtering tries for the lighter to catch and even longer for the papered tip to burn to a glorious red.

DeDe took a slow drag, and then handed it over as she exhaled. Lisa took a long pull, forcing the smoke deep into her lungs. She leaned her head back against the wall, letting the taste coat the inside of her mouth before she blew out.

"Bet your dad wants to see you, but your mom won't let him," DeDe said, taking back the joint. "Bet she's lying to you about not knowing where he is. Bet she lies to him, too, about you. Bet he calls wanting to see you and she tells him you don't want anything to do with him."

"Maybe he's some terrible person." Lisa had to relight the joint before she could take her turn again. She had had better, but not while she'd been locked up here.

"Maybe he's rich. Maybe he's remarried and has more children."

"Wonder what kind of house he lives in? Maybe one that's air-conditioned."

"Of course it's air-conditioned. Everyone has air conditioning."

Everyone but them.

Lisa's mother was in their room when they returned from the mystery meat feast. Sophie planted a kiss on her cheek, embarrassing her in front of DeDe.

"I'm going down to the rec room to watch TV," DeDe said as she gathered up her cigarettes and lighter.

Lisa wanted to watch TV, too. Instead she had to endure hearing all about her mother's day at the hospital. Lisa didn't care whether Margaret Chandler was in the hospital or not. Nor did she need the lecture about one of the nurses who came down with AIDS from a needle prick. Lisa wasn't going to get AIDS—she only shared needles with friends.

"It's a lovely evening out," her mother chirped as she waved DeDe a fond farewell. "Shall we go for a walk?"

Yeah, a walk would be great. Let the whole town see her with her mother. A block ahead of her mother would suit her fine.

Lisa could almost make out some lightning bugs in the bushes on the slope down to the bayou. Sort of like when you start noticing the lamplight, even though it really isn't quite dark enough to really need it. Lisa wished she had another joint.

"How was your day, dear?"

That was about the stupidest question in the world. A quip about it not being as bad as the nurse whose AIDS test had come back positive came to mind, but it would only inspire her mother to recite lesson eighty-seven.

She wanted out of this place. She'd missed so much school, that she'd never catch up. "Well, let's see. In algebra, I didn't work any problems on the board. In English, I didn't read *Macbeth*. In—"

"Lisa, stop it! Do you think I like this any better than you? Do you think I enjoy watching you suffer? Do you think I don't know how important it is to you to graduate with your class?"

"Yeah? Well you have a funny way of showing it." Lisa spotted a swarm of gnats by the bank and walked straight for them.

Her mother followed, swatting the air. "This is for your own good. You almost died! I'm trying to save your life."

"What for? You think I have such a terrific life that I'm going to miss it if I die?"

"How can you say such a thing? I've tried very hard—"

"To what? Ruin it? Not let me see my father?" Lisa could tell from the deep furrows on her mother's brow that she'd struck a sour chord. "I want my father. Maybe I want to live with him and his family."

Her mother crossed her arms and stood pat. But unlike all the other times her mother had taken her disciplinary stand, Lisa wasn't impressed. "He doesn't have a family," Sophie said.

DeDe was right. Her mother had lied about knowing where he was. "How do you know that, Mother? Thought you didn't know where he was."

"I just know," she said, too quickly. "He doesn't want anything to do with either of us. Just drop it, Lisa."

"How do I know that? Because you're telling me? Okay, I'll drop it . . . when I hear it from my father."

Chapter 41

Margaret

Josh was leaning over her when she woke up. He seemed so faraway, like looking through the wrong end of a telescope. His voice was like a bad long-distance connection. Now she saw. They were placing her *in* a telescope.

"Where are we?"

"In X ray."

X ray? What were they doing there? Her horse! She had to find her horse. "Did you see my horse?"

"Your horse is fine. Now be very still."

Noisy machines started around her. She sat up, banging her head on a light or something. "What are you doing to me?"

Josh lowered her to a rubber pillow. "Try not to move, Margaret. Your doctor wants some magnetic resonance images. Some pictures."

"What for?"

"God only knows." He said it more to himself, than in answer to her question. She giggled. He was so funny. "Margaret, try very hard to remain perfectly still."

"Yes, sir." She saluted.

He took her hand and strapped it to something cold at her side. That wasn't very nice. He didn't have much of a sense of humor when he worked. She could tell by the way he frowned.

"How do you feel?"

Funny. Everything seemed slow. One side of her body was numb and the other tingled like when a sleeping foot wakes up. "Did I break my leg when I took a spill?"

"You didn't take a spill. You were bit by a rattlesnake."

Now she remembered. They had met eye to eye. That's when she knew it was over. The pupils weren't round like the nonpoisonous kind, but long slits. It struck so quickly she didn't have time to do anything. "My contacts. Take them out of my eyes."

"This first."

"The horse threw me because of the rattler." She wondered if someone caught the horse. She wondered if the rattler got his fangs in the horse first. "My tongue tastes like metal." She held it out for him to see.

"It looks fine."

"Doesn't taste fine. Is there a piece of metal in it?"

Josh turned around to see who was coming in. Margaret saw it was Nana and the hospital administrator. Nana looked so worried. She called out to Nana that she was all right. Josh bent down and whispered in her ear. "Now you be a good girl and don't move until after I bring you out again. Will you do that for me?"

"I'll do anything for you. I love you."

The tunnel seemed to move around her, enclosing her. Nana sat next to the machine and stared at her through the window. Nana was having a time catching her breath.

The noise was making her stomach sick. She needed to throw up in the worst way. How could she? There was a metal rod sticking through her tongue. She held her tongue out to get a look at the metal rod. Her nose was in the way.

Josh pounded on the window and mouthed something to her. How did he expect her to understand him over the noise?

"Hi, Dr. Bell," she said when the telescope machine moved away and she could breathe again. "I'm in someone else's body. This one isn't mine. It feels funny."

He gave her a warm smile and pushed her hair off her forehead. "It's yours, child. It's swollen. That's why it feels strange to you. But you're going to be fine."

Why did everyone talk like they were far, faraway. "Is my face swollen, too?"

"Your face looks wonderful, Margaret," Josh answered.

"Good. I was afraid the tree branches had grown back."

Josh and someone in a white uniform were moving her to another bed.

Someone marched to her side. It was Bill Martin. "Heard you were here. How you doing?"

She held out her tongue for him to see. But he turned to Josh. "I'm leaving now. I'll take the beeper. Take call for you. It's been such a hectic day."

Josh had a strange look on his face when he turned back to tuck the sheet around her.

Nana stood over her. "You're going to be fine, Margaret."

Margaret showed her grandmother her tongue. "Can you take the metal rod out of my tongue?"

Nana looked at Richard, instead of taking the metal rod out of her tongue. It tasted so bad. Why wouldn't they take it out for her? She fought the sheet to find her missing hand. She tried to get hold of her tongue, but it kept slipping away.

"Josh! Take it out for me."

He cupped her chin. "Open wide." She saw him probe her tongue, though she couldn't feel it. "There, is that better?"

"It still tastes funny."

"That's from the venom, Margaret. We're fixing you up. You'll be fine."

She turned her head into the pillow feeling its crispness. "Thank you, Josh."

Chapter 42

Pam

"What in the world are you doing here?" Pam asked when Billy planted a kiss on her neck.

He sat down beside her at the Peds' nursing station. "Got called in on an aortic aneurysm."

She seethed.

Billy nodded. "We're waiting for Ellis to get here. He might as well live on the moon, as slow as he is getting back to town." He leaned over, demanding a proper kiss. Pam delivered an abbreviated version and slapped his hand away as it tugged at her elastic waistband. Juanita, the aide, was changing a wet bed in 108 and should be finished soon. "Rather spend the time with you than watch Rosa pace the floor."

"And I'm happy you came down to visit." It was time to give meds, but she'd wait. "So lonely at night." She ran her fingers over the back of his hand. "Be a long time until Saturday night."

"Tuesdays are slow. Only have a couple of therapy patients scheduled. Maybe I can slip away in the afternoon tomorrow." He tickled the back of her ear with his tongue.

"I'd like that." Crepe soles squeaked. She jumped up and leaned over the counter to have a look. Juanita was heading this way. Pam pulled a chart out of the rack and opened it up in front of him. "Look busy."

Juanita passed them on the way to the linen closet with her bundle of dirty sheets. More crepe squeaks.

Billy stuck his nose into the chart when Juanita came around the counter and disappeared into the supply room behind them, where she had been taking inventory before the LVN, Lori, told her to change the asthmatic's sheets.

Lori, a screaming baby over her shoulder, jostled her way to the supply room. She came out, struggling to uncap a bottle of soybean formula.

Pam took the baby from her. "I'd cry, too, if they made me drink that stuff." She stuck out her tongue and made an ugly face. The baby didn't appreciate it, but Billy did. When Lori was settled in the rocking chair with the ready bottle, Pam handed over her charge. "I'm going downstairs to get some coffee. Want anything?"

Lori shook her head as she shifted the baby to the crook of her arm and popped the nipple into his greedy mouth.

Billy shut the chart with satisfaction, as if he had solved the deep, dark secret that had puzzled the rest of them. He slid the chart across the counter toward the rack and followed her out.

The main corridor was empty, but he waited until they were on the stair landing before he pressed into her. "I love that perfume."

"Coral May gave it to me. A present for asking you to take her home that night at the Sundowner."

"Don't mention that woman's name."

That was still a sore subject with both of them. Not only did Coral May almost catch them together, but she'd talked his leg off after she got him home. Pam spent practically the whole night in their motel room all by her lonesome. And then when he got back, he was so tired, the only thing he wanted to do was sleep.

Billy pushed her up against the wall, his hands clawing at her uniform. "Wear a dress next time." He smeared the words over her neck and face. She heard one of the quarters she had in her pocket clang down the stairs.

"Don't," she scolded, pulling her pants back up. "I have to get back." After she found the quarter and bought a cup of coffee. "Tomorrow."

"Now, too." Greedy hands pawed her insistently.

A metal door above them opened. Billy freed her and disappeared. She twisted her pants back to their proper position and pulled her top down, settling it just over her hips.

"No coffee?" Lori asked as she burped the baby.

"Dropped a quarter down the stairwell and couldn't find it. I'll get a cup after I distribute meds." She hated nights. Her inner clock was still off. Billy was no closer to asking for a divorce. She'd have to see to it herself, she feared. She just didn't know how.

Chapter 43

Ellis

Ellis was showing Patrick the aneurysm X rays when Josh walked in. "What in the world has come over you?" Ellis asked. "No one's allowed to smile before eight o'clock."

"Sorry." Josh wiped the smile from his face. "I'll remember the rule next time." He looked at the films. "Where did these come from?"

"The elves made them while you slept," Ellis explained, scientifically.

"Bill see these?"

"Last night."

Josh outlined the aneurysm with his finger. "Marked dilatation. Fixing it this morning?"

"They're preparing the OR as we speak."

Patrick got to his feet. "Let's do it. We're not getting any younger." Ellis followed Patrick out of the reading room, leaving Josh to his own devices.

Everyone was in position when Ellis pushed through the swinging doors into the OR. Leroy, the anesthesiologist, sat on a stool at the head. Kathy, the EEG tech, and Gary, who ran the cardio-pulmonary bypass machine, monitored the equipment behind Leroy. Patrick on the left side fiddled with his mask. Vicki would move in beside Patrick after she gloved Ellis. Jennifer was on the other side of the table, inspecting the instruments and saving him the spot next to her.

Ellis stood over the well-toned, clean-shaven chest

scrubbed down with Phisohex. The owner was in his fourth decade and in otherwise good physical condition. Ellis poised his scalpel. "Let's rock and roll."

"Doesn't sound like rock and roll to me," Vicki teased in her usual deadpan. "More like musical stuff from *Miss Saigon.*"

"You're too smart for your little britches," Leroy admonished, one eye on the respirator.

"She hasn't ridden in the Little Britches for years," Ellis defended as he drew the scalpel down the chest.

"Gee thanks, Ellis." Her intonation contradicted her words. "Eight years to be exact." Little Britches was the rodeo competition for up to eighteen. That made her twenty-six.

"Now, don't be highfalutin miffed at me. I was being your white knight."

"I'm your black knight," Leroy wanted her to know.

"Saw," Ellis said to Jennifer to let her know he was ready for the electric saw. It was unnecessary. She already had it in hand. "Vicki, don't despair. We've got another couple years to find you a husband before you hit Old-Maid status."

"You do that, oh, knight of my days."

"A rich doctor," Patrick put in as he finished cauterizing the tiny blood vessels along the incision.

"You're crazy if you think I'd put up with a doctor on my own time."

"Even Leroy, here? Leroy's as good as they come." Patrick kept up the battle of the sexes so Ellis could concentrate on getting through the breastbone.

"That's the point." Vicki could jangle with the best of them.

Leroy whined about his broken heart as Patrick and Ellis pulled the ribs apart in a tug-of-war to insert the spreader.

"Look how far the lung has been displaced," Jennifer offered as she slapped scissors into Ellis's palm.

Ellis snipped through the pericardial sac. After a

perfunctory look, he made incisions for the bypass tubes. Ellis encircled the distal ascending aorta with an umbilical tape, while Patrick tested the bypass machine.

"Okay, let's do it." The patient was put on the oxygenating machine. The body's five quarts of blood would circulate through the machine, the blue blood being replenished with oxygen and pumped back through the body. Now they would work in first gear. No lollygaggers.

Ellis clamped the aorta and sliced open the aneurysm. "Okay," Ellis said when he was ready, "pour it in now." Jennifer poured the freezing fluid from the pitcher. "Pour in more," Ellis said when the stubborn heart refused to stop. Finally it was too cold to beat. Patrick and Vicki suctioned. Ellis snipped around the value leaflet to make room for the artificial valve.

He worked everything at the back first, for once the ascending aorta was reconstructed with Dacron cloth, he wouldn't be able to reach the back. He sutured the cloth around the Starr-Edwards' ball valve, the girls holding the ends until they'd spun a cobweb.

Patrick readied the prosthesis. "Reminds me of the weekend. Spent it trying to hook up our new dryer." He dangled the pleated tube that looked a great deal like the long, air filter on the back of dryers.

They worked it in, reconstructing the ascending aorta. Ellis sutured it, while Patrick readied a smaller tube. Ellis twisted it around behind the other and sutured it in place. He made a path for the exchange between the two and tied off the sutures, clipping them and dismantling the cobweb.

"It's waking up," Patrick said, after Ellis had noticed.

He nodded to the pitcher and Jennifer duly poured. Patrick and Vicki suctioned. The heart stopped and Ellis wrapped the aorta around the prosthesis and sutured it. It was more for a lack of knowing what else to do with it. The aorta was no longer functional, and would serve more as a protective covering.

Now they worked to get the air out of the heart. Air bubbles escaping into the body would cause tissue destruction. The less air, the better. No air was optimal, but nearly impossible.

"Think that does it." He took the defibrillating paddles from Jennifer and jump started the heart.

The bypass machine was turned off and Patrick removed the clamps, allowing the blood to flow into the heart.

"What happened to the music?" Ellis asked when he was satisfied that everything was in working order.

"Clicked off a long time ago," Leroy answered.

"Oh." Ellis uncranked the rib spreader. Once the ribs were back in place, Jennifer handed the stapler to Patrick. He would close while Ellis bore the good tidings to the man's family.

Chapter 44

Josh

Josh wasn't certain whether to stay or go when he saw Allison in Margaret's hospital room. He had avoided a confrontation with her since opening night at the spa when he had walked in on Allison and her man, Jinx, rutting about like animals in heat.

Margaret saw him at the door and offered a warm smile. It was enough to keep him from going. He had always felt a glowing affection for Margaret, but he hadn't been able to pigeonhole his feeling before. It went beyond the kind of relationships he'd had with women in the past. Spiritual was the wrong word, but it was the nearest he could come.

He couldn't deny that after her return from California, he had physically wanted her. But he could control those feelings. After all, Allison and she were sisters. The proper thing to do was to forget them both. If only he could eradicate his other feelings for Margaret—the happiness he felt simply talking to her, the way he wanted to protect her, the overwhelming fear he felt when Rosa told him she had been brought to the ER, and then seeing for himself how serious the bite had been.

The walk to the bed was immeasurably long. Each footstep echoed in his ears. He gave a nod to Allison. Allison looked through him as though he were the invisible man.

"How are you feeling?" he heard himself ask Margaret in a hollow voice.

"Much better. Though I wonder if the swelling will ever go down," Margaret answered, feigning keen interest in a hangnail.

Allison must have grown weary of the stimulating conversation. She collected her things and rose to her feet. "Margaret, I have to go now. The Hospital Auxiliary luncheon will be starting soon." She gave her sister a peck on the cheek, but forgot to acknowledge Josh's presence.

Margaret monitored her IV line as if the drip would stop if she turned away. "I look pretty bad, don't I."

"Not to me." Why was this so hard for him? He knew what he wanted to do, but was afraid of making a false move. "I'm sorry I ran her off."

"I'm sorry it bothers you. I assure you," she said, turning to look at him, "it doesn't bother Allison." Magnified and distorted by the thick glasses, her eyes no longer looked beautiful, only kind.

Why had it taken him so long to realize? "You were able to get your contacts out, I see."

She nodded. "Guess so. I was pretty out of it. Don't remember much." He looked for hidden meaning in her words.

"Remember your MRI exam?" His question had a hollow ring even to himself.

She shook her head. Good. Her declaration of love would have embarrassed her to no end. He wanted to save her that.

He reached out and touched her chin. "You have a nasty little scrape here." He bent over and kissed it. "That should make it heal all the faster." He touched the tender new skin over the scar. It blanched white when the rest of her face turned scarlet. "You embarrass so easily." She tried to turn her head away, but he held it all the firmer. "That's one of the many things I love about you."

She gave him a surprised look. Magnified the way her eyes were, it was meaningful.

He eased himself onto the edge of the bed and kissed her mouth gently, and then hungrily. This was how it was meant to be. He squeezed her tight to him, rocking her. She would be forever a part of him. "Oh, Margaret. Margaret. I was so worried for you. Don't ever do that again." Josh could feel her body shake with laughter, and then quiver with tiny sobs. "It's all right now, Margaret. *Everything* is all right."

A rap on the door, as the dietician brought in her lunch, sent him to his feet.

"Meat loaf, mashed potatoes, and beets," the woman said cheerily, as she uncovered the food like the curator of the Metropolitan Museum of Art would a new acquisition.

"Thank you." Margaret waited for the woman to leave, and then pushed the tray away. She braced herself against the headboard. She wore a look that said she had made a horrible mistake. Huge shame filled her eyes.

He stood over her, afraid to sit on the bed. "I'll keep my penny. I don't believe I need to hear what's on your mind for I know what it must be. Your sister and me." She bunched up the edging along her blanket. "I can only say that any feelings I might have had for her are over. And those fleeting feelings never had the breadth or depth of the love I have for you."

Margaret looked up at him, and then reached out to take his hand.

Chapter 45

Coral May

Coral May saw Allison come in as though the fall Hospital Auxiliary luncheon was in her honor. She looked around, trying to see which table of volunteers she would grace. She wouldn't be sitting at the table with Carolyn Wright, that was for sure. Because Coral May had already beat her to it. And to Mrs. Bell and Peggy Tilton.

Carolyn and Bubba had been so sweet to her after Jacob's passing. Sent her a potted plant and a nice card. Coral May still had both.

Allison sat down between Dr. Ken Steven's wife and the mayor's wife. Ellis's wife was at the table, too. Coral May couldn't think of a better person to inflict on Allison. She suspected she'd be seeing a lot of her once the trial started. Coral May wasn't so sure she wanted to spend all that time in court. Emma had admitted the hospital's fault in Jacob's death and paid up. But that arrogant sonovabitch Ellis couldn't admit that he was capable of doing anything wrong.

Boy, was he wrong about Jacob not signing the land over to Salty! She was there, guess she knew better than he did. And now look at the pickle she was in. The house was hers, but the girls got everything around it. Coral May wouldn't be a bit surprised if they drilled a well right on her porch and started pumping oil. She hated the sound of the black oil pumps, *swoosh-pop, swoosh-pop* every time the pistons slid up and down. Having one on the porch would drive her crazy.

The queen bee herself found her place at the head table between Karen Martin and Patti Thompson. Jacob would turn over in his grave if he knew how badly Emma was treating her. Coral May watched Patti suck up to Emma. Even before that, Coral May didn't think much of Patti. What kind of woman wanted to be married to a surgeon who worked with the likes of Ellis?

She'd heard that Margaret was in the hospital suffering from a rattlesnake bite. That was all too bad and everything, but she gave her word that that damned helicopter wouldn't bother her and it bothered her plenty. Sitting practically in her front yard. If she let the girls get away with that, she'd be listening to black oil pumps all night, every night, for the rest of her life.

Coral May excused herself and went over to talk to Allison. It took forever before the girl stopped yaking and looked up at her. Allison did it to spite her, Coral May was positive.

"Allison, I'm sorry about your sister's accident and all, but I want you to get that helicopter off my land. And I want it off today!"

"First of all, that isn't *your* land. It's Margaret's and mine. Second of all, Grandma dear, when Margaret gets good and ready to move it, she will. If you have a problem with that, I suggest you pick up your house and move it off our land."

The nerve of the girl! "First of all, Allison, I'm not your grandmother. I'm your grandfather's widow. Second of all, if I was your grandmother, I would have whipped you black and blue years ago for being such a turd." She started off, and then turned back to Allison. "If the helicopter isn't gone by morning, I'm having a bulldozer move it for you."

"You do that and you'll be buying a new one for Margaret."

Coral May could hardly eat her salad as upset as that girl made her. By the time the main course came, she

was able to pick at her baked potato and carrots, but
didn't touch her steak. She hated thinking of all those
cows at the ranch all being the girls'. Jacob was so
shortsighted about them. She was his wife, he should
have left them to her. She would have left everything
to the girls when she died. That would have been more
fair.

Her blood boiled thinking about those spoiled girls
getting all of Jacob's things. She might just call the
bulldozer people to move out the helicopter. Margaret
had no call to leave that blasted thing practically in her
front yard. Soon the oil pumps would be all around the
house keeping her up all night with their swooshing
and popping.

She only halfheartedly listened as Karen Martin
spoke in the microphone, going on and on about the
proposal to install cable TV in each of the patient's
rooms. It would cost ten thousand dollars, which
seemed an awful lot to Coral May, and they would
have a Christmas dinner dance to finance it. Coral May
had half a notion to get to her feet and suggest that the
Chandler girls donate the ten thousand dollars. She
didn't because, knowing them, they'd suggest she donate it from the money the hospital had to pay her for
the wrong they did her poor Jacob. So she sat back and
gave Karen her attention. Hard to believe Billy ever
married the likes of her.

Karen looked so old. If she wore some makeup and
colored her gray hair, that would help a whole lot. But
still, Billy deserved someone better. Karen sure didn't
deserve him. Look how she treated him, standing him
up at the bar and all. Not that Coral May minded.
Hadn't he taken her home and tucked her in? There
wasn't a soul in the world who could tuck a girl under
covers better than Billy. She could still feel his kisses
on her lips and everywhere else.

Poor Billy, stuck with a wife like Karen.

Everyone gave their reports and when it was her
turn, Coral May told how they'd spent the proceeds

from the gift shop buying toys for the pediatric ward. And then she got up to go to the restroom when Karen started talking about how the East Side Clinic in Houston had sent a nice thank-you note for the drugs the Medical Wives' Auxiliary, a branch of the Hospital Auxiliary, had collected at the doctors' offices and hoped that CMC's Hospital Auxiliary would remember them again.

The meeting was over by the time she returned from the restroom. Karen and Karen's big box of stuff she carried around pertaining to the Hospital Auxiliary were the only ones left.

"Here, I'll get the door," Coral May said. The box looked pretty worn. She'd be needing a new one before her term in office was up.

"Thanks," Karen said unpleasantly as she went through the door. "Nice perfume."

"Jacob always called it yummy. Where you parked?"

"Out back, unfortunately. By time I arrived, the front lot was filled." Karen must have been in a bad mood or tired or something. She sure didn't sound friendly.

"Me, too." It meant they had to trudge downstairs and out the hall between the cafeteria and the pharmacy. "I'm sorry you came down with a bug and missed the movie and all, over in Richmond that time," Coral May said to have something nice to say as they were walking to the staircase.

"When was that?"

"Month or so ago. Didn't Bill tell you I ran into him?"

She shook her head.

"It was plumb amazing seeing him at the lounge. The lounge at the Sundowner Motel. I used to work there, you know, and like to drop by every once in a while to visit with old friends. And there Bill was, waiting for you. We would have invited him over for a drink, but he was waiting for you."

Karen stopped and leaned her head on the box and

gave Coral May a funny grin. "Coral May, I don't know what your game is, and I don't care. I got your letter, all right, but you're all wrong." She started off in a huff.

Coral May caught up with her. "What letter? What are you talking about, Karen?"

"You think I didn't recognize that perfume you're wearing? You really think Bill is going to leave me for you?" Karen juggled the dilapidated box to hold up a scolding finger. "Let me tell you something, Coral May, he's never going to leave me. You know why? Because I'm his protection. I'm his excuse. He doesn't want anyone else. He wants *everyone* else."

She had found out about Billy and her somehow. But what was this about a letter? Did she write a note to Billy? No, she was sure she hadn't. Coral May chased after Karen. "Wait a minute!"

Karen turned around at the top of the stairs. "Coral May, you must have me confused with someone who gives a damn. Now, if you'll excuse me." She turned back around but somehow missed the step and tumbled down to the landing. The box of papers and pamphlets scattered everywhere.

A nurse coming up the stairs from the basement got to Karen before Coral May did. "Is she all right?" Coral May asked.

"Don't touch her," the nurse said, real haughty-like. "I'll be right back." Coral May wasn't going to touch her. She just wanted to know if she was all right. The nurse ran down the stairs the way she'd come. Karen had landed flat on her face, wasn't moving, and looked dead. This was awful. Coral May's heart was going so fast, she could hardly catch her breath.

"Where is she?"

"Up on the landing."

She recognized the tall scrawny man in white, coming up from the basement two stairs at a time, as the nurse who was with Jacob in the emergency room. The nurse followed him. Dr. Morgan came up the stairs behind the nurse, but he was poking along on account of his accident with the bull last spring. People were coming down the stairs behind her. Suddenly, people were all over the place. Now she was being squeezed against the wall as people finagled to get a better look at Bill's wife. Everyone was talking and shouting at once. It was hard to follow everything, even if she had understood what they were talking about.

"What happened?" Dr. Morgan asked her after he gave orders for someone to bring a board and a cervical collar.

"She tripped up there," she answered, pointing at the head of the stairs, "and tumbled down. She was carrying that box." Coral May looked over the rail and pointed to the box that someone had thrown all the way down the next flight.

They were stepping on the papers and pamphlets, making a mess of them. Coral May started picking up the ones by her feet, but someone took her arm and led her up the stairs, telling her they'd take good care of Mrs. Martin. The nurse didn't give her the chance to say that she wanted to go down the stairs.

Coral May looked up and down the hall. Down the hall someone was racing toward the stairs, so she went up the hall toward the elevator. Now she really wished she'd gotten there early enough to park out front.

She sure wasn't able to make heads or tails out of what Karen had been saying. She sure had been acting crazy. Coral May turned left to the lobby phones instead of the elevator. Surely Pam was up by now.

Chapter 46

Sophie

Sophie had found Cole having a late lunch in the cafeteria and was about to ask him to meet her after work, when Vicki came back in to say that Karen Martin had fallen down the stairs. It was her bad timing not to have asked Cole before he rushed out. Now, an hour later in the ER, watching Bill standing helplessly by, waiting for Karen to be taken to surgery, she still hadn't asked Cole.

She was at her wit's end over Lisa. Neither Sean nor Meredith was pleased with Lisa's recovery. Sophie had painted herself into a tight corner and didn't know what else she could do.

Jennifer pushed a gurney through the double doors. Ellis would operate on the fractured rib and collapsed lung first, and then the orthopods would pin Karen's leg. They had already set the green-stick fracture in her right arm. And Cole had ordered an ice pack for her complaint of tenderness over the trapezius and latissimus muscles of the left shoulder and upper back. Her face was bruised and contorted, but it was all superficial.

Bill kept eyeing the area of suspected concussion. Karen was more concerned with how long it would be before she could ride. Cole assured her she wouldn't be riding in the Columbus Day Parade this year. Veteran's Day was iffy.

"Thanks for your help," Cole told her after Karen had been whisked away.

"You're welcome."

He grinned boyishly, showing the tops of his capped front teeth. "Gee, Sophie, you sound so formal."

"Sorry, didn't mean to. I was just building courage to ask you something."

"Ask me what?"

"Would you meet me after work?"

He flashed another smile. "Sure, why wouldn't I?" He turned serious. "Something wrong, Sophie?"

"Yes, something's wrong," Sophie answered, hours later as he sat on her sofa in the living room. "Lisa." She took a deep breath to sharpen her senses. "Cole, I don't even know where to begin."

"I have all night, and I have a good ear."

She stood at the window, arms crossed, and looked out on to the empty street. The streetlights made the decaying neighborhood look so vulgar. "I'm at the end of my rope with that girl. She is so willful and belligerent. She has decided she wants her father."

"That doesn't seem so unreasonable. Would he be a danger to her? I mean ... you married the guy, he couldn't be all bad."

Too many memories, most unforgiveable. "John Drummond, you mean. No, it's not that. He wouldn't hurt her, I'm certain. It's just that he doesn't want anything to do with us."

"Not even if you explained about Lisa and what's she's going through?"

Sophie turned around and looked him straight in the eye. The time for telling lies was over. Lisa's life was more important than what Cole, or anyone else, would think of her. "You don't understand. He's ..." Her resolve gone, she turned away, her unfocused eyes out the window. "John's a nice guy. Friendly to everyone. Every Wednesday he would stop by the clinic I was rotating through spring semester of my senior year. He always had something for me. A cup, a pen, a note-book."

"All imprinted with his pharmaceutical's logo, of course." He was still bitter, that was apparent.

She turned around to look at him. "You're missing the point, Cole."

"Well, do go on. I love walking down memory lane." His eyes were cold.

"And I thought you had a good ear," she snapped.

He got to his feet. "It's hot in here. I've changed my mind about that beer you offered." He found the refrigerator, not to mention the kitchen, and helped himself to one of the cold cans she'd bought on the way home from the hospital. He chugged away before he sat back down and motioned for her to continue.

"Anyway, back to John Drummond. He was always teasing me, saying, 'If you're not doing anything this evening, let's get married.' One day I said yes. And what's more, a week later we did. I don't know why he married me, but I know why I married him."

"All right, I'll bite. It's a question I've been asking myself all these years. Why *did* you marry him when you were engaged to me?"

"Because I was pregnant. And I knew if I told you, you'd do the honorable thing and marry me instead of waiting until you were through medical school as we had planned." How vividly it all rushed back to her. That spring vacation when she tried to tell him, but couldn't muster the courage. Remembering his father's threat after high school when they wanted to marry, that if they did, he wouldn't pay for college. "You would have quit school. I couldn't let you do that."

"You could have told me! Let me make my own decision!" He got up and came toward her, hatred etched in every line on his face. "How could you've waited all these years to tell me that Lisa is my daughter? Especially after I moved back." She hadn't expected him to be this angry. He was swearing. She clutched the edge of the drapes, afraid of what he might do.

She screamed as his fist punched through her wall. His hand was throbbing red, swelling up like a balloon, and he wasn't even looking at it.

"How could you do that to me, Sophie?!" The muscles in his face moved, he was so angry.

Sophie couldn't keep the tears back. "I was trying to protect you."

"Protect me? You ruined my life!" If he would only calm down. His hand. How could he not notice it? "There was only one thing in the world I ever wanted. You. I wanted you to be with me. My life has had no meaning without you." He wrapped his arms around her, his anger replaced with shared regret. "All of our plans. Why couldn't you have told me?"

"Can't you understand? Please, Cole, understand."

He held her tight, their tears merging together as if one. "Oh, Sophie, I do understand. That's what hurts me the most. You've sacrificed our hopes and dreams, and Lisa's life for the notion that humanity couldn't survive without Cole Morgan, M. D. There were scores of equally qualified medical school candidates. Any of whom could have been every bit as good a doctor, if not better. And how do you know I wouldn't have gone on to medical school had we married? Student loans. You could've worked. And as it turned out, I joined the military program, which paid my tuition and books and a generous stipend. We would have gotten by. We could have been a family all these years."

For the first time she realized the magnitude of her mistake. It hadn't mattered that she had suffered over her decision. She deserved the hurt of John's friend coming to take Lisa and her home from the hospital, explaining that John had a bad cold and had moved in with him for a while so he wouldn't be exposing the baby. She should have known then that he'd never come back to their apartment. She didn't deserve better than the formal letter from his attorney. She had tried to deceive him. But, in the end, she couldn't. Her conscience had gotten the better of her after she'd held the baby in her arms, and she'd confessed. But that was pain she brought on herself. Pain she learned to live with day after day. It was only now that she realized the horrible pain she had caused Cole. That it could have lasted like hers. She thought he'd gotten over her years ago. She thought it was different with men.

"I'm so sorry, Cole. I was so young and stupid. I only wanted to protect you."

He kissed her tears. "And I only wanted to love you. We were at cross purposes, it seems." A torturous groan came from deep within him. "And now all I want to do is pick you up and carry you into the bedroom—" He collapsed his head on her shoulder. "But it's all my damned leg can do to carry my own weight."

Sophie found herself laughing. That was so like her old Cole. He seethed as she took his hand—she bet it did hurt—and led him into the bedroom.

The clock, that had ticked away their youth, stolen their ideals and rose-colored glasses, rolled backward. They were as before, entwined together in shared longing.

Later, as she lay peacefully nestled in his loving arms, stroking his swollen hand, she said, "Maybe you should go to the hospital, get your hand X-rayed."

He held his hand up and inspected it. "I've seen worse. It can wait till morning. Nothing's forcing me from this bed tonight."

She pushed away. "Cole, I have to go to the rehab center. Visit Lisa."

"No." He drew her back and cuddled her in his arms. "Leave her be. We have to think this through."

Chapter 47

Ellis

Ellis sideswiped the magnolias with his Suburban as he turned into his circular drive to avoid Will's bike. Will was so careless with it. The drive back and forth to the house was a long one, but the one thing they could be thankful for was that there was no pilfering to speak of. Ty had had a problem with something being missing, though Ellis couldn't remember what it was. Hillary told him, but he hadn't been listening.

It was late and the only light that seemed to be on was the porch light high between the two-story white pillars. A dim light was spilling out from the kitchen. It was over the stove and led him to a plate of beef stroganoff. He poured himself a drink instead and went out to the swimming pool.

Ellis crunched what he suspected was a cockroach underfoot as he crossed the flagstone path in the dark to turn on the Jacuzzi jets and lights. He started to turn on the underwater lights to the swimming pool as well, but decided against it. He knew how many strokes it took to swim its length. He left his clothes on the lounge chair, his drink next to the Jacuzzi, and slipped into the wet darkness of the swimming pool. He needed this workout. Not only to tone his body, but to clear his mind.

He felt like the man who had struggled up the mountain to find that there was nothing more to climb, only a mesa to traverse and drop off on the other side. He dove down, kicking harder and harder, propelling himself faster and faster through the water like an armed torpedo.

Later, in the Jacuzzi, Hillary slipped up on him and dropped her robe where his glass had been. Her thigh brushed his shoulder as she slid into the Jacuzzi. "You swam an extra lap tonight." She was counting his laps? "Bad day?"

"Had an emergency thoracotomy this afternoon that set my office hours back." He set his drink down and twisted around until his shoulder was receiving therapeutic benefits from one of the jets. "Then Robert Copeland called to say that he would be down next week to take my deposition." He watched her round breasts skim the top of the bubbling water as she lifted her hair and leaned her head back against the blue tiles. "And then Rosa caught up with me while I was rounding to ask me to look at one of her patients."

Hillary sat up straight. "I just bet she did!"

"What's that supposed to mean?"

"You and Rosa having a little hoochy-coochy. How stupid do you think I am, Ellis?" She pushed herself out of the water and onto the edge. Her legs were split and he was getting an eyeful, but he had no interest in starting anything with her like this.

"Pretty stupid if you think that. Look, Hillary, I work with Rosa. That's all there is to it."

She laughed hysterically. "So how do you explain going dancing with her?"

"Going dancing with her? Oh, you mean when she picked me up at Saint Luke's." He shrugged. "We stopped at the Barn for a hamburger. That's all there was to it."

Her face contorted in hatred. The Jacuzzi lights shining up like footlights on a stage transformed her into an ugly harpy. "Then why didn't you tell me? Why did I have to get another letter to find out?"

"I'm sick and tired of hearing about those mysterious letters." Ellis downed his drink, and then scrambled out of the water. Between Bill kibbitzing over his wife's surgery like he knew what he was talking about and Hillary's insane accusations, Ellis had had all he could take for one day.

Hillary came running after him. He felt her fingernails dig into his arm. "Don't you walk away from me, you bastard!"

"Be still. You'll wake the kids." He ripped her hand from his arm.

"Oh, let's not wake the kids! Let's pretend we're one happy family. You don't think they know you're having an affair with that Mexican? Everyone knows. They're all laughing behind my back!"

"Well, then the joke's on everyone, because I'm not."

She slapped him across the face before he was able to grab her wrist. It was dark, but not so much so that he couldn't see the fire of hatred in her eyes. Her pain-filled gasp made him aware that he was squeezing her wrist. He freed her.

"I'm sorry, Hillary. I didn't mean to hurt you."

"Hurt me?" she hissed. "You think sleeping with Rosa doesn't hurt me?"

"I meant your wrist. I'm not sleeping with Rosa. How can I apologize for something I'm not doing?"

"Stop denying it! I have letters that prove it!"

"Hillary, you're insane."

"Insane! I'll show you insane! I'll drown myself if you don't admit it." She marched to the pool and stepped off the edge, water splashing over the side.

He stood in the puddle and watched her float facedown for a creditable length of time. He looked over his shoulder to the second-floor windows for signs that Amy and Will might be watching. He saw nothing, but still hopped into his pants. He squatted down, wondering if she'd sneaked a breath, and called quietly to her. "Hillary, please don't be like this. I need you. The children need you."

She wasn't moving. He was beginning to worry. "Hillary, for pete sakes. Hillary?" He dove in. She took a choking breath as she struggled with him. He was the stronger swimmer and forced her to the side and out of the water. He carried her scratching and biting into the house where he threw her naked and wet onto her precious couch. He pinned her down with the bulk of his body, one hand struggling to secure her flailing ones while the other clamped over her mouth. "Be still, Hillary."

They struggled for God only knows how long. When the fury faded from her eyes, he said, "I'm going to give you something to calm your nerves . . . so you can sleep."

His reward was rows of teeth marks on either side of his hand.

He threw her over his shoulder like a sack of potatoes and carried her screaming and kicking and pounding up the stairs. Amy came to the head of the steps, rubbing her eyes.

"Go back to sleep, baby." Ellis could only imagine what she thought. A naked mother, a half-naked father dripping wet and clamoring through the house.

"No!" Hillary screamed. "He's going to kill me!"

"I'm not going to kill you, Hillary. I'm going to give you a sedative and call your doctor." He threw his head toward Amy's bedroom, ordering her to do as he instructed. She pressed up against the wall so he and his burden could pass.

Will was peeking out of the crack in his door. After Ellis settled Hillary down, he would have to go in and reassure Will. Reassure him of what? That his mother would be fine? That his anguish wasn't justified? That they were a typical American family?

He threw Hillary across the bed and went in search of his black bag on the top shelf of the linen closet. He took it down and went back into the bedroom. Hillary was gone. He raced out the door. Hillary was nowhere to be seen. Amy was looking over the railing. "Where is she?"

Amy stared at him as if *he* were the dangerous one.

"I'm not going to hurt your mother," he said in a tone meant to reassure her, supposing that the outward signals he had broadcasted in his anxiety and frustration had not inspired faithful and everlasting allegiance from his daughter. "Where is she?"

Amy cast her eyes on the carpet. "She went to the VanFleets to call for help."

"Did she have anything on?"

Amy pinched her lips together so tightly they disappeared entirely. She shook her head.

He pulled her gently into his arms as she gave way to her tears. He stroked her tangled hair. He started to tell her that her mother would be fine, but thought better of it. "We'll get through this." He said it over and over again like a broken record. When her sobs mixed with gasping, an indication that the crying jag was ending, he said, "Honey, I have to call her doctor. Could you check on your brother for me? I'm sure this has been as hard for him as it has us."

Ellis watched her slink down the hall and disappear into Will's room as he descended the steps. He noticed the front door standing open. Hillary, in her right mind, would not have given the sea of insects their chance.

He found the doctors' list in the junk drawer in the kitchen and dialed Meredith's number. The voice that answered was unmistakably Sean's. "Sean, it's Ellis. I must have dialed the wrong number. I was trying to reach Meredith."

" 'Tis no mistake. I'll tell her you're on the line. She's in the shower, so be patient."

Ellis heard the phone bang on the table as Sean put it down. Ellis tried to calm himself. He needed to act professionally. How would he explain it to Meredith?

What would she recommend? The children would need some sort of counseling.

What was Sean doing at Meredith's this time of night?

Chapter 48

Pam

Pam took notes as she was given report from Bonnie, the evening-shift RN. If she could judge from the evening shift, things were going to be about as pleasant as her afternoon.

Coral May's visit had left her unable to go back to bed and she didn't function well on five hours of sleep. Nor did she like the news Coral May brought. Not that she minded hearing about the accident. She only wished the woman had broken her neck and died. That would have solved one of her problems.

What nagged at her was what Coral May said Karen told her about Bill never leaving her.

Pam hoped she acted naturally concerned enough for Coral May's feelings when she started whining about being found out. How Bill was coming out to the ranch to "tuck her in" almost every night. That bastard!

"The Garcia baby," Bonnie said, looking at the rough floor map of squares she'd drawn. Each square represented a patient bed and the little scribbles around each, things she needed to do. Those not checked off were now things Pam needed to do. "Dr. McNamara wrote orders to try him on five percent glucose. See if his projectile vomiting ceases."

Pam wrote it down on her yellow legal pad.

She had gone up to ICU on the pretense of visiting Avon and telling her how much everybody missed her in Peds. Karen was there, all right, and so was Bill.

Sitting next to her bed. Holding her hand like the concerned husband. She hated him more than she could say.

"Charles tumbled out of bed. He somehow managed to get the rail down."

Keep a eye on Charles, Pam wrote.

"I noticed his IV line was clogged with blood clots when I changed his dressing, but I wasn't able to get back to it."

Didn't look to Pam like Bonnie got much work done at all. She added *Flush Charles's IV line with heparin* to her list of things that needed doing.

Bonnie picked up the Kardex, which documented the distribution of all medications from aspirin to narcotics. She looked it over and put it down. Apparently nothing was amiss there. "Lori was off the floor for treatment this afternoon and is now off-time three hours."

Nine, one, five, and nine was the regular meds schedule. Pam made a note to give Lori hers at midnight.

Pam was burnt to a crisp about Bill. She meant no more to him than any other woman. Women were good for one thing only as far as he was concerned, that was clear enough.

It was when she was flushing the heparin through Charles's IV that the idea took hold. She was thinking about that time on Three North when the new LVN prepared the heparin for an IV flush that would have killed the patient. How could she forget that evening? That little thieving daughter of Sophie's stealing from the meds led to Pam's ruination. Now there was a black mark on her record. Well, she didn't plan to be around for her annual performance evaluation. She planned to be building a radiology out-patient clinic across the street. And she knew just how she was going to do it. So Bill liked having a wife to protect him from all his women friends? Fine. But she was going to be that wife.

Pam waited until Juanita and Lori were both off being busy somewhere else before she went into the back room and took out the bottle of heparin. She filled two syringes with undiluted heparin and shoved them into her pants' pocket. She filled the heparin bottle with saline solution. It would take a sharp eye to tell the difference.

"I'm going down to the cafeteria for a cup of coffee. Either of you want one?" Pam asked a little after one o'clock when they were all sitting around the nursing station.

Juanita shook her head. Lori started digging in her pockets for some money.

"My treat," Pam said as she took some change out of her purse in the drawer. "How about a Coke, Juanita? Be happy to get it?"

She shook her head again. "No, thank you."

Pam's heart pounded in her ears as she climbed up the back staircase. The ICU was built on the south end of the third floor in a horseshoe to provide for two entrances in case of an emergency code. Karen was in the room closest to the main entrance on the right. Pam took the left branch of the hall. It was the old lady in the far room that she was interested in. And the trick was to get onto the floor and off without being noticed. The best way was to cause a diversion.

She opened the back door a crack. No one was in the hall. She slipped in. Her head throbbed with a splitting headache. She was wet with perspiration. She wiped her hands on the sides of her uniform. She needed them dry so she could do her work. She reminded herself what Aunt Emma had done to her family. This was the means to revenge.

Pam could hear the nurse at the nursing station talking to someone. According to the daily admission sheet, three patients were in the ICU. The RN was most likely alone. She was probably on the phone.

The lights were never turned off in the ICU, but the old lady was asleep, her even breathing assured Pam.

Pam walked, as though hypnotized, to the bed. She stooped down and pulled the plug to the respirator and ran out, accompanied by the screeching warning signal. She didn't look back until she was in the hall. The nurse was hurrying to the patient's side.

It wouldn't take her long to realize that it wasn't a true emergency, only a cord that had worked itself loose. Pam raced to the other door and then calmly into Karen's room. Karen looked up at her.

"You're awake, I see," Pam said as if to her own patient. Karen turned her face away as Pam pushed enough heparin into the IV line to kill her. "You should try to get some rest," Pam added as she walked out of the room and off the unit.

She raced down the stairs. Her breath was short by time she got to the basement. She poured two cups of coffee, stuffed a packet of creamer and three sugars in her breast pocket, flipped the change into the donation basket and hurried back to Peds. She would toss the used syringe in the red container, according to the new AIDS directive, and no one would be the wiser.

Chapter 49

Cole

Cole sat behind Meredith's desk. No, that was too formal. He moved to the other side of the room. The warmer side. To the chair beside the chaise loungue. The clock told him it was after seven-thirty. He had to be in the ER by eight to relieve the physician assistant. What was keeping Sean?

He moved back to the desk. He would start there, with the intention of moving if Lisa warmed up to him.

The rap on the door needed no reply, for Sean opened the door a nanosecond after. He ushered Lisa in.

She looked so small and vulnerable standing beside the giant man. "Where's Dr. Fischer?" she demanded of Sean. "I thought she wanted to see me."

"You heard me wrong. I said you were wanted in Dr. Fischer's office." He motioned to the straight chair on the other side of Meredith's desk.

"So where's she?" she asked cruelly as she flopped down onto the chair. Cole was glad he'd decided on the desk. He could see now that he wasn't going to waltz into the child's life and straighten her out in half an hour.

"She's in Houston. Transferring a patient." Sean pulled a Kleenex out of the box on Meredith's desk and handed it to Lisa. "For the matting in your eyes." She smirked and dutifully dabbed at the corners of her eyes. "You know Dr. Morgan?"

Lisa played with the used Kleenex. "Yeah."

"Then I'll leave the two of you." She started to jump up in protest. Sean patted her shoulder. "We'll see that you get your breakfast. Don't worry."

"Send it to Africa with my compliments," she said to his back. When he was gone, she turned back. She slumped down in the chair and crossed her legs like a man, ankle to knee. She started picking at the fray at the knee of her worn jeans. "So what do you want? To dump me in ice water again?"

"It's not so much what I want, it's what you wanted. You told your mother you wanted your father." He stood up. "So here I am."

She stopped pulling threads to look him over. She was a tough little cookie and showed no emotion. "You're not my father. My father is John Drummond."

"No, your mother's ex-husband is John Drummond." He rounded the desk, a hand on the edge for support. And not solely for his game leg. "Your father's name is Cole Morgan." He leaned against the front of the desk as casually as he could manage and put his bad leg on the arm of her chair, trapping her. He explained as candidly as he could, assuming the brunt of the blame while defending Sophie's actions and honor. He had rehearsed the long night through.

There was nothing to read on her face when he finished. "That is the past. Now I'll tell you the future. Your mother and I are going to be married and you have several options. You may rot in here, kill yourself with drugs, or be a part of our family . . . a non-dysfunctional family."

She bit her cuticle. "Frank know this? He's sleeping with her, you know."

He was thankful Sophie had someone to lean on and felt somewhat sorry for Frank. Although she visited him a couple of times while he was recuperating from his warehouse-fire injuries, she had broken off with him that night last month after Lisa's overdose had made it perfectly clear that she had never loved him and wanted nothing more to do with him. Cole felt she was irrationally upset over Frank's search of Lisa's room. He was doing his duty, Cole had tried to remind her.

Sophie didn't see it that way and it worried him that she might end up hating him, too, for taking a hard line with Lisa. So far she was allowing it and perhaps she felt Cole had a right, being the girl's father. Sophie had had nearly seventeen years to work through the idea of his being Lisa's father and no doubt held preconceived notions and contingencies. She had him at a disadvantage.

"I'm afraid that's his misfortune. I've reclaimed her. I was her first love and will be her last." Sophie had changed so much in the years between. Besides carrying a few more pounds, which rounded her nicely, she was considerably more experienced. His one regret was that they hadn't gained their experience together. "But that's neither here nor there. You, young lady, have no business talking about your mother that way." He would like to give her some fatherly advice dealing with her highly gossiped-about sexual exploits, but would put that on the back burner.

She looked up at him as he let his foot drop away. If he had gotten through to her, she sure wasn't letting on.

"You know, you and I are much alike. Your mother is the nice one in our family. Too nice for her own good. And for yours." Sophie had lost the girl's respect by trying to please her. He wouldn't make the same mistake. "You and I are both selfish people and are going to have to come to terms with our relationship. We are both in for some drastic changes." He walked around her and over to the window, passing the clock. He was late for work. "Personally, I'd like to have a daughter. And I hope you come around." He stared at the back of her hair, which could stand a good brushing. "I'm late for work. If you want to talk to me again

. . . and I mean, with you doing your share of the talking, let me know."

Cole didn't look back when he walked out.

Sophie was standing in the outer office, next to Sean. She looked as small and vulnerable as Lisa had beside him. It was Sean's doing, for Sophie hadn't been small since seventh grade. Her vulnerability was Lisa's doing.

"What did she say?" Sophie asked.

"Nothing."

Sophie swallowed hard. "How did she take it?"

"Stoically." Stoic shock was something he'd seen frequently in the military. It was easier to be indifferent to the horrors of war than to react. Though it usually didn't last long. He hoped Lisa would crumble soon, so they could get her on the road to recovery and be the happy family he wanted for them.

Sophie looked up at Sean. "Should I go in?"

"Let me talk to her first."

Cole and Sophie watched him go in. He could see Lisa hunched over in the chair picking at her jeans. He didn't know what to think. What he wanted to do was gather Sophie in his arms, but not in front of Meredith's receptionist.

Instead he took her hand. "I better get to work." He gave her a peck on the cheek. "I'll see you later."

She gave him an impish smile. It raised his spirits.

Chapter 50

Rosa

Rosa picked up Mrs. Crawford's chart and swirled around in her chair. "Mary Jo?" The nurse looked over her shoulder. "Do you know anything about this notation?" She slid the chart across the nursing station counter.

Mary Jo read it. "I did hear something about it in report. Mrs. Crawford's respirator came unplugged. No one was in her room. It probably worked itself loose is all."

Rosa took back the chart. The notation said that the respirator was down less than a minute. The patient looked as well as could be expected and didn't seem to have suffered any ill-effects from the respirator failure. Still . . . she would report it to Richard Bell.

"Rosa?" Bill Martin was standing over her, blocking the morning sunlight. "I wonder if you might look at Karen for me."

His wife was Richard Bell's patient. "Does Richard know you're asking me?"

"I'll tell him. Just a quick look. As a professional courtesy."

Professional courtesy? She wondered what he meant by that. Most doctors' idea of professional courtesy was waiving their standard fee, sometimes billing the insurance company to see if they'd pay anything and usually under the pretence that their claim would reduce the patient's deductible. Bill went on record at the first County Medical Society quarterly meeting Rosa attended, by saying he would bill all patients alike, that the IRS considered professional courtesy barter and, therefore, he would have to discontinue the practice.

Rosa closed Mrs. Crawford's chart and got to her feet. "All right. I'll be happy to look at her. As a professional courtesy." She slid the chart into the metal carousel as she went by. Now that she was having a close look, Bill seemed very, very distraught.

No wonder. Karen's blood was seeping out of every orifice. Her nose, ears, the scratches on her face, and around her IV casing. Droplets of blood leaked from needle punctures.

"Look at the sutures on her chest," Bill whispered so as not to wake his wife.

Rosa pulled back the covers. Bill untied his wife's bloodstained hospital gown. Karen moaned and called his name, but she wasn't fully awake. Blood oozed out of the sutures. Rosa pulled the covers lower and saw a wide ring of blood, which she assumed was rectal, not menstrual. She pulled the covers up and left.

Bill followed.

Rosa pulled Karen's chart to get her vital signs' reading, and to see if Richard or Ellis or the orthopods had her on Coumadin or any other anticoagulant. She didn't see an order, or an indication for its usage. No venous thrombosis, pulmonary embolism, or myocardial infarction.

Bill was looking at the chart over her shoulder. He seemed genuinely concerned. Rosa hadn't known that he had it in him. She handed him the chart. "You aren't having any of the same symptoms?"

He shook his head, sweat flying.

"Is it possible your wife ate something that had been killed with Decon?"

"Like what?"

"Rats come to mind. But I suppose that's not a staple food in your household."

Bill pulled her around the side to the back hallway

where the crash cart was kept. He opened the door out of the ICU. She'd never actually gone out the back door before. He then made sure no one was coming. "She's going to die, Rosa. What am I going to do?" His eyes were watery. Rosa was getting a whole new slant on the man. She had always seen him as one of those people who subscribed to the belief that the person with the most money and possessions when he dies wins. To see him as a concerned husband was very touching.

"Let me go down to surgery and interview Ellis and Leroy, see if they know anything about this." She headed toward the elevator, Bill following her like a lost puppy.

"Ellis isn't here today," Bill said as she punched the down button.

She found it somewhat amusing that Bill kept tabs on his archenemy. "Where is he? I'll call him."

"Try the psychiatric hospitals."

"The psychiatric hospitals?" The elevator dinged. She'd still go down and see if she could find Leroy.

"Meredith and he drove Hillary—"

Rosa put her hand on his sleeve telling him to wait a minute. Someone was getting off the elevator. It was the new LVN. Rosa nodded to the girl. She'd forgotten her name. The only thing she remembered about her was how hard Sophie had to work to get her orientated. How calm Sophie had been when the LVN poured undiluted heparin—

She gripped Bill's arm tightly and pulled him back into the ICU. "Let's try something."

"What?"

Rosa ignored his question. She had one of her own. "Mary Jo, see if you have some protamine sulfate, and if not, call down to pharmacy." She would draw the blood herself. "Come on."

Karen was awake. Bill took her hand and caressed it. "How are you feeling, sweetheart?"

She gave him a weak smile.

"I'm going to draw a sample of blood, Karen, if you don't mind."

"She doesn't mind, Rosa," Bill answered for her. "She's going to find out what's making you bleed," he said to Karen.

Rosa drew the sample and left Bill swabbing the blood from the needle puncture. Rosa hoped she was right. The protamine sulfate was sitting on the counter of the nursing station. Mary Jo was in with Mrs. Crawford.

She mixed a couple of drops of blood with protamine sulfate. The blood clotted. She made a guesstimate of how much protamine sulfate to give. A large dose to be sure.

The question she kept asking herself as Bill and she monitored Karen's treatment for the next hour was how it had happened and what they were going to do to prevent such a mistake from recurring.

Chapter 51

Josh

"Impression . . . negative for fracture."

"Dr. Allister, do you have a minute?" the tech called from the door of the reading room.

Josh turned off his cassette recorder as he ripped down the two ankle films. "Sure, come on in." He put the films in the jacket and tossed it in the "read" pile. He pulled another flat film from its jacket. A chest. He slapped it under a clip on the light box and twirled around in his chair. "What is it, JoAnn?"

"This." She held out a Nuclear Medicine X-ray jacket. "I'm clearing out the pending bin and need to know what to do with this set of films. Dr. Martin said not to file them with the patient's other X rays. Should I throw them in with the seven-year-olds we're selling?"

They were legally obligated to keep X rays for seven years before they could be destroyed. Or rather, sold for their silver content. "How old are they?"

"Four months."

"Let me see them." They were Jacob McQuade's. The initial films of a Gallium Scan. "Where are the others?" Follow-up films were taken as the radioactive dye settled into the lymph nodes.

"There weren't any. He checked out of the hospital before they were finished. That's why they're pending."

"Dr. Martin knows about these?"

She nodded.

"Leave them with me. I'll speak with him about them." Josh threw them across the counter, out of his way. He wanted to finish the flat films before lunch. They were sending Margaret home after lunch and he wanted to get up there before she left.

He found Emma in Margaret's room. The door to the bathroom was closed. "Hello, Mrs. Chandler. Nice to see you."

"Josh." Her voice was cold and she nodded in that noble way of hers. He took it to mean that Margaret had told her about them and she didn't approve. A pity, because he planned to be with Margaret always.

"Margaret in there?" He nodded to the bathroom. The toilet flushed before she had to give any kind of answer.

Margaret opened the door and came out. She looked dreadfully ill and was still wearing a hospital gown, because her side was too swollen to allow for comfort in any of her own nightware. Then her eyes sparkled and her teeth flashed when she saw him. Her whole being glimmered and pulled him to her like a magnet.

He showered her with kisses. "You were asleep when I dropped by this morning. Feeling better?"

She held out a swollen arm to let him judge for himself.

"The edema's down a bit. You'll be out of the saddle a few more days, but you'll recover."

Margaret gave a little smile, and modestly holding the gown together in the back, hobbled over to her bed and sat on the edge. "That's what Carolyn Wright said when she came for a visit this morning."

"Well, I'll have to give her a glowing recommendation if she ever wants to get into medical school."

"What was Carolyn doing here?" Emma brushed past him and took a yellow blouse and a denim skirt, plus an assortment of underwear from an overnight case and laid them out on the bed beside Margaret.

"Meredith cancelled her appointment, so she came

here instead. She brought those flowers." Margaret motioned to the large bouquet that dwarfed the single rose in the bud vase next to it that he had purchased down in the gift shop.

"It might not hurt her to stay home with her husband once in a while instead of gallivanting all over the country," Emma snapped.

Josh was clearly in the way. "Rest up." He gave Margaret a peck on the cheek. "I'll call you tonight."

He didn't feel much like eating lunch, but bought a Pepsi out of the machine in the main corridor. A candy bar in the adjacent machine caught his eye. He fed the machine a couple of coins and retrieved his goodie. Maybe the sugar would ease his disappointment and improve his mood.

The X-ray technicians were in the cramped lounge taking turns with the microwave. Josh went down the hall to the reading room to eat away his misery in solitude. A call-report film was sitting there waiting for him. He turned on the light box and slapped up an AP view of a chest and then the lateral view.

He unwrapped his Snickers while he was waiting for Sarah's office to answer the phone. She was out to lunch, so he left the message that the child had pneumonia.

Josh didn't like this left-out feeling, but wasn't sure what he could do about it. Maybe he should have a little talk with Sean, to help sort out his feelings.

He took down the chest films and shoved them into the jacket and tossed it across the counter to start another finished pile. The Nuclear Medicine jacket fell to the floor.

It was curious. Why didn't Bill want it filed with the rest of Jacob McQuade's films? He took the films out and slapped them up on the light box. The uptake was normal. Oh, yes. The lymphoma. Bill didn't want everyone to know he'd been wrong about the lymphoma.

He thought about how hard all of this had been on Margaret. Her grandfather's recovery would have been a sight easier without Bill initiating invasive and expensive tests to rule out a lymphoma that he thought he spotted on a pre-op chest X ray.

At least Rosa had believed Josh about the spot being nothing but old scar tissue. Not that it did any good. Bill had stuck his neck out on it and ordered the tests himself. That is, in Ellis's name. At Ellis's expense. And here were the films that proved Bill wrong. No wonder he wanted them destroyed.

Josh decided to buck Bill and issue a report to be filed in the patient's records. Bill hadn't ordered him not to. And if challenged, Josh would simply say they were in the pile of films to read. So he did it.

He picked up his recorder and flipped it on and held the mike to his mouth. "Gallium scan films taken one hour after injection of radioactive dye shows normal uptake. Impression . . . Negative for lymphoma or any other infect—"

Josh flipped off the recorder and picked up the phone, adrenaline coursing through him. "Is Ellis in?" he asked after the customary chit-chat with Valerie, Patrick and Ellis's office receptionist.

"He's in Houston. Cancelled all of his appointments for today. And postponed a bypass surgery."

"Tell him to give me a call ASAP. Tell him it's important."

Chapter 52

Lisa

The potter's wheel was spinning out of control, her pot was leaning and threatening to tumble. She brought both fists down on it, reducing it to a clump of clay, screaming at it.

Everyone was looking at her.

She got up and ran from the room, the instructor calling to her. An orderly tackled her in the hall. She clawed at the floor, streaking it with clay until she was blinded by tears.

They hated her. Everyone hated her.

People were circling her like vultures waiting for their pound of flesh.

Sean's arms went around her and she was lifted into the air. He told everyone to go back to what they were doing.

"Everyone hates me. Everyone hates me," she cried into his chest.

"No one hates you, Lisa. We love you and want you well."

It wasn't true. Her mother wanted Cole Morgan, not her. They were going to get married and live happily ever after and leave her stuck in here. He was making her mother turn away from her. He had come between them. Nothing was ever going to be the same. She wanted a nice father who had an air-conditioned house, and other children. Someone who would buy her nice clothes and give her money. She didn't want someone to come in here and tell her what she had to do. "No, they don't. They want me out of the way. I hate him. I hate her."

Sean carried her to the women's wing. "Man on the floor," he called out. He kicked the restroom door open and set her down at the middle sink and ran her hands under the water. "The only person you hate is Lisa Drummond." He worked up a pathetic lather and scrubbed at the clay. "Why else would you try to kill yourself? And you are so wrong about yourself." He pulled one coarse, brown paper towel after another out of the wall dispenser and scraped the clay from her arms and face. There must have been some on her neck, too. Why couldn't they buy soft paper towels? "You are a worthwhile person who has much to offer the world. We just have to find a way to make you realize it."

Lisa didn't want him saying these things. She wanted to be left alone. She wanted to die. "Mom and I were fine until *he* came along."

"You're lying to yourself, Lisa." He turned her to the side and twisted her down so he could run a strand of hair under the faucet. "Neither of you were fine. You were abusing your mother and she allowed it because of her guilt over the circumstances of your birth. Your father wants nothing more than to straighten out the mess your life is in, as does your mother. 'Tis for your own good."

"It's not for my own good!" She jerked away and looked at her hair in the mirror. She pulled a lump of wet clay down the strand of hair, but it only made it worse.

"This must be what they mean about having a bad hair day. Let me see what I can do." Sean took some paper towel to the gummy mess.

"They'd get me out of this place if they wanted to do what was good for me."

"So you could kill yourself with drugs?"

"It's *my* life!"

"And we want you to do something constructive with it. Channel the energy you're expending on your hate into something meaningful." He went into one of the stalls for some toilet paper and made her blow her nose on it. "I told you once before you'll get nothing but hard love here. Nor does your father suffer slackers lightly. He is dishing up the same course because he wants to do what's best for you. You have to respect him for that. A lesser man, given his circumstances, might take the path of least resistance and buy your affection."

"What would be so wrong with that?"

"You know the answer as well as I. A good parent knows a child needs vegetables, even though 'tis easier to get candy down his gullet. Your father is a good and decent man who, like your mother, wants to see you grow strong and live a productive life. You might as well give in, lass, because none of us will."

"I hate him! I hate him! I hate him!"

"What you hate is losing control." He looked at her through the mirror. "Can't you understand that your biggest fear has been realized? You can no longer control your mother. You're out of control." He squatted down so they were at eye level. "The irony is that you've been out of control since your drug addiction took control over you. You've only been kidding yourself."

She fell into his arms. "I'm so scared, Sean. I'm so scared."

"'Tis a start, sweetheart. We're all here for you. We'll walk the road to recovery together, supporting you and carrying you when you can't do it yourself. 'Twill take time and effort, but at the end of the road will be your golden future."

He patted her back as she sobbed. "Life is scary, Lisa. For all of us. But hiding from life in drugs isn't the solution. You have to get beyond wanting drugs as the center of your existence. You have to want to be free of drug dependency."

"Sean, I don't know what I want. I don't know if I can do it. I'm so tired and confused."

"Then it's time for us to carry you. To tell you what you want. You want to get well. You have to want to get well. Say it. Say it with me. I want to get well."

"I want to get well. Yes, I want to get well."

Chapter 53

Ellis

"Do you want me to send Sean to your house to talk to Amy and Will?" Meredith asked. "He has an unique rapport with children. Especially teenagers."

Ellis nodded, his eyes on the road ahead as the Suburban ran full throttle. But instead of the broken white line, he saw the hatred on Hillary's face when she realized he was leaving her there.

He couldn't blame her; it was an awful place. If that was the best of the lot, he'd hate to see the worst. Her narrow room with its narrow bed and bare mattress, the barred window too high to look out, and the door without a knob. They had taken all precautions against their patients hurting themselves.

Echoing over the engine were Hillary's screamed words to Meredith. "It's a conspiracy! You're taking his side because he's a doctor. Can't you see how he's manipulating you?" Ellis couldn't let himself think about her or he'd drive himself crazy. That would make Sean's job a sight more difficult, explaining to the kids that both their parents were crazy.

"How long before I can stand seeing her like that?"

"It'll take a number of visits to become desensitized, I fear. I know it wasn't easy for you, or for anyone leaving a loved one in a psychiatric hospital. Your only defense is that it was in her best interest. She needs full-time professional help, which she shunned despite your best efforts when she was an out patient."

He couldn't remember ever feeling this bad inside. He had always enjoyed this stretch of the road between Houston and Chandler Springs before. Now all he could see were miles and miles of emptiness. He wanted to be transported in time and place. So far in the future that this hurt would be forgotten. Or transported back to better times. Better times! He couldn't remember a time when Hillary wasn't, to a far lesser degree, disturbed. Maybe if he'd paid more attention to her.

Ellis looked to the wide open spaces on either side of the highway, trying hard to recapture its beauty. The last time he felt a semblance of affection for his home state was when Rosa had driven him back to Chandler Springs after delivering the Kilpatrick baby to Saint Lukes. It had been a futile trip as the infant had died not long after.

Rosa knew so little about Texans and their ways. But she was one damned smart doctor and he held her in high esteem. She had a sense of humor, too, once you got her away from the hospital. And she'd been a good sport about the Barn and dancing. She was beautiful to boot. He could certainly see why Robert Copeland had taken a romantic interest in her.

Robert Copeland. Ellis wished he hadn't triggered that memory. The lawsuit was hanging like an albatross around his neck. And now Hillary. What had he done to deserve this? How much longer could he tread water before he drowned in the turbulent sea of his troubles?

"We have reason to be optimistic, Ellis."

He waited for Meredith to elaborate. She didn't. Her silence told him more than her vague assurance.

Ellis offered Meredith a smile. "Thank you for coming with me. I don't think I could have done it alone."

Her smile was quite pretty. She didn't smile easily, so he had never noticed before. He hadn't actually seen before what an attractive woman she was. Blond, graceful—if somewhat rigid—carriage, proportional facial features. It was a lesson he'd learned in anatomy. Average, or proportional, was the makings of what was generally termed beautiful. A big nose, a small chin, thin lips, fat lips would draw attention away from the whole. Meredith's beauty had not been lost on Sean, apparently.

"Sean answered the phone last night at your home."

"Are you asking if there is something between us?"

He shrugged. "Not if it's politically incorrect. Like calling a Latino Mexican. I wouldn't want to do that."

"I'm not overly political. In answer to your implied question, we're dating. Though I doubt anything will come of it."

"Why's that? I thought the purpose of dating was to find a compatible partner. Someone to share your life."

"Compatible." She sighed. "There is a nine-year difference in our ages."

"So what? Ty VanFleet is about that much older than his wife. It doesn't seem to bother him."

"Because he's a man. It is one of the double-standard cultural values society adheres to rigidly. Besides, Sean wants children."

"You can't have children?"

"I suppose I could, but I'm straddling the upper boundary of my childbearing years." She gave him a jab. "And it's none of your business."

"Sorry. I only wanted to repay you in kind for coming with me. I, for one, hope it works out for you and Sean. I hope to be the best man, if not godfather."

Josh's message said it was important. So Ellis detoured to Radiology on his way to the surgical theater where a bypass was waiting in the wings. He found him in the reading room with Rosa.

"Ellis, am I ever glad to see you," Rosa said. She tapped the film Josh and she had been discussing when he came in. "Bill's wife. We're treating her for a massive overdose of heparin."

"Heparin? I gave Recovery standard orders for prophylactic Coumadin—"

She held up her hand, stopping him. "Slow down, Ellis. No one ordered an anticoagulant. The heparin must have been a nursing error. I've already run it by Sophie. She's going to have a training session on the appropriate heparin-lock flushing of blood clots in the IV lines. That's a nursing problem and has nothing to do with us. What we want is your opinion. There is a great deal of blood in the pleural space, but the bleeding is now under control."

Josh outlined the involved area.

"What should it be, Ellis?" Rosa asked. "Another emergency thoracotomy, which Bill is insistent upon, or a more conservative closed thoracotomy with intercostal tube drainage?"

He picked up the magnifying glass and gave the chest film a good look. "Let's try a needle aspiration first."

Rosa took the magnifying glass out of his hand and gave the film a careful study. "I would never have expected that of you, Ellis. I thought the surgeons' motto was 'a chance to cut is a chance to cure'?"

Josh swallowed his grin.

Ellis had nothing to offer in his defense save a wry smile. "Actually, Tilton's giving me a chance to cure as soon as I can get down to surgery. His patient has been waiting all day. A needle aspiration is about all I have time for." He took Rosa's arm and led her to the door. "Fifteen minutes for Karen won't kill him. You may assist."

"Oh, Ellis," Josh called him back. "I think you'll want to see . . . where did that go?" He rifled through a stack of X rays.

"Hi, Margaret," Rosa said. "Mrs. Chandler."

Ellis turned to see Emma pushing Margaret's wheelchair over the threshold. Margaret's eyes were filled with pain until she saw Josh. Now they danced. Josh's did too as he dropped everything and rushed to her side. That boy had the worst case of runaway endorphins Ellis had ever seen. The girl wasn't immune to love, either. But what of the other Chandler girl? He was confused.

"Am I disturbing you, Josh?" the girl asked.

"No, not at all." He took her hand and bent over to give her a kiss. "You going home now?"

She nodded, her eyes glistening like diamonds in bright light.

Emma's eyes were well under control.

Rosa met Ellis's gaze and smiled. He thought he knew what she was trying to communicate. The laser surgery. Or maybe how touching love was. She was right either way. Though battered and swollen, Margaret looked wonderful. Ellis moved to the side to have a better look at the girl's reconstructive surgery. The only telltale sign was the coloring. Ellis gave Rosa the thumbs-up sign.

"I wanted to say good-bye," Margaret said, embarrassed.

Josh patted her hand. "I'll call you tonight."

"Hey, is this where the convention is being held," Cole said, more than asked, as he stuck his head around the door.

"Well, you look chipper for a gimp," Rosa told him.

"That's because he's getting married," Ty explained as he pushed Cole forward and stepped in after, a box of donuts in hand. "Hello, Mrs. Chandler. Margaret. We're celebrating. Have a donut."

"Better not, Dr. VanFleet. But thank you all the same," Emma said.

"Anyone we know?" Josh asked as he took a donut after Margaret had declined.

"Sophie," Cole announced jubilantly.

Someone should test the chemical content of the water fountain, Ellis thought. Phenylethylamine and endorphins seemed to be running amok. Everyone was in love. Ellis looked in the box, but he didn't see a donut with his name written on it.

Emma backed Margaret out of the increasingly crowded room. Ellis needed to scoot along too, if he intended to aspirate Mrs. Martin's lung and get down to surgery before Jennifer came looking for him with a pistol. "Josh, I'll come back later."

"No, hold on." Josh stepped to the intercom and raised the reception clerk. "Do you know what happened to Jacob McQuade's nuclear medicine study that was lying here on the counter earlier?"

Ellis's interest was piqued. As was Emma's and everyone else's in the room.

"I didn't pick it up," said the voice over the intercom. "I'll ask JoAnn and get back to you."

"Thank you." Josh turned back to Ellis as if they were the only two people in the room. "The study was quite interesting, Ellis. It was done on the day Mr. McQuade left the hospital and shows that he didn't have an infection. I think your attorney might like to see them, don't you?"

"You're off the hook, Ellis," Ty declared.

"Where are the films?" Ellis asked, more greedily than he intended.

"Bill's coming down the hall," Cole said with a look of innocence, "maybe he knows where the films are."

That was a pretty safe bet. Ellis threaded through the crowd to get out to the hall. Rosa put a warning hand on his arm, but he brushed her off.

"Bill, what did you do with Jacob McQuade's nuclear medicine study?" Ellis noticed everyone had followed him out like gas filling a void.

"I'm sure I don't know what you're talking about."

"The films that were on the counter before lunch," Josh said to refresh Bill's selective memory. "The Gallium Scan that proves Jacob McQuade didn't have an infection on the day he was discharged from the hospital."

"The day he left CMC," Ellis corrected. He wasn't discharged; he left against medical advice. According to Copeland, that was to be a big part of Ellis's defense.

"Oh," Bill said, his neck blotched red around his

white collar. "The study wasn't finished. I don't know how you can say it proves—"

"Is this what you're looking for?" Rosa held up an X-ray jacket as she came out of Bill's office.

Ellis took his best shot. An uppercut to Bill's jaw. His head jerked back, but Bill managed a glancing blow to Ellis's neck before he rocked back on his heels. The wall shook as Bill landed against it.

"You goddamn bastard! My family has gone through hell over this lawsuit and you've known all along that he became infected after he left the hospital." Someone screamed as Ellis lunged at Bill. They crashed together on the tile floor.

No one stepped in to pull them apart this time. Ellis felt Margaret's wheelchair at his back as Bill and he rolled across the floor like circus tumblers.

"Stop them!" Rosa shouted. "Ellis has a patient on the operating table."

Cole sandwiched in, locking Ellis's arms back and sending a twinge through his shoulder. "Okay, Ellis, that's enough. Don't want to get those talented hands of yours mangled."

Josh pinned Bill down to keep him from throwing a final punch. It was a lesson he'd learned at Ellis's expense the last time he and Bill went at it.

Ellis felt a bit hazy, but he didn't feel as bad as Bill looked when he pushed Josh aside in favor of getting to his feet under his own steam. Bill wiped blood from the corner of his mouth.

"Josh," Emma said calmly, breaking the stillness, "that study you were talking about. It proves that Jacob was well when he left Chandler Medical Center?"

"Yes, ma'am." Josh crossed to Margaret and put his hand on her shoulder. "The radioactive dye that was injected into his system was taken up by his nodes evenly. If he had had an infection, the dye would have been concentrated in the infected area."

Emma nodded. "I see." She looked at Bill. "Did you

know this before Chandler Medical Center settled out of court?"

"Dr. Morgan to ER," the voice boomed out of the hall speaker. "Dr. Morgan to ER." Cole hurried off.

Bill dabbed his mouth with a blood-speckled handkerchief. "No, and I don't believe it now. The study was for a suspected lymphoma."

"Doesn't matter what it was for," Josh explained. "The uptake was normal. Normal for everything."

Bill looked like he could strangle his "partner." Though with Margaret in Josh's corner, Bill no longer had the upper hand.

Rosa crossed her arms over her chest. "Wasn't it lucky *I* ordered a Gallium Scan?" She looked at Josh as if in premeditated orchestration. "I *did* order the Gallium Scan, didn't I?"

Josh looked at the order form. "No, Ellis did."

"I thought I did." Ellis suspected that was lost on Emma. He, of course, hadn't ordered it. Bill had. He'd ordered it in Ellis's name, like he had all of the other exams, including the lymphangiogram that had fostered the lawsuit.

"Good thing you did," Rosa said to rub it in, "you saved your skin. If you hadn't ordered that Gallium Scan, I don't know what you would have done."

Bill looked sheepishly at his handkerchief as he excused himself and started into his office.

"Oh, Bill," Rosa called compassionately, "Ellis and I are on our way up to ICU. Ellis is going to try a needle aspiration on Karen. Why don't you come along with us?"

He nodded. "Go ahead. I'll be up in a minute."

Rosa and Ellis left the department. Rosa started toward the elevator, but he pulled her toward the stairs. "Real Texans use the stairs."

"Sorry, pardner, I was thinking of your welfare. I wasn't the one rolling on the ground like a wild Indian."

"Rosa! 'Wild Indian' is not politically correct."

"I stand corrected." She sighed. "I hope this works. For Karen's sake."

"I hope it works for mine. Going to be a hell of a long afternoon if I have to work her in for an emergency thoracotomy. Got one on the table now that's been waiting since six this morning."

"They said you were in Houston with Meredith today." It was more a question than a statement.

"We committed Hillary."

Rosa lost her footing momentarily. "I'm sorry, Ellis, I didn't know. If there's anything I can do. . . ." Her voice trailed off.

He nodded his thanks. "Sophie and Cole. Did you know about them?"

Rosa stopped and looked up at him. "Ellis, you're going to have to get here a little earlier in the day if you want to keep up on all the—"

"All available medical personnel to the ER. Multiple incoming. ETA five minutes. All available medical personnel."

"You're right, Ellis. It's going to be a hell of a long afternoon."

Cole Morgan, M.D., was the happiest man alive. And why not? Today was his wedding day. He'd waited a lifetime for this day. Seventeen years to be exact. That was when Sophie had married someone else to give *his* daughter a name. She did this seemingly without compunction, or without so much as informing him of her plans. They would have been happily married all these years if only she'd turned to him instead of foolishly protecting him, fearing he wouldn't go to medical school if he were saddled with a wife and child. All that was behind them now, and tonight she finally would be his bride.

Wednesday was an odd day for a wedding, but it was Halloween and Lisa, their daughter, thought it would be cool to have a masquerade wedding. They could wear masks and no one would know who was getting married. Oh, he'd recognize Sophie, all right. Though she had a penchant for marrying the wrong man. No matter. If Lisa wanted a masquerade wedding, they'd have one. It was high time Cole said yes to one of Lisa's requests. He would have rather eased into the responsibility of having a teenage daughter had fate not deemed otherwise, but he was determined to be the best father he knew how to be.

He swung his pickup into the *doctors only* parking area, noting that everybody and his uncle were already there. Most doctors start rounds between seven and eight, and he figured it was after eight now. He'd gotten a late start this morning—if he did nothing else, he was going to build a second bathroom onto the ranch house—and then had to sit on the county road ten minutes waiting for a freight train to pass.

Cole checked the rearview mirror and repaired the damage the wind had done to his sandy hair. He was probably the only person in east Texas who didn't have air conditioning. Well, he had it in his Mercedes, but Sophie was driving it. Lisa wasn't keen on being left with Sophie's dilapidated Datsun, and Cole had promised that he'd trade it for the first Sherman tank that came on the market. In that light the Datsun didn't look so bad.

He slid out of the cab and came down on his good leg. Six months and his game leg still hadn't mended to his satisfaction.

The ambulance was in the bay outside the emergency room. Usually it was kept at the funeral home where Pokey, the mortician/ambulance driver, spent his time.

Pokey and he crossed at the bay door.

"Have another run ... out at the shooting range," Pokey said in a lingering Texas twang.

Was a slow day in the E.R. too much to ask on this particularly spectacular day?

Inside, Cole found Doctor Rosa Sanchez, a cardiologist, straddling a man who looked to be in his seventh decade. If the old guy hadn't presented in full arrest, having the dark beauty on top of him, her skirt up to her waist, could have.

Dennis Green, the E.R. registered nurse, cupped his hand over the phone's mouthpiece as Cole passed him at the nursing station. "Good thing you're here. I was just about to call a code."

The second hand of the big clock over the head of treatment table number one had swept away thirty-five seconds. The patient's face was ashen. Cole took over cardiac compressions. The skin was cold and clammy to the touch.

Rosa climbed off the table and pulled down her skirt.

"Got another coming, I hear," Cole said in lieu of a howdy.

Rosa's eyes were focused on the unspooling strips of

electrocardiogram readings, monitoring the electrical activity of the heart, her hand squeezing the black ambu
bag. "Not for you. The way I heard it, a woman shot herself on the recoil." Her index finger stabbed her forehead.
"Be Ty's patient." Ty VanFleet, the pathologist, would
perform the autopsy.

Cole, head of the emergency department at Chandler
Medical Center, Chandler Springs, Texas, would concern
himself with the here and now. Namely, stabilizing this
patient. He was certain the oxygen hooked up to the ambu
bag and being forced down the polystyrene endotracheal
tube was 100 percent. And he was the one circulating the
oxygen to the vital organs via compressions. A liter of
Ringers lactate, a solution of electrolytes and glucose,
was hanging on the pole beside the patient, running down
the IV line and through the plastic tubing under the wrin-
kled skin of the forearm. The electrical leads were attached to the circular patches taped to his sunken chest.

"X ray's coming and lab's on its way," Dennis told him
as he cast his long, thin shadow over the examining table
and inflated the blood-pressure cuff wrapped around the
patient's withered arm. "Eighty." A normal blood pressure is one hundred and twenty millimeters of mercury
systolic, heart contraction, and eighty diastolic, heart re-
laxation. Their immediate interest was in the systolic rate.
Hence, eighty was systolic.

Cole deepened his compressions, cracking the xiphoid.
No matter. *If* they stabilized him and *if* he lived long
enough, the surgical team would be cracking *all* of his
ribs.

"Ninety."

Rosa turned on her penlight and directed it at the patient's pupils. Satisfied, she pushed ten milligrams of ep-
inephrine into the IV tube. "Let's try another amp of
bicarb."

Dennis turned to the crash cart and opened the meds
drawer for the sodium bicarb.

Rosa took in a deep breath and let it out slowly. "And
atropine."

A young woman from the lab rushed in to draw the

blood gases. The X-ray tech was on her heels. Cole stopped compressions and stood back long enough for the girl to take a single-view chest X ray. She pushed the portable machine out of the way and hurried out to process the film. The lab tech had hightailed it long before and the E.R. was back to a cozy three. Four, counting the patient.

Rosa shook her head as she looked at the ventricular fibrillation rhythm on the green-grid cardiac monitor. Cole's eyes were on the clock. The first five minutes of a cardiac arrest were golden, and they were coming to a hasty swan song.

"Okay, let's zap him." Cole picked up the defibrillator paddles as Dennis swabbed two gel patches on the patient's torso to keep from scorching the skin. "Two hundred on three."

Dennis duly set the voltage to two hundred-watt seconds.

"Stand back," Cole warned, "one, two-everybody-clear, three." Cole touched the paddles to the gel patches. The convulsing body jumped up off the table like a frog.

They watched the monitor for signs of a stabilizing heart rhythm.

"Sumbich," Dennis said, shaking his head.

Cole's unarticulated feelings exactly. Rosa's too if Cole could go by her scowling brow. "Three hundred on three."

Dennis upped the voltage.

"Stand back. One, two-everybody-clear, three." Cole jolted electricity through the patient. The monitor spiked, and then zigzagged across the screen. Cole threw the paddles onto the crash cart in disgust and resumed compressions.

The phone was ringing. Dennis ran to answer it in the likelihood that it was the lab reporting the blood gases. He called out the PO^2, CO^2, pH, potassium, and sodium results. Rosa and Cole stared at each other in shared knowing. The numbers were not good. Only one in ten patients who landed in the E.R. in full cardiac arrest survived. He didn't have much of a chance at being that one.

Rosa prepared a nine-inch cardiac needle and angled it into the heart.

Swishing from the automatic bay doors made Cole turn to look. A cowboy in a dusty black Stetson carried in an unconscious young woman. Dennis directed him to treatment table three, but the man settled the woman gently on the examining table next to them. Both the newcomers were drenched in blood, which covered her face like a grotesque mask. Head wounds were famous for their gross external bleeding, so it was hard to tell the extent of the injury.

Cole divided his attention between the two patients. "What happened to her?"

The frightened cowboy glanced over at him, and then turned back to the girl on the table as if his watchful eye kept her safe. "I was learning her to shoot. It kicked back on her while she was still squeezing the trigger."

Dennis took a gauze pad to the blood, which pulled away in tacky strings. Cole wondered what kind of cannon the man had put into her hands to make such a noteworthy depression in her skull. Must have been a semiautomatic to report twice.

"At the shooting range?" Rosa asked.

The cowboy nodded absently, worry etched on his sweaty face.

"You didn't wait for the ambulance?" Rosa glanced at Cole, silently corroborating what he had already guessed, that this was Ty's patient.

"You the doc?" the cowboy asked Dennis in a frantic voice.

"Black," Dennis reported. Black was the triage term for dead. Cole turned back to the old guy who, unlike the woman, had a good ten minutes of life left in him.

Rosa ran a hand over the old guy's blue earlobe. "Let's call Ellis, see if we can get him down here and crack him open for a heart massage."

"You the doc?" the cowboy asked again.

"The nurse." Dennis tried to pull the curtain between the two stations, but the cowboy stopped him.

"Where's the doc? Sally needs the doc."

"I'm the doc," Cole said, continuing compressions. "Dennis, page Ellis."

Dennis started toward the phone, but the cowboy hooked his arm and twirled him around. "No, you take care of Sally!"

"Let him go," Cole cautioned.

"We do things here by priority," Dennis explained. "Let me make the call, and then we'll see to Sally." Dennis broke away.

"No!" the cowboy spun around wildly, grabbed Rosa around the waist, and brought out a semiautomatic that had been hiding under his jacket. "You see to Sally, now!"

There's an epidemic with 27 million victims. And no visible symptoms.

It's an epidemic of people who can't read.

Believe it or not, 27 million Americans are functionally illiterate, about one adult in five.

The solution to this problem is you... when you join the fight against illiteracy. So call the Coalition for Literacy at toll-free **1-800-228-8813** and volunteer.

Volunteer Against Illiteracy. The only degree you need is a degree of caring.